BLACK
PRIVILEGE
PUBLISHING

ATRIA

# ALSO BY ANITA KOPACZ

*Shallow Waters*

# THE
# WIND
## ON HER
# TONGUE

A NOVEL

# ANITA KOPACZ

BLACK PRIVILEGE
PUBLISHING

ATRIA

New York | Amsterdam/Antwerp | London | Toronto | Sydney | New Delhi

An Imprint of Simon & Schuster, LLC
1230 Avenue of the Americas
New York, NY 10020

First Black Privilege Publishing/Atria Books hardcover edition January 2025

BLACK PRIVILEGE PUBLISHING / ATRIA BOOKS and colophon are trademarks of Simon & Schuster, LLC

For information about special discounts for bulk purchases, please contact Simon & Schuster Special Sales at 1-866-506-1949 or business@simonandschuster.com.

The Simon & Schuster Speakers Bureau can bring authors to your live event. For more information or to book an event, contact the Simon & Schuster Speakers Bureau at 1-866-248-3049 or visit our website at www.simonspeakers.com.

Manufactured in the United States of America

1   3   5   7   9   10   8   6   4   2

Library of Congress Cataloging-in-Publication Data has been applied for.

ISBN 978-1-6680-5221-1
ISBN 978-1-6680-5223-5 (ebook)

*To my mom, dad, and sisters:*
*Sharon, Yvonna, Michelle, Nikki, Jatiana, and Dani,*
*for putting up with me as a child.*

*To Sheldon, Sadie, Tela, and Mayan for putting up with me as an adult.*

*This book is also dedicated to my cousin Leonie Shorte Nicholls,*
*my sister Michelle Kopacz, and my dear friends,*
*Domino Kirke-Badgley, Sebrena Tate, Lori Land Lastra, and Rachel Gomez-Wafer,*
*whose experiences with multiple miscarriages and stillborns*
*inspired me to tell this tale.*

All that you touch
You Change.

All that you Change
Changes you.

The only lasting truth
Is Change.

God
Is Change.

—Octavia E. Butler

## Mid-1500s

*Stories of Oya, Shango, Ogun, Yemaya, Obatala, Oshun, and several other Orishas are brought to the New World by enslaved Africans through the transatlantic slave trade.*

## Late 1840s

*Mary Ellen Pleasant (often referred to as Mrs. Ellen Smith or Mammy Pleasant) practices social etiquette and voodoo under Marie Laveau in New Orleans for a few months. She establishes herself as a main player in the Underground Railroad, helping enslaved Africans escape slavery in the South.*

## 1863

*Lieutenant Colonel (Dr.) Alexander Thomas Augusta becomes the first Black doctor in the U.S. Army.*

## 1860s

*Marie Laveau II, Marie Laveau's daughter, is known for practicing a more theatrical style of voodoo. Many people think she is her mother, so it's hard to distinguish between their works during this time. Like her mother, Marie II practices voodoo, rootwork, conjure, and Native American and African spiritualism.*

## 1830s

*Marie Laveau, one of the best-known voodoo queens in New Orleans, leads public voodoo ceremonies in Congo Square and private rituals along the banks of Bayou St. John and Lake Pontchartrain.*

## 1852

*Mary Ellen Pleasant sets sail for San Francisco during the gold rush (1848–1855).*

## 1852

*Thomas Bell meets Mary Ellen Pleasant on the four-month journey at sea to San Francisco. They become business partners, and in the next three decades they procure millions through investing in banking and mining interests.*

## 1865

*Congress passes the Thirteenth Amendment, which abolishes slavery in the United States, but slavery continues in some areas for years to come.*

## 1867

Streetcars in New Orleans are segregated from inception, first by separate trams. The "Star Car," marked with a black star, is available for Blacks to use, but whites can also board. Then sections become segregated with Blacks in the back. In 1867, New Orleans residents protest the segregation of streetcars in a weeklong series of demonstrations. They remain integrated until 1902, but many Black people still prefer to ride with each other.

## 1877

Mary Ellen Pleasant builds her thirty-room mansion in San Francisco on Octavia Street.

## 1877

James D'Arcy, one of the founders of a national Workingmen's Party, is elected to run the workers' meeting that turns into the San Francisco Riot of 1877.

## 1870s–1890s

Harriet Tubman speaks at events about freedom and the women's suffrage movement. During the Civil War (1861–1865), she serves as a nurse, spy, cook, and scout in the U.S. Army; she helps rescue more than seven hundred enslaved people.

## 1870s

Jesse James and his gang hold up trains, rob banks and stagecoaches, and steal horses. Because of his many Southern sympathizers, he is never caught by the authorities.

## 1877

Lew Hing, the founding father of San Francisco's Chinatown, marries Chin Shee in San Francisco. Lew amasses his riches from creating many successful canning companies.

## 1877

During the San Francisco Riot of 1877, the white population of San Francisco wages a three-day riot against the Chinese immigrants, killing four people and demolishing several Chinese homes and businesses.

# AUTHOR'S NOTE

A friend of mine named Yurie, who happens to be Japanese, shared with me a captivating mythical story from her culture that was widely known among her people.

"You are so lucky that you were taught that," I remarked.

"What do you mean?" she responded.

Ancient African religions and folklore were concealed from many African Americans under the guise of being demonic. Enslaved Africans across the diaspora faced brutal punishment, including beatings and even death, for practicing their original religions. When you strip a people of their gods, language, and medicinal stories, you can break their spirit.

We are now in a time of reclaiming our heritage. For Africans in the diaspora, rediscovering African religions and folklore means reconnecting with who we truly are. We are piecing together parts of ourselves that were deliberately obscured.

*The Wind on Her Tongue* is my tribute to Oya and to historical figures who continue to be demonized today, such as Marie Laveau and Mary Ellen Pleasant. Oya is the Orisha of the storm, wind, and weather. In the Ifá religion of the Yoruba people in Nigeria, Orishas are divine spirits that embody aspects of nature and serve as intermediaries between God and humanity.

Oya is depicted as the daughter of Yemaya, a relationship affirmed not just in my interpretation but in ancient parables. Known as an invincible warrior and the "mother of nine," Oya earned this title after enduring nine stillbirths and miscarriages. As the Orisha of weather and storms, she brings about change and transformation.

In certain societies, the sacred stories and parables about the Orishas are referred to as Patakis. With deep reverence and respect, this Pataki about Oya delves into the realms of racism, colorism, and classism as she confronts her own identity and abilities, striving to carve out her place in a society rife with challenges and complexities. *The Wind on Her Tongue* offers a compelling exploration of resilience, heritage, and the unwavering spirit of a young woman finding her voice amid the tumult of American history. The sequence of events within this novel are not completely accurate. I have included a timeline to note most of the historical occurances.

As we immerse ourselves in this narrative, regardless of our ancestral backgrounds, may we reconnect with our true selves and remember who we really are.

# FOREWORD

In the vast landscape of literature, few stories resonate with the spiritual depth and transformative power of Anita Kopacz's *The Wind on Her Tongue*. This novel is not just a tale woven from historical threads; it is a profound journey that bridges the seen and the unseen, the past and the present, the mortal and the Divine. It also beautifully demonstrates and reflects the essence and tapestry of Anita's unwavering commitment to her spiritual growth, our cultural heritage, and the art of storytelling.

I have had the privilege of knowing Anita for over a decade and have witnessed her dedication to her spiritual study and work. Our journeys together, including our meditative sojourns to the sacred pyramids of Egypt (hosted through Agape International Spiritual Center's travel ministry), have been a testament to her deep connection to the divine and her remarkable ability to channel wisdom from the ancestors. As a spiritual psychologist and retreat leader with the Goddess Wisdom Council, Anita has facilitated the emotional healing and empowerment of women. Such work affects countless individuals on a vibrational level and opens us up to the possibility of creating a truly civil society in which love and compassion are at its foundation.

Anita is also a longtime cultural beacon, sharing the voices of Black people in mainstream media. During her tenure as the editor in chief of *Heart & Soul* magazine, she elevated numerous narratives, including mine, spotlighting the importance of spiritual and emotional wellness in our community and beyond. I've even had the honor of sharing some of the wonderful insights contained in one of her previous books, *Finding Your Way*, during several Sunday sermons.

Anita's exceptional storytelling and writing transcends mere fiction—it is a sacred act of bringing forth ancestral wisdom into contemporary consciousness through stories that evoke healing and transformation. This is evidenced in *The Wind on Her Tongue*, a medicine story that connects us back to our ancestors, reminding us of the resilient and enduring spirit that reside within us all.

In this compelling narrative, we are introduced to Oya, born in Cuba and gifted with otherworldly powers from her Yoruba Orisha lineage. This lineage, rich with the legacy of her mother, Yemaya, imbues Oya with a dual nature: the potential for healing and the capacity for destruction. It is this duality that lies at the heart of Oya's journey and serves as a powerful metaphor for our own lives.

Through Oya's eyes, we experience the turbulence of her powers, the trials of her identity, and the ultimate realization of her purpose. Her struggle with her destructive powers and quest for balance mirrors the inner conflicts we all face. Oya's narrative also reflects the collective journey of those who have faced oppression and sought to reclaim their power.

It is through Oya's trials that we learn the importance of embracing our full selves—both the light and the shadow. Anita's portrayal of Oya's evolution is a potent reminder that True power comes from within and that our greatest challenges can be our greatest teachers. It also reminds us that we are all connected by the threads of our ancestors and that our voices, like Oya's, have the power to shape the world.

*The Wind on Her Tongue* is yet another avenue for Anita to help heal the emotional psyche of anyone who reads her words, especially Black women.

As you immerse yourself in the pages of this book, I invite you to reflect on your own journey. Consider how you are connected to the wisdom of the past and how your actions today shape the future. Let Oya's story inspire you to embrace your own power, to seek wisdom from within, and honor the sacredness of your path.

With deep gratitude and admiration,
Michael Bernard Beckwith
Founder and CEO, Agape International Spiritual Center
Author of *Life Visioning* and *Spiritual Liberation*
Host of the *Take Back Your Mind* Podcast

# PART 1

# WHIRLWIND

# CHAPTER 1

*Pull yourself together. Pull yourself together.*

The drums that once seemed so all-encompassing now merely echo in the distance. Everything feels like it's reverberating. The multitude of voices mumble together into a soup of sound. I keep my eyes closed, afraid of what I might see. *Was I poisoned? I never signed up for this.*

With my eyes still clamped shut, I touch the tips of my fingers to my thumbs, counting, *One ... two ... three ... four ... four ... three ... two ... one ...* My mama taught me that when I was a child. If I ever needed to bring myself back from too much emotion, *One ... two ... three ... four ... four ... three ... two ... one ...* Silence.

It all stops. The sounds. The echoes. The voices.

I slowly open my eyes and see that I'm still here. In the corner. Everyone is still here, but it's silent. They are laughing, drumming, eating—but no noise escapes them.

I'm seated in the middle of the ceremonial altar in the crook of the ballroom. Candlelight gleaming all around me. I'm not used to being the center of attention. Though there are many revelers dancing about the great hall, I can't seem to hear a thing. A wooden crate draped in purple velvet cloth props me slightly above the ground but affords no cushion. I can feel the splintery wood and small gaps between each plank on my buttocks, but I've been told to keep my legs crossed and not to touch the floor until the ritual is over. I have seen statues adorned in this way, with nuts and fruits as offerings, but never a human.

Lace dyed lavender has been cloaked along the walls of the altar, and the floor-to-ceiling windows around the room reflect the hundreds of flickering tapers adorning buffet tables brimming with food. Platters of shiny coral-colored crawfish, silver bowls of steaming hot jambalaya, gumbo, and red beans and rice. I can smell the delectable yeasty puffed beignets above all the other heady, spicy, mouthwatering aromas. In spite of the celebration, I feel in no shape to participate. The superbly costumed guests swirl and twirl through the room in their ceremonial garb, the women in long flowing cotton skirts in various shades of purple with multicolored headwraps, and the men in loose white tunics cinched at the waist.

Purple and white confetti floats through the crowd as the drummers beat with increasing intensity. Their muscles pulsate as I feel the vibration, yet I still cannot hear a thing. Those dancing begin to move as if they are in a trance. I notice that the red candles, which are only at the altar, have burned down almost to stubs. Marie, bedecked in gold jewelry encrusted with precious gems as befits a queen, approaches and whispers something in my ear, but I can't hear her. She motions for two of her servant women to remove the melted tapers.

A gust of wind rushes past us and blows out a few of the candle stubs before the women can change them. They turn to Marie, wide-eyed and visibly unnerved. The draft swells and picks up speed, traveling around the room until all the candles have been extinguished. The dancehall is now only dimly illuminated by the light of the gas streetlamps glowing through the large windows. The wind returns to my corner and surrounds me, encircles me as a tornado might, but I am calm in the eye of the storm. I begin to drift off, nodding my head back. The line between my imagination and reality now becomes increasingly blurred.

*⚡*

DING! DING! DING!

"Get the midwife, I can't feel her heartbeat!" they yell.

My eyes are still glued shut. I don't want to see them. I don't want to feel what this reality has to offer. Against my will, I peel my eyes open.

*⚡*

There she is. Sitting behind her heavy, ornately carved dark oak desk with a feather pen in hand. *How did I get here? What was that ringing I heard? And the call for the midwife?* I think I might be going mad. The smell of old smoke only slightly obscured by lavender oil chokes me. I try not to cough.

The window behind her encapsulates the life of this town. Horse-drawn streetcars roll down the wide tree-lined boulevard, past the colorful two-story houses with their curlicue wrought-iron gates, gingerbread embellishments, and ubiquitous white-columned porches. Negro and Creole women walk about in high fashion, garbed in brightly colored silks and satins; long dresses with puffy sleeves, tight bodices, full skirts, and bustles; bonnets with wide ribbons, elaborate bows, and feathers. *Are they headed to a ball or just out for a stroll?* It's hard to tell.

I blink hard and look back at Marie. She is a Negro, but her color seems to have faded with age. Her thick, white wavy hair is pulled up into a loose bun, and her purple satin dress appears to be uncomfortably tight around the bosom. I assume she is wearing a corset, something I am grateful I've rarely had to squeeze into. In Cuba, we almost always have loose cotton sundresses that flow in the sea breeze and feel like we are clad in close to nothing at all.

Marie's judgment shows through her deadpan expression. She forces a slight smile as she deliberately places her feather pen back in its well.

"I think it's time we try some herbs. Nothing permanent, just something to help you through this rough patch. What do you think?"

*I don't know what I think?* My mother sent me here because she said that Marie has a special interest in my well-being. She says I am connected deeply to the spiritual work that she does. Marie handles me as one might a newborn child, she is so careful. I can tell that her handmaidens, dressed in white, who seem to attend to her personal and business affairs, and servants, dressed in black with full white aprons, have the utmost respect for her. Or perhaps it's fear, so hard to tell. Regardless, I know Mama would not send me to anyone who would mistreat me, so I try to trust her. Apparently, I met her when I was young, but I do not recall.

"I came to New Orleans because my mother said you would know what to do with me," I whisper.

Marie lifts her gaze from the parchment and meets my eyes. "I am of the mind that you know exactly what to do with yourself, I am only here to help you find that answer."

She asks one of her servants to make me the prescribed herbal tea. I rub my still-tender and somewhat distended belly and swallow my unbearable grief as I think of my baby girl. The winds come again, strong enough to rustle the thick dark green velvet curtains framing the grand windows, which happen to be closed. I try to hold back my emotions, counting backward in my mind. Marie looks up but does not seem startled by the breeze.

She walks over to me and places one of her hands on my stomach and the other tight around me. My body automatically stiffens with the touch of this virtual stranger, but then, without thinking, I find myself responding to her nurturing kindness, softening and folding into her embrace.

"*Nou pral rive,*" she whispers. "We will get through this."

The winds settle down in Marie's dark room as she comforts me. Dusk has fallen, and the servants have not yet lit the candles. The only light comes from the full moon that peeks through the slits between the velvet drapes with its faint yellow glow. Marie is the first person other than my mom who doesn't seem frightened by my powers. One of her handmaidens walks in with a steaming cup of liquid in a delicate porcelain teacup. She places it on the wooden desk and then retreats to the corner of the room, where she stands quietly with the other handmaidens and servants.

"This tea has a mix of herbs that will both heal your wounds on the inside and calm your nerves."

"But my mother already healed me," I inform her.

"Yes, these will heal your emotional wounds, my child."

I take a sip of tea and have to call upon my full restraint not to spit it out. I gag on the wretched bitterness and almost choke on the loose bits of herbs that have not been strained.

"You will get used to it," Marie states in a flat tone, her eyebrows furrowed with more worry than her voice indicates.

She walks over to her handmaidens and whispers something to them.

I let the water cool before I take another tiny sip of the disgusting brew.

Without warning, two handmaidens, either my age or younger, walk up to me. I notice that they are identical twin sisters, their resemblance striking, as they stare intently at me. Their dark, mysterious eyes have a glint of wisdom beyond their years. Their skin is smooth, like the melted chocolate my mother would prepare for me on special full moons. Their lips are almost heart-shaped, with a deep bow in the middle and full bottom lips. They are so uniquely beautiful that it is hard not to stare back.

"Madame Oya, we have been tasked with watching over you."

"You're the most gorgeous woman we've ever seen, isn't that so, Cosette?"

They both giggle, and Cosette replies, "Oh yes. You're an angel! Exquisite—your hair is so big and curly! Women here never wear their hair loose like you. And—"

They pull me to my feet, and Cosette stands on her tiptoes and says, "You're so tall!"

Their candor and sweetness completely disarm me.

The other twin curtsies awkwardly and says, "I will perform the spells and prepare your herbs. My name is Collette."

"And I will help with your everyday chores until you are settled in. I'm Cosette."

I know what the herbs are now, but what does Collette mean by "spells"? I don't want to come off as completely ignorant, so I decide not to ask. I reach for the tea.

"Collette and Cosette, that's easy. Thank you," I say.

Collette flashes a mischievous smile and whispers, "The hard part is telling us apart."

Cosette pours me a fresh cup of steaming tea before they both curtsy awkwardly, giggle, and hurry off. I hold my nose and take a swig of the tea, forgetting that it is freshly poured and scalding hot.

*

"Oya! Oya! You can't catch me, you're too slow!" my brother, Obatala, yells as he runs in front of me.

*How did I get here?* I am running as fast as I can in the hard wet sand and trip over my own two feet, landing headfirst in the surf. Obatala sprints back to me. He looks to be around eight years old, making me just four.

"Oya, are you hurt?" He pulls me up and brushes off my face.

I spit out crunchy grains of sand and feel his strong arms holding me up. "I'm good," I say, sniffling.

Obatala walks me over to the shore. *I remember this day. I remember what happens.* Still, I can't seem to stop this nightmare, and, even worse, I can't stop my participation. Obatala spots a glistening orange starfish on the beach. He runs up to investigate and sees that it is still alive. I can feel the deep urge inside me to keep it.

"I want it!" I demand.

"No, Oya," he says, "it will die. We must put her back into the ocean."

"No!" I yell. "I want her!"

We feel the winds begin to pick up. Obatala puts me down and grabs the starfish. He shields his eyes to protect himself from the stinging sands that the building squalls are throwing about. He runs to the ocean to put the starfish back, but the waters have already begun to swirl.

"No!" I yell again. "That's mine!"

A huge wave advances over Obatala and crashes down on him.

⚡

The dainty teacup crashes onto Marie's desk and splashes hot tea everywhere.

Cosette runs up. "I'll take care of it, miss." She hurries to fetch a rag.

I stare at the steam rising off the spilled liquid, watching the symbols forming in the vapor. They seem to be telling me something.

"Do you see it?" Marie walks in with a rag.

I jump like a child being caught doing something naughty. *Is she talking about the steam?*

"You can read it too; you can read any element speaking to you in form. You can read water, stones, fire, smoke, clouds—everything in existence is trying to commune with you." Marie reaches over and wipes off the table. "It would be a shame if it ruined my desk, though." She laughs.

Her face is as smooth as a baby's cheek, but I know she must be in her seventies. Her hands show the life she has lived. They are a shade darker than the rest of her body, with wrinkles gathering at each joint. Her veins are raised, purple and green, and her skin has a shine as if it might be wet.

"Are you reading my veins?"

"I'm sorry, I'm sorry," I mumble, lowering my gaze. I realize that I think I've seen something she doesn't want me to see. *Has she been through the same thing I have? Has she lost a child?*

Marie reaches for me with her wizened hands and lifts my chin. "Don't you ever bow your head to anyone. You are not like others on this earth. We are fortunate to be on your path."

"But you are the queen." I had heard some visitors refer to her as such. I hope I do not offend her.

She smiles. "If I am the queen, then you are a god."

*But she is the queen.*

While wiping the final spot of tea, she holds her other hand out to me. "Come on, now, don't be shy."

I grasp Marie's hand and, with the strength of a large man, she pulls me to my feet. Startled, I stumble forward and almost fall. She steadies me.

"I don't know my strength," she says with a crooked smile. "Collette will bring more tea to your room. You should have a cup of this at least three times a day until I deem you healthy. There is nothing you need to do here but heal. Rest, my child."

She walks me down a long narrow hallway lined with rows of large portraits in ornate, heavy gilt frames. The paintings depict a wide array of people from different backgrounds. A Negro woman clad in European wear, a white man in military gear, an old Native woman holding a child, three mulatto children sitting by a toy train. Candles in brass sconces cast eerie shadows that bring the portraits to life. Their eyes seem to follow me as I walk slowly down the hallway staring in wonder. Such different people. *Who are they? How do they all belong here?*

"My ancestors," Marie says, noticing my stare. "They help guide me. I keep their light burning by honoring them. I do rituals and spells to keep them happy."

*Rituals and spells?*

I'm startled when she seems to read my thoughts.

"Not to worry, you will understand all of this mumbo jumbo before you know it. Time for you to get some rest."

Marie guides me to my bedroom on the second floor. The hefty dark wooden door creaks as I slowly push it open. Marie smiles and slightly bows her head as she turns back toward the ancestor hallway and leaves me to explore my new room. As I step inside, my gaze is immediately drawn to an arresting painting of the Black Madonna hanging over my bed. I recognize her instantly, a figure my mama introduced me to long ago. In all the depictions I've seen of her, she wears a solemn expression, as if burdened by the baby Jesus. Mama told me it wasn't sadness about having Jesus in her arms but, rather, sorrow for all the injustices he would endure in his life. *But how did the Madonna know?*

I stretch out on the plush lavender bed and take it all in. The lace canopy reaches the floor, and though it is pulled back and contained by soft satin ropes with long tassels, it flutters and shimmies as I settle in. The room smells delightful, like lilies and orchids, and is decorated with delicate lightweight wooden furniture—an armoire, a vanity, side tables, and high-backed upholstered chairs—painted white and pale pink, with carved edges embellished with gold. It feels like a young girl's quarters. Soft and pretty. Fine and elegant. But I can't shake the feeling that this room doesn't quite belong to me. I wonder if it was one of Marie's daughters'. It is so distinctly different from the rest of the decor in the house: heavy, dark, and serious. The only thing in my bedroom that seems out of place is the painting of the Black Madonna. Her intensity permeates the room in spite of the lace and pink and gold.

Though the space is charming and bright, I feel a chill and pull the feather comforter over myself. The houses here feel cold, not only in temperature but in spirit. There is an air of repression and restriction, with the city's wrought-iron gates and proper dress, that I never sensed in Cuba. I hate the feeling that I must control myself, must contain my energy.

*

The waves crash upon my feet.

"Obatala!" Mama comes running down the beach with clouds of sand following her.

I clutch the orange starfish to my chest and stare into the waves that have just swallowed my brother. I'm unable to move, but Mama dives into the ocean and grabs Obatala. She pulls him out, and I see that his body ragdolls like bundled scraps of cloth. His arms are completely limp. Mama gently places him on the sand and puts her ear to his chest. Her face tightens as strings of pearly silken threads flow out of her hands and surround Obatala in a soft cocoon.

Mama mumbles some words I don't understand. A golden light flashes all around the cocoon, and it begins to shudder. Obatala's little hands emerge from the woven shell as he coughs up a gush of water.

"Obatala!" Mama jerks him up and pulls him into her arms. "Obatala, now, now, child, everything is going to be all right," she says as she wipes away the webs.

Obatala coughs in her arms and holds her tightly. I slowly walk up to them. Obatala spots the starfish in my hand. He weakly whispers, "Put her back, Oya, you don't want her to die."

I look at Obatala, then back to the ocean. Mama encourages me to go. I drag my feet in the sand, creating long, curved lines with my toes until the water washes away my marks. I kneel in the surf.

"Bye-bye, star," I say as I place her in the water.

N

"Her water broke!" Marie yells as she pulls me away from a very pregnant, very young woman laboring in her back room. My hands shake as I attempt to steady myself in this reality. The waves, Obatala—it all feels so real. *How did I get back here?* Through the blur of my tears, the details of the room slowly sharpen into my vision.

The space is perfectly outfitted for birth, with its soft colors, sterile bed and birthing stools, basins, and gleaming silver birthing instruments all lined up on a clean white cloth laid out on a long enamel cabinet.

"Go fetch some hot water and towels. Collette, go help Oya." Flustered, I almost trip headfirst into the wall. Collette catches me and directs me down the long, dark, narrow hallway to the kitchen, large and opening out to the verdant herb and vegetable garden behind the house. Last night's dinner of roast chicken lingers in the air, and I realize that I'm hungry. Only a few candles are lit, as it is now the middle of the night, and most of the servants are asleep.

"I'll go put the water on the fire, and you get the towels from the washroom," Collette commands. She is confident and sure, the opposite of the giggly young handmaiden I met before. I follow her orders.

The washroom is a separate small building behind the main house with a water pump and laundry basins. I speed out the back door and onto the shadowy path that takes me to the washroom. I don't have a candle or lantern with me, so it takes a minute for my eyes to adjust to the scant moonlight. The streetlamps have already been extinguished, so I imagine that the entire city of New Orleans is dark. I've heard this is a place known for its nightlife, but when three or four in the morning rolls around, there aren't any souls on the street. Marie calls it the witching hour. I like the darkness and the quiet. They calm my nerves.

"Oya!" Collette shouts. "Did you find the towels?"

She startles me, and I yell, "I'm looking!"

I haven't yet explored the washroom, so I fumble around in the darkness, unable to locate the towels. I see a light bobbing on the path outside, and

Collette busts the door open with a lantern in hand. The light reveals a tidy, whitewashed interior, tile floors, and several barrels for washing, as well as a hand-crank clothes wringer and hanging racks. Collette heads straight for a trunk in the back of the room, swings it open, grabs the towels, and runs out. I follow close behind.

Cosette meets us in the kitchen with a pot of hot water. She carefully walks toward the back room. I feel a bit useless; I couldn't find the towels, and now Cosette has the water.

"It's not about you," Cosette says, as if she can intuit my thoughts.

I am silent, but I stay close in case they need me. By the time Cosette and I arrive, Collette has already given Marie the towels. Cosette hurries over and places the hot water at her feet. There is so much blood. My knees begin to buckle. Cosette runs up to me and whispers again, "This is not about you, remember. We are here to serve right now. Remove your self-importance. Just for the moment."

I feel like I should be offended by her words, but they make so much sense. I see the woman, who appears to be my age, writhing in pain as she struggles to find a position to push. "Lorna May, do you remember the breathing exercises I taught you?" Marie asks as she pulls Lorna up off the bed and guides her onto her feet.

Breathing in tandem with her patient, Marie holds Lorna's arms as she instinctively squats in pain. Marie encourages her to breathe in time with her contractions, and Collette positions herself in front of Lorna, ready to catch the baby.

I can feel my spirit needing to leave this reality.

Cosette whispers, "Stay here with us, I know it's hard, but it's—"

"It's not about me," I interrupt. "I got it."

As much as I want to believe that it's not about me, I can't help thinking of the baby I lost. The dream I lost. The life I lost. Tears well up in my eyes, and before I can wipe them, Marie commands, "Oya, come."

I rush to her side. Marie lays the woman on the floor and positions me and Collette on opposite sides of her body. Lorna lifts her feet and bends her knees. Marie instructs us to place her feet on our shoulders, and when it's time to push, we counter-push her legs back.

"I have to push, I have to push!"

𝒩

"I have to push!" I yell, even though my mama and the midwife are close by.

Sweat drips into my eyes, but all I can feel are my intense contractions.

"Something is not right," I mutter.

"This is all natural. Keep breathing," the midwife reassures me.

I blow fish lips, as my mother would call it. She said it would help me relax during labor. The contractions subside for a moment. I begin to wail uncontrollably.

"Mama, something is not right, I feel it! I feel her leaving."

Mama holds me from behind and wipes the tears from my eyes. "There, there, now, child. There, there," she says to comfort me.

But nothing can relax me. I can feel my baby saying goodbye to me. I can feel her giving up, and there is nothing I can do.

The contractions start again. The midwife can sense something is wrong now.

"It's time to push," she says.

I push with all of my might, but nothing happens. I push again, using every bit of strength I have left.

"We have the crown!" the midwife yells.

Mama begins to cry with joy, but I already know. A dark cloud begins to loom inside of me and outside of our house. Mama looks out the window and sees the weather shifting.

"One . . . two . . . three . . . four . . . Come on, breathe with me."

I push once again, and my baby flops out. There is silence. The midwife holds her upside down and taps her on her bottom. Still no sound. The midwife looks at my mama and shakes her head. Mama rushes over and tries to heal her. Webs form on her hands, but it is already too late. The silken threads flutter to the ground as my beautiful baby girl, my Kitari, rests in her lap. Mama traces her face with the tips of her fingers. She's more beautiful than any baby I've ever seen. Her skin is smooth, and her black curls are shiny. She has a birthmark on the side of her arm that looks like a misshapen heart. Mama kisses her cheek and slowly hands her to me.

*⁄*

Marie hands me the baby girl.

"Good job," she whispers.

I am visibly shaking, but I hold on to the precious life. Collette and Cosette hurry to me. "Let's wash her and get her back to her mama," Cosette says as she offers to take the baby.

I oblige. My arms are weak, and I can't seem to handle whatever cruel trick my mind is playing on me. I feel like I'm going to break.

Collette holds my arm and leads me to the kitchen, where we will wash the baby. I can hear the wind howling outside. *One . . . two . . . three . . . four . . . four . . . three . . . two . . . one . . .* I take a deep inhale to try to calm down. The last thing we need tonight is a hurricane. Collette lights a candle and burns some herbs. She starts chanting over a small red thread bracelet. Cosette is on baby duty. She takes some of the water we warmed and mixes it with cold water. While holding the baby in one arm, she dips a rag in the bowl and wrings it out with her other hand. As Cosette washes the baby, Collette says a prayer over her and blows smoke from the herbs onto her body. The baby begins to wail.

"She is telling the ancestors that she arrived," Cosette says with a smile.

When Cosette finishes washing the baby, Collette puts the red bracelet around the baby's wrist.

"This represents her connection to the ancestors. It also lets them know that she wants to continue that connection throughout her journey in this world," Collette explains as she ties the knot.

"Let's get her back to her mommy," Cosette exclaims, and they hurry out.

I fall to the ground, too weak to continue. Tears fall incessantly from my eyes.

*◢*

I feel Mama embracing me from behind. I hold on to her arms and let it all out, the grief, the rage, the searing pain. I keen, scream, howl, and weep as the rain outside our house pounds the tin roof. Though I am being dismantled from the inside out, we are contained within the eye of my storm—but God protect the rest of the island!

# CHAPTER 2

With my eyes still closed, I hear them whisper over me.

"We're lucky it didn't turn into a hurricane before she passed out."

"Was it really her that did it?"

"Let her rest."

My eyes flutter open, and they all stop muttering. Marie's handmaidens surround me, dabbing me with rags drenched in cold water. There is a spark in their presence that I have never felt before. They speak like regular folk, a bit of worry and fear, but there is a protective energy encircling them, like an invisible whirlwind. The power holds them together until I begin to move; I feel it dissipating as I stir in the bed.

"Welcome back, miss—" Cosette says.

"We knew you were going to be okay," Collette adds, finishing Cosette's sentence.

But they didn't know. I could tell by the sweat trickling down their faces on this chilly night. *Why is it so cold?* Cosette runs to the corner of my room to get a blanket to cover me.

"We have been praying for you all night," Collette says.

"Hush, child, don't make her feel like a burden," Marie says, startling us.

The handmaidens jump simultaneously and line up against the wall. Marie walks up to me with a steamy cup of herbal tea. I slowly sit up in the bed, slipping on the pale pink silken sheets. I feel so weak.

"Why is it so cold?" My voice shakes as I inquire.

"Your fever broke, and you released a storm before you passed out."

I can feel the emotions stirring inside of me again. Not anger but deep shame.

Hesitantly, I ask, "Was anyone hurt?"

"No, child, it wasn't anything we couldn't handle," Marie says as she hands me the tea.

My shame feels like a switch to turn on my insecurities. I didn't feel like a burden when Collette said they prayed for me all night, but as soon as I found out that I caused a storm, those tables turned. I could've seriously hurt or even killed everyone here.

"I'm sorry." I choke through my closing throat, trying to hold back my tears.

As my wind rustles the lavender lace canopy above me, I watch as Marie's white hair dances in the breeze. Around us, the handmaidens begin to chant a prayer, their voices soft and melodic but loud enough to hear over the whistling of my squalls. Though I can catch only fragments of the words, the sounds they produce remind me of the prayers chanted by the Babalawos during my mother's ceremonies.

Suddenly, I feel a palpable shift in the air—a circle of charged energy, invisible yet undeniable, begins to form around me. It feels like a warm embrace. As the handmaidens continue their chant, my winds gradually subside.

"What is happening to me? It's never been so bad," I say to Marie.

"Nothing is bad, my child. You are just becoming more powerful with the deep life lessons you are learning, and now you need to learn to wield that power. Hone that power. Control that power. Before it controls you," she says, rubbing my head. She encourages me to sip the tea.

"I'm not fully here," I say as I bring yet another hand-painted porcelain teacup to my lips. I notice that this one has the image of a fancily dressed woman with a large hat painted on it.

"I know, I can tell when you are gone. The tea will eventually help you stay present."

I sip the brew, and the bitter taste still chokes me, it's as if my body is completely rejecting it. I push down my desire to regurgitate and take another swallow. The ladies continue to chant in the corner. My eyes roll to the back of my head.

*

"Think about it, Oya, when does the weather change around you?" Mama asks.

I'm on the beach again, dressed in one of my favorite sundresses, a worn peach-colored cotton shift with holes in the bodice, not something I could ever get away with wearing in New Orleans. I'm barefoot, standing in the surf, allowing the cool water to bathe my feet as they sink slowly into the soft sand. I can feel the wisdom of the ocean and the wisdom of my mama speaking to me at the same time. I listen intently.

I'm older, maybe twelve, and Mama is teaching me how to control my powers, because ever since I began to bleed, I've had less and less rule over the storms, which have been coming more frequently. She asks me when the weather responds to my emotional state.

I don't have to think about it. I say, "When I'm angry."

"Good, any other time?"

"I think when I'm sad."

"Yes, yes, good. When my healing powers started, I had no idea what they were. I would just wipe the webs from my hands when they formed. It took quite a while for me to realize their properties."

"But my powers are not healing, they're killing."

Mama swallows as if she is trying to find the perfect words, treading carefully as if walking on eggshells around me. I've noticed this cautiousness before—it's as though everyone fears triggering my anger. Rightfully so, I suppose. But amid it all, I observe something—Mama never seems afraid for herself. She remains steadfast, her composure unwavering.

"We are learning what your powers are. If you are a healer, then your powers will be used for healing. It is not the power but the person who wields it who determines its fate."

That sinks in for the very first time.

*It's up to me.*

"I'm a healer, Mama, but not in the same way as you. I'm a warrior."

∗

Images of Mama and the ocean flicker back and forth in my mind, interspersed with static pictures of Marie, her hands steady as she tries to prevent me from spilling my tea. Slowly, I settle in before her, cradled in my lavender canopy. With gentle care, she peels my fingers off the teacup and takes it away from me.

"Where were you?"

"With Mama. We were practicing my powers at the ocean."

"Good, good. Take a deep breath," she says as she places the tea on my side table. "There are some exercises you can do when you begin to feel yourself drifting away. You are jumping to different times and places because your spirit and emotions do not want to deal with what is happening in the present. That is normal when something as traumatic as losing a child has happened."

With the ladies still chanting softly in the background, surrounding me in the protective prayer, I allow myself the freedom to release a tear. As it falls, I sense no change in the weather, so I let my emotions flow. As their chanting gradually crescendos, Marie moves in and embraces me.

"I want my baby," I cry.

I daydreamed about her a thousand times when she was inside me. Even then, I could sense her presence—the sweetness of her essence, like the scent of fresh mangoes lingering in the air. I imagined the softness of her touch, the gentle tickle of her black curls against my arm as I cradled her in my dreams. Her face was etched in my mind long before I laid eyes on her. She was so vivid, so alive.

Marie stands by quietly, allowing me the space to empty my tears. The handmaidens, like warriors, stand in position until my last tear falls. It's a cathartic release, one I've never allowed myself without concern for everyone's safety. My eyes feel sore and dry, and my nose is stuffy from the torrent of emotions unleashed.

It all feels so surreal. Just weeks ago, I was basking in the warmth of the Cuban sun, rubbing my pregnant belly. And now here I am, in this cold French villa, surrounded by people who seem overly invested in my well-being.

"Your mind may not be your friend as you heal," Marie says. "The tea will help. And if you feel yourself moving to different times, do the counting exercise I taught your mom when you were a child, or call out specific objects you see around you, like 'purple canopy, pink sheets, white desk.' That should bring you back pretty quickly."

I hesitate, unable to find the words to express what I'm feeling. I can't bring myself to tell her that my mind moves so swiftly between different times and places that I doubt any exercise could anchor me in the present. Instead, I find myself drawn to her deep brown eyes, which seem to hold a wisdom beyond anything I could ever comprehend. She is always reading everything, like she told me before. The elements are always talking to us.

"Will you read me?" I ask.

"Not now, darling, you will not like it. The predictions are sometimes affected by how you are feeling; this is why I tell people not to wait until they are in crisis to get a session. Those are simply surface readings, though. The more we learn, the more we realize that everything has already happened, and we are just obeying the laws of time and experiencing life in a linear fashion."

Though I don't quite grasp what she's saying, some comfort settles within me as she speaks, as if my soul understands everything, even if my mind doesn't.

As the days pass, I find that they blend into one another, the sharp edges of my grief gradually softened by Marie's tea. Though the flashbacks grow less frequent, there remains a deep sadness within me, an ache for my lost baby.

Yet I find solace in helping others. Marie teaches me much about midwifery, and together with her handmaidens, we tend to the needs of many pregnant women. Night births have become a regular occurrence in our household, and I'm now adept at providing care and comfort to mothers in their time of need.

But not every woman leaves with her baby in her arms. I share with them the same teas that have helped me find peace, crafting special packages of herbs for them to take home. In caring for these bereaved mothers, I find a sense of purpose—a healing balm for my own wounded soul. At first I worried I would feel broken, experiencing others' pain, but it gives me hope, like my suffering has gifted me with wisdom and the sense that it was not all for nothing.

The twins teach me everything I need to know to be a beneficial member of this household. All of the foreign concepts and languages feel like second nature. They often speak to me in French or Creole, and slowly I begin to catch on.

"*Gade w, kounya w ap fè remèd ou pou kò w,*" Collette says as she brings in a bundle of fresh herbs. "Look at you, you are making your own medicine now," she repeats in English.

Collette sets to work, meticulously separating the herbs strewn across the counter. I recognize some basics: oregano, basil, sage, and rosemary, but there are a few that I am still learning. She deftly ties a red string around each fragrant bunch. Meanwhile, the water simmering on the stove seems to be taking an eternity to boil.

"Has Madame Marie said how much longer you need to drink the teas?"

"No," I say.

Collette's question strikes a chord within me, stirring unease that I hadn't fully acknowledged before. I find myself contemplating my dependence on the herbs. Will I need them forever?

"I actually don't mind it anymore," I say defensively. "It doesn't even taste bitter."

I haven't had a flashback in weeks, and even then, it was so faint that I managed to bring myself back using the technique that Marie taught me.

"I've been meaning to ask you something," Collette whispers.

She places the last herb bundle on the counter and grabs the top of my arm, the way one might an elderly grandmother to cross the street. She leads me to the back washroom and closes the door, looking around, plagued with paranoia.

"*Sa w genyen?*" What's wrong? I ask, one of the few phrases I picked up in Creole.

"On the contrary, nothing is wrong," Collette whispers, giving me her all-too-familiar mischievous smirk. That's how I tell the twins apart now: Collette always looks like she is up to something.

"Did your mom ever tell you about Moses?"

"Yes. She didn't tell me many stories about herself, but she did share about Moses. She helped Mama on her journey north. Mama said that Moses kept going back to the South to help free enslaved Africans."

"There is a meeting—"

A loud crash from the street interrupts Collette. She snaps her head violently and stares in the direction of the noise without blinking. A cat squeals behind the wall.

"It must've been a trash can falling over," I say to calm her nerves.

Collette takes a deep, long breath and whispers, "There is a meeting tonight that I want you to attend."

"What has you on pins and needles?" I ask.

"Madame Marie must not find out about it. She would forbid us to go if she knew."

Now I'm intrigued. I have always been one to break the rules, but I thought differently of the twins. Even though Collette seems a bit prankish at times, they are both such do-gooders, obedient to Marie and the other handmaidens.

"What kind of meeting?"

"We can't talk about it here. Just meet us around the corner by the great willow tree. Do you know where that is?"

As a matter of fact, I know exactly where that is. It's on my favorite path to walk during the day. Secretly, I slip off my shoes during the stroll to revel in the sensation of the earth beneath my feet. It's so different from Cuba, where I often wandered barefoot along the sandy beaches. Here, the earth is damp and springy. I particularly relish the feeling of mud oozing between my toes after it rains, accompanied by the pungent, earthy aroma of damp leaves.

I snap out of my reverie and respond, "I do, but what if Marie asks me about my outing?"

"Just say that you are coming to help us care for the elderly couple in town," Collette says, as if she has already thought of every scenario.

It's hard to contain my excitement. "I'll be there."

Collette smiles. "Now go get your tea, I'm sure your water has boiled."

She grabs my hand, opens the washroom door, and leads me back through the tangled foliage of the overgrown garden, retracing our steps toward the kitchen. We skip on the stepping stones, from one rounded rock to the next, laughing every step of the way.

# CHAPTER 3

The willow tree has billowing blooms, its delicate petals clinging to the drooping branches like wisps of dissipating clouds. I lean on her trunk, hidden from the world behind her dangling canopy. As a gentle breeze rustles through the leaves, I hear the familiar sound of the rainsticks. The men in Cuba would use them with their drums to conjure songs for the spirits. I feel the ancestors with me under the tree, their souls intertwined with mine, just like the energy evoked by the handmaidens' prayers.

The breeze picks up, and a break in the leafy curtain reveals the twins, standing side by side, staring at me. I let out an involuntary yelp, immediately feeling embarrassed. They run toward me, consoling me in unison. "We didn't mean to startle you."

They each grab one of my arms and Cosette says, "We saw your feet by the trunk."

"But it's a good hiding place, especially in bloom," Collette adds.

I wasn't really trying to hide, but I don't let the girls know. They are on high alert, so the more cautious they think I am, the better.

"Where are we going?" I blurt out.

The sisters rarely answer me without a whole story attached.

"Where do we begin?" Cosette asks.

"Do you know about the Underground Railroad?" Collette inquires before Cosette can continue.

"Yes," I answer, "that's where my mother met Moses. It was a group of people who helped enslaved Africans north to freedom."

"Correct," Cosette says. "And some of those people are still around and still fighting."

"But slavery is over," I say.

Collette and Cosette look at each other.

"Did you know that our mother was a slave?" Cosette asks.

Before I can answer, Collette blurts out, "Madame Marie's slave."

The blood runs cold in my body. *Marie? How could she own slaves? She's a Negro herself.*

"I told you this would be too much, too soon," Cosette says to Collette, comforting me with an embrace.

*Are all the handmaidens slaves?* I'm hurt and angry and confused. I try to hold it all in so the weather doesn't change, but nothing seems different. Perhaps the twins are surrounding me in prayer to prevent the storm.

"Are you her slaves?" I hesitantly ask.

"God, no," Cosette says.

"We are free to leave whenever we please, but no place is as good as the madame's," Collette explains.

*Am I her slave?* Everything feels tainted in a way that is hard to understand. I feel violated, like someone has broken into my house and stolen my most valuable possession. Not one that is worth money but one that has an intimate connection to me. Now there is an empty space in my house, in my heart, where that valuable object once stood. Marie was one of Mama's closest comrades. She knew my father gave his life to protect Mama from that servitude. My mind is spinning.

*How am I feeling so much and the weather is stagnant?*

The twins gaze at me, eyes brimming with compassion, their empathy so palpable it seems poised to spill over at any moment. They must be surrounding me with the energy to prevent the weather from changing. I allow myself to feel, knowing that the twins are here for me. A surge of anger claws its way from my stomach to my throat, finally granting me the ability to speak again.

"I hate her!" is all I can muster.

"Oh, dear," Cosette says, "we mustn't hate her, because she can intuit that. She feels any extreme emotion."

"I really don't care what she knows or feels."

Cosette and Collette stand in front of me. "She is very powerful," they say in unison, this time without a smile.

Collette continues, "We have seen her control people's actions and words.

We have seen her turn rich white women into obedient slaves who take off their own wedding rings and pearl necklaces and hand them to her."

I sneer. "I don't even want to go back to that house."

"Come, let's bring this fire you are feeling to the meeting," Cosette says as she takes my hand and leads me down the street. There are few people about, as it is near dinnertime, and almost everyone seems to be inside with their families. The sun is setting, and the streetlamps are being lit as we walk.

The bountiful trees that usually speak to me of beauty now look like scribbles in a child's drawing. I trip on the cobblestone road, unable to find my footing. Collette grabs my other arm and leads me silently to the corner.

"We will wait for the streetcar here," Cosette whispers as if Marie can hear us.

We stand in silence. A whirlwind of thoughts plagues my mind. The twins stand guard, protecting me and the weather. A steam-powered streetcar pulls up. It's painted green and red, with the top half made up only of windows. Stern white faces stare at us as the streetcar squeaks to a halt.

The twins look at the driver and shake their heads. He pulls off with no question.

"Why didn't we get on?"

"That was the white folks' train," Collette says.

"But he stopped for us," I contest.

"We still don't get on," Cosette says, then she mumbles something in French.

A horse-drawn streetcar pulls up. This one is also painted red and green, but the surface is faded and scratched in several places. A black star is painted on the front of the car. A few windowpanes are missing, but when it pulls up, the uniformed Negro driver has a wide smile on his face. He's an older gentleman with a graying beard and a tobacco pipe hanging from the side of his mouth.

"Well, if it ain't the three most beautiful gals in all of New Orleans." His deep voice rings through the neighborhood.

The twins lead me up the stairs and onto the streetcar, their giggles infectious as we navigate through the crowded tram. Despite the tight quarters, people smile warmly and graciously make space for us. Folks are laughing. Chatting. Humming to themselves. The glow of the streetlights makes it feel like perpetual daylight. An older, kindly woman, cradling her grandchild, sings a gentle French lullaby, her soothing voice weaving through the crowd. Entranced, I close my eyes, allowing her melody to transport me to my inner peace. This orchestra of soulful sounds seems to chip away at the tension we were all feeling. The twins are laughing with each other, and I lean on Cosette, resting in this jubilant chaos.

A bell rings and the driver yells out, "Last stop!" He looks at us and adds, "Before I turn around and start all over again." As he laughs, his belly jiggles and his pipe miraculously stays in place.

We sidestep down the narrow metal stairs of the streetcar onto the compact dirt road. All of the streets I've seen here have been cobblestone, so I know we are far from home.

"We are close now," Cosette says, still in a whisper.

We turn down a dark, narrow alley that reeks of spoiled food and alcohol. I trace the bricks on the back of the building to guide my way. It seems as though the twins can see in the dark. They are walking and chatting as freely as they were with the streetlights on. There is a faint glow emanating from the doorframe of one of the back entrances. Red paint is peeling from the wooden door, and a seemingly useless, small faded awning juts out above the frame.

Collette walks up and knocks four times. The person behind the door raps back three methodical taps. Cosette runs up and does a final two pounds. The door creaks open, and we all slip in without saying a word.

The man at the entrance seems to be three heads taller than we are, with muscles almost bursting out of his pale blue button-up shirt. A thin line of beard creeps down the side of his jaw, giving his face even more definition. His lips are full and distinct, as if outlined, and further accentuated by a small goatee. His eyes, deep rusty brown like Mama's molasses jar, flit past us as he ushers us in. I want to ignore him, but I can't. We follow him downstairs, and he passes us on to an older woman. He rushes back upstairs without uttering a word.

The twins catch my gaze and share a knowing laugh before the older woman guides us down a dimly lit hallway, the musty scent of mildew lingering in the air. Eventually, we reach a metal door with rust creeping up from the bottom like inverted rain tracks. With a rhythmic knock from the older woman, the doorknob trembles, signaling the unchaining of a heavy lock. As the door creaks open, it reveals an industrial space illuminated by flickering candles and oil lanterns. Inside, a diverse gathering of people spanning various ages and ethnicities, clothed in simple dark work attire, is assembled. They occupy mismatched seating—a collection of weathered wooden chairs, aged church pews, and worn-out sofas.

The crowd makes space for us at the front of the room. I can hear quiet gossiping behind us.

"Is that Yemaya's daughter?"

"She seems so normal."

"Maybe she doesn't have any powers."

I look at the twins, and they don't seem to hear the whispers. *I don't want to be here anymore.* Before I can fall too deeply into regret, the metal door opens and a tiny, frail woman walks in. She has a printed scarf wrapped around her head, showing only a small tuft of hair in the back. Her crimson jacket seems too heavy for the humid heat of the South. She glides to the middle of the room with her lips perched up. I can't help but to feel like she is judging us.

Silence. Everyone seems to be holding their breath.

A man speaks from the side of the room. "Please give Ms. Moses a big New Orleans welcome! There are people who didn't want this meeting to happen, people who tried to intimidate us, but the good Lord was on our side!"

Cosette pinches my leg, and with wide eyes, she motions for me to look at the other side of the room. Marie is sitting there with two other handmaidens. Cosette tears up, and her breathing becomes shaky. My hatred is so strong that I can't even muster up any fear of that decrepit crone.

Moses speaks. "Forget who you were yesterday; do not tarry in the past. All that matters is today. All that matters is right now. All that matters is this very moment. They say that freedom was granted to us, but what freedom do they speak of? Freedom to starve? Freedom to be homeless? We are still in shackles as long as the white children are given the means to succeed while our Black children struggle."

Moses, looking over the crowd, fixes her eyes on me and pauses. "My Lord, are you Yemaya's fruit?"

Heat rises from my neck and floods my face. If my skin could turn red, it would. "Yes," I mutter, "I am Oya, daughter of Yemaya."

Moses holds her heart. "You are a copy of her, not a hair different. You even have her dimple." She guffaws to herself. "I hear she made a life for herself as a free woman in Cuba."

I am shy to answer, not wanting the gossiping women to know of my family.

"We will talk later, my dear," Moses says, sensing my discomfort.

She walks over to Marie. I hold my breath, and I think the twins do too.

Marie hands Moses a clunky metal cup unlike any of the fine china in her house. Moses takes a sip and walks back to the center of the room. *Does Moses know of Marie's dreadful history of owning Africans?* The twins and I look in Marie's direction. She picks up the cup, refills it with water, and glimpses our way. We snap our heads back to the front of the room. If Marie can really read extreme emotion, then consider us read.

Moses continues to talk about freedom and what it truly means to be liberated. She tells us stories of the Underground Railroad and shares with us visions of a free future.

She yells out, "Who are you?"

"We are free!" the congregation answers.

"What are you?"

"We are free!"

"I can't hear you! Who are you?"

"We are free!" the people yell with vigor.

"And what are you?"

"We are free!"

The crowd bursts into soulful cries and grandiose affirmations.

"That's right!"

"Preach!"

"Speak it, Moses!"

Moses removes her heavy jacket and passes it to Marie, whispering something in her ear. Marie gives Moses a handkerchief to wipe the sweat from her face. Moses walks back to the middle of the room with her arms up, waving them in the air, shouting, "Settle down, settle down."

The crowd is silenced as fast as a hungry baby getting a teat. No one wants to miss a word Moses says.

"Remember, when we walk out of these doors, we are in charge of how people treat us. We are not the victims; we are the great authors of civilization and of our lives. Do not fight to be the biggest victim in the room. You come from kings and queens. We will fight until every one of us is free!"

The crowd erupts into cheers and yelps of joy and determination. I glance over at Marie, and she is smiling at the people celebrating. She turns my way and locks eyes with me. My body freezes. Try as I might, I cannot lift a finger. Air moves in through my nostrils, down my throat, and into my lungs, but I have no control of it. My eyes feel stuck, much like they do when I daydream. A sense of deep calm floods my body, and I slowly stand up. The twins stare at me in dread: They know what is happening; they have seen this before. Both Collette and Cosette summon their courage and follow me over to Marie.

People have started filing out of the crowded room, so Marie is surrounded by plenty of empty seats. I sit right in front of her. As I settle in, the spell lifts. My anger returns tenfold. *How dare she try to control me?*

"I know that you are not happy with me," Marie says.

My breathing becomes heavy and my jaw clenches, trapping my words inside. "Not happy" is an understatement. I am furious.

"I don't usually put too much weight on people gossiping." Marie looks at Collette and Cosette. They lower their gaze. "It usually says more about the people gossiping than it does about me."

"They didn't own slaves!" I blurt out.

Marie's face becomes stern. "Before you go around accusing people of such horrendous acts, you should always get the whole story."

Moses walks over to us and stands by her. My eyes dart back and forth, feeling an overwhelming sense of confusion. I look to the twins, and they don't seem to be holding me in prayer, but there is not one inkling of a breeze in the room.

"I bought my fellow African people to help set them free."

"What?" I look back at the twins. "But what about their mother?"

"Some people chose to stay with me. We had a route up north on the Underground Railroad, and many of the Africans I purchased took that path to freedom. Moses and I have been working hard to free our people for longer than you have been alive." Marie turns to the twins. "And what is this? Your first meeting and you're causing all of this ruckus? Did your mother tell you that she was a slave?"

"No, ma'am, we found her purchase papers, and they listed you as her owner," Cossette says, lowering her gaze.

"We are terribly sorry," Collette adds in a shaky tone. She seems to be on the verge of tears.

"I know the consequences of Oya's emotions, I wanted to clear this up for all of our sakes."

I don't tell Marie about my powers feeling weak, especially because I think the twins are helping me keep them at bay. I would hate to get them in deeper trouble. Moses, standing slightly behind Marie's chair, has been staring at me during the entire conversation. The handmaidens help Marie pack up her belongings and guide her slowly to the door. Collette and Cosette follow close behind.

"I'll be staying with you tonight. Can we walk together for a moment?" Moses asks.

"Why, of course," I respond as I slowly stand, still a bit dizzy from the spell.

"I see the apple didn't fall far from the tree," Moses comments. "How old are you? Seventeen? Eighteen?"

"Eighteen, ma'am," I respond.

"I knew it, your mother was around your age when I met her, and you are just as fiery as she was."

*Is my mother fiery?* She has always been a place of calm for me; a place for me to rest when my emotions flare up. I want to know more about those days. Mama didn't tell me much, perhaps for fear of upsetting me. I know my father was killed during their fight for freedom, but that was years before I was born.

Moses smiles at me. "Let's catch up with the others, and I'll tell you about your mother."

Moses wraps her thick coat around her shoulders and takes hold of me. She leans on my arm, and I am entirely surprised at how heavy this tiny woman is. We head toward the door.

"Your mother, she saved a child you know. She saved plenty of people, but one child stood out to me."

Moses goes on to tell me how my mother ripped a young boy from the jaws of a wolf and healed him with her webs. She healed him in front of a group of runaways, a group whose fear of her was palpable. They screamed and wailed while my mother stayed wrapped up with the child, healing him.

"Why were they scared of my mama if she was helping?"

"That's the question of the year. Often people who help to create tremendous change are feared. I am feared. Your mother is feared. Marie is feared."

*I am feared.* That's why I was sent away.

"It has never bothered me. People's fears. I am guided by a higher power that cuts through such trivial emotions. If people walk with me, we call upon that power with every prayer, with every breath."

When we reach the back alley, Marie, the twins, and the other two handmaidens stand by the entrance. My eyes must've already adjusted, because the dark back street seems illuminated by the moon now. A black horse-drawn carriage detailed with gold trim awaits Marie, Moses, and the handmaidens. I am struck by its grandeur, and as the footman opens the door, I can see that the inside is just as elegant as the outside. The seats are upholstered in dark burgundy velvet, and the windows are covered with heavy matching lace curtains.

The twins and I stand watching while the ladies board the carriage. The sound of the horse's hooves hitting the packed dirt road echoes throughout the alleyway as they disappear into the night. We walk to the streetcar, kicking stones and wishing there were room for us in the fancy carriage. I'm anxious to spend more time with Moses. She seems excited to share information and stories about Mama. My heart pounds in anticipation. I never realized how curious I was about her history. Perhaps this is the first time that I've had the space to wonder and inquire.

# CHAPTER 4

Cosette pounds the keys on the piano, her eyes closed and back arched, her head swinging to and fro. At times she curls in close, her face nearly kissing the keys. Red wine and bourbon tip to the edges of the glasses on the dance floor, yet they never seem to spill. Marie's prized handwoven rug withstands our twists and turns. Collette slaps the sides of the piano, beating out a rhythm in time with the song. She hums along in harmony with her sister, both riding a melody guided by an unseen force.

Moses and Marie are precious, their movements are small and a bit stiff, but you can tell that the music feels to them like a needed respite. Collette makes her way to me across the cerulean, gold, and forest green Persian rug, shaking a coconut shell rattle to the beat of Cosette's song.

"I really made a fool of myself earlier," Collette says with boisterous laughter. "But I'm glad we cleared that up. My sister and I have been bearing that burden for quite some time. We never really felt comfortable here because of that. So some good did come of it." She raises her arms and spins around in a circle.

Collette tosses the rattle to another handmaiden and grabs my waist with one arm and my hand in the other. She leads me in a dance the way a gentleman might.

"Just relax and follow my lead."

Collette spins me around the dance floor while Moses, Marie, the handmaidens, and the servants clap and hoot and holler.

*BANG! BANG! BANG!*

The window shatters.

The music stops.

Cosette falls to the ground.

I dash toward her, and horror grips me as I observe the gunshot wound piercing her chest. Without hesitation, I yank her away from the danger, dragging her out of the living room just as a fiery torch hurtles through the remnants of the once stately Victorian window. As flames erupt, engulfing the space, Collette remains frozen in the living room, seemingly in shock. Another handmaiden rushes in, bravely plucking Collette from the brink of the inferno, sparing her from the merciless flames.

I haul Cosette out to the back of the house, seeking refuge by the washhouse. Collette's eyes widen in shock at the sight of her sister, and she bolts toward the front of the house without a second thought. Despite attempts to detain her, a few handmaidens trail after her in futile pursuit. Clinging to Cosette, I feel her weakening breath against my skin. My heart is heavy with worry. From a distance, we strain to hear the sound of Collette's voice carried on the wind.

"You should've hidden your faces! I see you! I know who you are!"

As the unmistakable sound of horses' neighs fills the air, I ask one of the handmaidens to hold Cosette. Summoning every ounce of power within me, I surge forward to confront the attackers. With a primal scream echoing from my lips, I unleash my fury, channeling my energy to knock the assailants off their feet. But to my frustration, not a drop of rain or gust of wind heeds my call. The men quickly mount their horses and flee into the night. One of the attackers, heavyset and burdening his mount, struggles to maintain control, while the others, more agile and reckless, taunt us with erratic maneuvers and gunfire before disappearing into the darkness.

The trees are still.

There is no breeze.

Not a leaf stirs.

No clouds form.

No rain falls.

No thunder or lightning.

No storm.

Collette slowly turns around and looks at me. She is covered in soot and tears. Filled with dread, we make our way to the back of Marie's house. The handmaidens diligently bring water to put out the fire. Through the smoke, we see Cosette lying in a pool of blood. The handmaiden attending to Cosette looks at us, her face drained of color.

Collette's knees buckle, but she finds the strength to run to her sister. She grabs Cosette and lets out a guttural wail, an otherworldly sound unlike anything I have ever heard. Collette clutches Cosette's arms and tries to wrap them around her, but they limply fall to the ground.

She begins to hum the French lullaby that the woman was singing to her grandbaby in the streetcar. Collette caresses her sister's face as streams of tears fall to the ground. I embrace Collette from behind and sit with the twins. I summon all of my strength to be there for her, even though I want to fall to the ground in tears.

As the frantic flurry of handmaidens fetching water gradually subsides, a somber calm descends on us. With weary steps, Marie and Moses approach the washhouse, their empty buckets hanging low in their hands. Marie's gaze meets mine, and I shake my head. *Cosette didn't make it.*

She drops the buckets, hurries over to us, and begins to pray in another language. It's not French or Creole. As she prays, a purple orb of light begins to faintly glow around me, encompassing the twins. A spark raises from Cosette's chest and fuses with the purple orb around me, then it fades away altogether, leaving Cosette's lifeless body in our arms. No one seems to notice the light.

Collette silently weeps over her sister as Marie ushers the rest of us in the house.

"Ba I yon ti tan," Marie whispers. "Give her some time."

My head is spinning. *How could this have happened? What was that purple light? Why didn't my powers work?* I know the twins were not holding me in prayer. *The twins. My God. Cosette is gone.*

As I drag into the house, the floors wet from the buckets of water rushed to put out the flames, one of the handmaidens walks up to me with some hot tea. "I think it would be good for you to lie down."

The lingering scent of singed animal hair permeates the air. Though most of the smoke has cleared, the oppressive stench remains. It looks as if the fire did not travel far from the rug. There is a blackened circle right in the middle of the room. I begin to feel nauseated, thinking of Cosette falling from the piano bench. Unable to bear the sight any longer, I flee upstairs, desperate to escape the haunting memory of the living room below.

I slam the door, and the painting of the Black Madonna dislodges from the wall, tumbling to the floor with a soft thud. I slowly reach down to pick her up, and I see it—I see her grieving for Cosette, I see her grieving for her son, I see her grieving for all who are suffering.

There is a knock on the door.

"*Rantre,* come in," I say as I lean the painting against the wall.

The door slowly creaks open, and Marie comes in with my tea. "You must've left this downstairs."

"*Mèsi,*" I say as I reach for the tea. "Can I ask you a question?"

"Of course," she says as she sits at the foot of my bed.

"I tried—" My throat closes up from my emotion. Trembling and tearing up, I take a deep and shaky breath. "I tried to knock the men from their horses with my storm, and there wasn't even a breeze." I huff, feeling the heaviness of everything that just happened.

"I noticed that change at the meeting, there was no reaction in the weather to your anger. Perhaps it's the herbs. They work to calm your nerves and keep you present. I wonder if it is dampening your gifts."

I look at the steaming tea on my bedside table. The vapor swirls from the cup look like a whirlwind. It seems to be calling my name.

"I have to stop." I swallow audibly. "If I can't protect those I love, then what am I here for? I could've taken those men down with one blow!"

"I know that is your anger talking, but taking a life is not something you want."

"I've already taken many."

"But not intentionally, Oya. Not murder."

"What's the difference?" I whisper under my breath.

Marie walks over to the side table and picks up the cup. "I will have Josephine make you some chamomile tea; that won't be as strong."

It has been so difficult for me to learn the other handmaidens' names. I believe Josephine is the one who gave me the tea in the first place. *I want to go home. I want Mama.* I feel myself rocking back and forth. Marie scurries by me with the steam from the tea blowing against her white tresses. I know that, inside, she is grieving, but she won't show it.

Collette is sobbing outside my window. Slowly, I approach the thick velvet curtains and cautiously peer outside. There, in the dim light, I see her swaying back and forth, her mournful hum mingling with the night air. Suddenly, she pauses, and a sense of unease washes over me as I instinctively withdraw from view. With a furtive glance around her, Collette retrieves a small glass jar from her pocket, swiftly collecting some of Cosette's blood. My breath catches in my throat as I watch in disbelief. A knot forms in the pit of my stomach. In a hushed exchange, Collette whispers something to her sister's lifeless form before hastily concealing the bottle beneath her dress as Marie and Moses emerge from the house.

Marie looks up at my window, and I duck farther down. Sweat tickles from my armpits, and my breathing becomes shallow. I know she saw me, but what does that matter? My nerves are just on edge. *How could life be so fragile?* I close my eyes and count: *One . . . two . . . three . . . four . . . four . . . three . . . two . . . one.*

For the first time ever, I can feel the calm pour down my body from the top of my head down to my toes. With a gentle sigh, I sink to the floor and sit at the foot of the window. I keep my eyes closed as I listen to Moses and Marie join in song with Collette, their voices rising in unison, a reverent invocation to the ancestors telling them to welcome their precious child into the afterlife.

# CHAPTER 5

"Do you mean to tell me that you know who did this?"

Several days have gone by since the passing of our sweet Cosette. The funeral was breathtaking, an all-day celebration of her life. From dawn till dusk, the streets echoed with the lively procession as crowds of mourners and revelers alike flooded the thoroughfares. It seemed as though every Negro in New Orleans was in attendance, with a second line band behind Cosette's coffin. Folks were dressed predominantly in pristine whites, adorned with matching umbrellas. We could spot the people who had traveled from out of town, clad in all-black ensembles, veiled in lace with skirts too tight to dance. But by the end of the day, even the most reserved mourners found themselves swept up, their dresses and skirts hiked high enough for them to join in the celebration.

The attack garnered all sorts of attention because, apparently, several well-to-do Negroes have been murdered as of late. Even entire towns have been burned to the ground if it looks like they are making more money than whites in neighboring settlements.

"I saw them as plain as day," Collette says to me, then whispers, "They were the scrappy-looking white boys who work on the docks. They're always giving Madame Marie a side-eye when she hops from her carriage. I think the bullet was meant for her."

"What did you do, Collette?" I ask.

"You never mind what I did, they will get what they deserve."

A part of me feels relieved. Feels satiated because Collette has the guts to do what is needed. I'm unsure of the details, but I know she—

My thoughts are interrupted by a thick newspaper thrown between me and Collette.

"What in the heavens?" Collette exclaims as we look up at Marie.

Wearing a floral dress with mud trimming the bottom of the frock, Marie looks as if she has steam coming from her ears. Her usually tamed locks are teased out of her bun, and she is breathing heavily. "Look at the story."

We slowly turn toward the front page of the paper, and there are sketches of three missing white men who have been declared dead because they were lost in the Mississippi River.

"*Asé* Yemaya," Collette whispers.

"No!" Marie grabs the paper. "This was not Yemaya, it was you!"

*How did my mama get mixed up in this?*

Marie takes a deep breath and slows down. "I know that you are hurting, so I am going to start at the beginning. Are these the men who killed your sister?"

"Yes, ma'am."

"Did you do a root on them?"

Collette looks at me like she's drowning, but I'm not sure how to save her.

"They deserved it," I say.

Marie cuts her eyes at me. "That might be the case, but if Collette here had anything to do with the speeding up of their natural karma, their divine justice, then she will have to deal with the spiritual consequences. Any spell, any root, any energy that you put out into world, comes back to you three times. If Collette has taken these men's lives, we will need to make it right as soon as possible."

Tears begin to stream down Collette's face.

"What did you do, Collette?" Marie insists.

Through her tears, she manages to mutter, "Blood."

"*Excusez-moi?*" Marie exclaims.

"I used her blood," Collette declares.

Marie begins to talk to herself in French, Creole, and a multitude of other languages. She makes the sign of the cross, the way the people do outside of the Catholic church, and I think she might be speaking in tongues. Collette and I are frozen by a mix of fear and intrigue. Finally, Marie stops her tirade and bends down to come face-to-face with Collette.

"A blood ritual is extremely hard to reverse. A blood ritual with human blood is almost impossible to break. We must find a way to placate the spirits before they come for you."

*What is happening right now?*

Marie walks away talking to herself.

Collette nervously begins to wring the rag she is holding back and forth. Whatever she did must be unforgivable. Although I am slightly lost, I don't see the harm in her exacting revenge. Those men would likely do that again. Collette saved us all.

"I acted in haste," Collette says as she bows her head.

"I respect what you did."

"No." She shakes her head. "It doesn't deserve respect. I should've shot them myself. I brought spirit into this, and now I'm in a tangled web."

"It would be just as tangled if you shot them." I immediately regret saying that: Collette is in an extremely fragile state, and the last thing she needs is my judgment.

There is a knock on the side door. "Hello, is anyone home?"

The door swings open, and a stately, extravagantly dressed Negro woman glides across the hall. Her maroon dress is the latest fashion, with puffed sleeves and a large bustle. She is carrying a matching umbrella and wearing a jauntily cocked bonnet with long drooping feathers. As she makes her way through the house, she absently fondles her pearl choker.

"What is this?" she exclaims as she passes by the charred carpet in the living room.

Collette looks at me like a scared deer. I can tell that she is in no state for company. I bend over and whisper, "Go rest in my room. You can have privacy there."

Collette scurries up the stairs, avoiding eye contact with this entrancing stranger.

The side door opens again, and a somewhat harried, slightly disheveled, though impeccably dressed white man enters. "Ellen, you forgot your spectacles."

"You know I only need them for reading. You hold them," she demands in a way I have never seen a Negro address a white man before.

He tucks her spectacles into his chest pocket and scurries over to Ellen. They both look at the burned floor, then up at me.

"What in the heavens?" Ellen says. "Is Marie around?"

As if summoned by the question, Marie enters from the hallway that leads to the kitchen. Her voice is shaky and weak as she whispers, "Ellen?"

They run to each other and embrace. Marie collapses into Ellen's arms and begins to wail. This is her first show of emotion since Cosette's passing. Even at the funeral, she held it together. Ellen and her white man lead Marie to the couch. I sneak up the stairs as they comfort her. I'm sure we will have a proper introduction later. Now is definitely not the time.

I knock on my door, and Collette creaks it open as if she were waiting for me.

"I feel sick to my stomach," Collette moans.

I lead her to my bed and sit her down. The sunrays shine into my room and illuminate the specks of dust in their wake.

"You haven't eaten since the funeral, do you want me to get you a baguette from the kitchen?" I ask.

"I can't." Collette looks up at me with dark circles around her eyes. She holds my hands and squeezes them. "Can I tell you?"

"You can tell me anything."

Collette swallows hard. "That night, when I was with Cosette, holding her— that's when I took her blood."

I remember that, but I don't tell her I was spying from the window.

"I saw the boys. I knew exactly who they were. Like I told you before, they were those rowdy boys from the docks. I remember their faces because they were harassing me and Cosette for a good moment, saying that they wanted to be in a nigger sandwich with us. Cosette was so innocent that she didn't understand. I made sure that we never walked home by their docks after that."

"I'm so sorry," I say, without knowing what else to offer.

"Well, I took her blood and did a root on their boat. I had no idea that it would work so quickly. I really did it in haste. I hated to see that they would get away with it. The white men are never convicted for killing Negroes, never."

I think she has run out of tears. I think she has run out of emotion. She speaks to me as if she were an empty shell. Searching my brain for what a root is, I deduct that it must be some sort of spell, which Marie has explained to me as words spoken together to enact change. "Some call it magic," Marie said to me, "but it's really just a law in the universe. We speak things into existence."

"I don't know what to do anymore," Collette says, exasperated. She falls back on my bed and stares at the top of my canopy.

I hear Cosette's voice in my head whispering, "This is not about you."

I lie down next to Collette and stare at the draped purple fabric with her. I have no words, but just being there by her side somehow feels better.

# CHAPTER 6

The mourning doves seem to mock the owl's hoots with three extra calls. Did we sleep through the night? As I stir awake, Collette slams her arm around me and holds me tight. I remember seeing her and Cosette cuddle at night in the same manner. I hold my breath; she must think I'm her sister. I don't want to wake her into this nightmare.

The door swings open, and Ellen and Marie stand there in what look like matching lavender nightgowns. I can't read their faces. As they walk closer, I see that Ellen's gown has tiny white flowers embroidered throughout the fabric, and the collar is made of white lace. My wide eyes fail to blink as they approach. Marie waves her hand in front of my face as if to check that I am alive, or perhaps just simply awake.

"Good morning," I whisper, still trying not to stir Collette.

"We have much work to do today, ladies, if we are to reverse the root promptly and properly," Ellen says with conviction.

Collette jumps awake and notices that her arms are tight around me. She releases her embrace and unsteadily looks at Ellen as she tries to orient herself. Collette rubs the sleep from her eyes as Ellen continues to relay the plan.

"We must find the spot where you did the root and walk backward to the house. That is only the first part. We mustn't look behind us as we walk, so we will have Oya here as our guide." Ellen pauses for a moment. "Nice to finally meet you, Oya. I am a big fan of your mother. Oh, I don't know if 'fan' is the right word, but let's just say that I wouldn't be who I am today if it weren't for her. But back to the task at hand." Ellen straightens her gown and takes a deep breath. "We must go to the graveyard and gather some dirt from your sister's plot and hope to find a coffin nail. If we are lucky, the spirits will gift us one without us having to borrow one, respectfully, from a local resident."

*Is she talking about stealing a nail from a dead man's coffin?* I feel like I've entered unfamiliar territory. The confusion must be evident in my eyes, and Marie seems to sense it. She reaches out, touching my shoulder, offering a reassuring connection amid the unfamiliar.

"Moses had to leave. She sends her love to both of you. She doesn't stick around for the dirty work with the spirits," Marie says.

"I don't blame her," Ellen adds without pause.

Marie rubs her delicate hands. "We must hurry before the root becomes irreversible. We are in what I call the sweet spot. Collette is genuinely remorseful, and the spirits have yet to come for their due."

I look at Collette. "'Come for their due,'—what does that mean, exactly?"

"Well, it's hard to say. It's always different, but oftentimes it comes up as an illness of the mind so that the spirits can have dominion of the soul."

*An illness of the mind? Is that what my teas are meant for?* I find myself pondering these questions as I absent-mindedly rub Collette's head. She is staring blankly at Marie. Perhaps the illness has already taken hold. Leaning down, I rest my head beside Collette's. *"Ou anfòm?"* I whisper in Creole.

Collette turns to me with a vacant look in her eyes. "I'm fine, I'll be okay."

She sits up, even though she has barely any room with the three of us surrounding her.

"I need to use the bathroom," Collette says as she shimmies her way through us and out the door.

"Of course," Marie says. "We all should be getting dressed for the day. Be sure to wrap your heads, we don't want any stray spirits coming home with us." She grabs Ellen's hand like a child claiming their best friend, dragging her from the room.

They slowly make their way down the Victorian steps, gossiping like schoolgirls. Ellen knows of Mama's powers, and most likely about mine, yet she shows no fear. Like Marie, the twins, and all the handmaidens, they treat me like an everyday person. Back in Cuba, Mama's protective measures kept me away from others to avoid causing harm. My interactions were limited to Mama, Obatala, and Oshun, my little sister. Sometimes I even thought Mama would take them away from me too. The looming dread of losing them never materialized; instead, I found myself shipped off. I get it all—the isolation, the precautions, the pain. Yet, despite the understanding, the hurt lingers. Marie is the first person to make me feel completely welcome and like I am not a disaster on the horizon. In her home, I feel accepted exactly as I am.

The silken sash from the bed's canopy whips across my face, and my breath catches in my throat. The winds in my room begin to pick up. The weight of my sadness about Cosette's death and Collette's grief lifts as I feel the exhilarating dance of the swirling breeze on my skin. I twirl around in circles, arms outstretched. The winds, though born from sadness, now stay for my joy, and I delight in their playful company. I open my window and usher them out with a wave. They kiss my cheek as they're set free to play in the leaves of the trees in the backyard.

The winds seem to sweep out the sullen energy that has plagued the house since the attack. I hold my hand out in front of me, and for the first time I pull a current of air from within me without being controlled by anger or sadness. Inspired, I blow the cleansing breeze down the ancestral hallway, and it extinguishes the candles lining the walls. An idea forms in my mind. Making a series of gestures with my hands, I command the currents, pushing them from side to side, causing them to swell and fade. I have never done this before, yet it feels so natural, like a homecoming.

"Oya!" Marie yells from downstairs. "*Se te ou menm,* was that you?"

"Yes, Madame! It was me. They are back. My winds are back!"

Marie walks up the stairs with her white mane dancing in the breeze. She makes no attempt to shield herself from the gusts. With a subtle gesture, I guide the invisible currents, directing them toward an open window at the bottom of the staircase. The surrounding curtains billow and dance, the sheer fabric twirling forcefully as the winds pass.

Marie's steps quicken as she reaches me, her face etched with a mix of pride and sorrow. In an unusual gesture of vulnerability, she wraps her arms around me, drawing me into an embrace that makes me feel like a cherished treasure. While I have found deep comfort in her presence, she is not overly physical with her love and compassion. I can feel her grief, not only from Cosette but from all that she has endured in this life. Slowly, Marie pulls away, her eyes shimmering with the remnants of her tears.

"I'm not sure what happened . . ." I tell her.

"Wisdom rarely comes with instructions. It appears, like a gift from a stranger." Marie holds my hands to her chest. "Now go get yourself dressed and wrap your head. We have work to do."

I know she is right, but I want to find Collette. I want to show her my new control over my powers, to dance with her in the breeze. I glance down the stairs.

"*Ale non,* go ahead, tell her," Marie says as she stands aside.

I rush down to Collette's quarters, flinging open the lightweight door and halting in my tracks. Her room, which is usually spotless, is a scene of disarray and chaos. It's as if a tornado swept through, turning everything in its path up-side down. A thick mildew scent hangs in the air. There is an eerie stillness in the room, as if it has been abandoned, frozen in time for centuries.

My gaze flickers to a haphazard pile of garments at the center of the room. Amid the chaos, my eyes lock on to a wrinkled, faded pink frock, one that I recognize all too well. It was Cosette's favorite, reserved for Saturday outings, always impeccably cleaned and pressed.

"Collette!" I yell.

I dash outside to the outhouse in the backyard. Midstride, I trip on the stone path that winds through the garden. I catch myself before landing flat on my face. As I glance up, the latrine door stands wide-open, and Collette is nowhere in sight. The tips of the garden plants rustle in a wave of wind. I take a moment to control my breath. With determined hand gestures, I gather up the gales and send them soaring high into the sky.

"Oya?"

I turn around to find Marie and Ellen dressed and ready to go. Disheveled and a bit off balance, I rush over to them. "Collette—"

Marie cuts me off. "We know, we can't find her anywhere either."

My throat tightens, and I well with frustration that my "almighty" powers, which I was so excited to share with Collette, are utterly pointless. They can't help us find her.

"Marie, can you find her?"

"My dear, she is like my daughter. Maybe even closer. I cannot intuit anything with so much emotion or so much attachment around it," she says without any signs of emoting.

Marie begins to teeter and sway, and Ellen catches her before she falls to the ground. We lay her gently on the grass, and Ellen places two fingers on her neck.

"She'll be fine. Her pulse is strong." Ellen sits on a rounded garden path stone and lifts Marie's head onto her lap. "She actually used to faint like this years ago, after she led ceremonies in Congo Square."

I turn my gaze to Ellen, eager for her to continue. Much like Mama, Marie seldom delved into details about her early life. Despite the silence about her past, it's clear that she commands immense respect. Whenever we ventured into town, people presented her with gifts, some even bowing at her feet in reverence. At the French Market, a vendor almost tripped over her table of wares to give Marie one of her handcrafted jewelry boxes. I think she repeated "For saving my daughter's life" in Creole, but I didn't quite understand.

Throughout my time in New Orleans, I've noticed Marie attending Catholic Mass every morning. I accompanied her once and was awed by how the priests acknowledged her presence, but the rituals left me confused and somewhat bored. Marie nudged me halfway through because I had unintentionally started snoring, drawing a few chuckles from those around us.

"That's actually where I met her, in Congo Square," Ellen continues. "It must've been 1849 or 1850, I was just heading out to California—"

"You've been to California?" I interrupt.

"Child, I live in California."

"Ellen!" the white man from yesterday calls from the kitchen door. "Is everything all right?"

"Marie just had one of her fainting spells. We need her if we are to find Collette and reverse the root. Come out here and meet Oya."

The pit in my stomach grows as I think of Collette out there on her own. My mind is protecting me with so many distractions. The white man strides toward us with a peculiar blend of nonchalance and self-assurance, not a bit alarmed by Marie's state.

"I'm Thomas." He extends his hand, delivering a handshake of unparalleled strength that leaves my palm throbbing. He smiles and looks at Ellen. "I'll be in the kitchen if you need anything."

I massage my hand as he turns about-face, just like a soldier might, and marches back into the house. I see Ellen stealing a glance at Thomas as he walks away; her cheeks blush as she looks back down at Marie. "Is he your husband?"

"Oh dear, no! My business partner. Such a kind man nonetheless."

Ellen checks Marie's pulse once again and looks back at me. "As I was saying, it must've been 1849 when I first met Marie. I was a free Negro living in Nantucket at the time, working with the Underground Railroad. It was becoming increasingly dangerous, and I was developing an irresistible urge to head out west, where it felt like the boundaries were yet to be defined. I stopped in New Orleans on my way there, and my life was transformed. I was walking in Congo Square one day, and I saw this beautiful woman standing before a huge oak tree, leading upward of three hundred Negroes in a ceremony. Everyone was wearing white headwraps, cotton skirts, and loose pants, sweating profusely. There was a large caldron steaming in the front of the congregation and, to the right, a fire with chickens and goats slow-roasting above it. The laughter, the music, the jubilation, outshone anything I had ever experienced, especially in a public square. I must've looked like a fish out of water, standing there staring at the folks in complete awe. A young man walked up to me and gave me a shot of rum. He held my hand and led me to the front, where Marie was performing miraculous healings. I saw, with my own eyes, a crippled child stand up and walk!"

Marie begins to stir, and I feel a twinge of disappointment knowing that the story is about to be cut short.

"Go fetch her some water," Ellen says as she checks Marie's forehead with the back of her palm. "And don't worry," she calls out after me, "we will finish the story later!"

I dash up the winding stone path that leads to the kitchen entrance. Gripping the handle, I swing the door open with reckless fervor, nearly slamming straight into Collette. Streaks of mud and grass stain her once pristine white cotton dress. I barely have time to collect myself as I move cautiously toward her. She holds a glass jar filled with dirt in one hand and a large rusted nail in the other.

# CHAPTER 7

In the opulent bathroom, Collette sits in the middle of the copper tub with her back upright and rigid. The tub's polished surface gleams warmly in the flickering candlelight; its clawed feet are designed with complex details, resembling the talons of a mythical beast. Large windows, covered with thick velvet drapery, enhance one wall. The burgundy curtains are drawn closed, their heavy folds blocking any glimpse of the outside world and keeping the room cloaked in intimate darkness. The only light comes from numerous candles placed strategically around the room.

Marble countertops line the walls, inlaid with delicate patterns of gold and silver. Crystal decanters filled with fragrant oils and perfumes sit atop them, their facets reflecting the candlelight in a myriad of sparkling colors. Ornate mirrors with gilded frames hang above the countertops, their surfaces slightly fogged by the steam rising from the bath.

Patches of mud from the graveyard still cover Collette's skin. I can't imagine what she was thinking while she dug through the dirt atop Cosette's grave. Marie moves gracefully about the tub, sprinkling the water with a carefully measured blend of aromatic oils, salts, and a colorful assortment of blossoms. Marie's wizened hands stir the concoction into the water, and a harmonious mix of floral and earthy notes swirls about the room. The oils glisten on the surface of the water, casting iridescent reflections that dance in the dim candlelight.

Watching her, I'm perplexed by how swiftly she's recovered from her fainting spell, especially considering her age. Nonetheless, here she is, attending to Collette as if nothing happened.

Meanwhile, Ellen adds to the ambiance with a resonant, deep hum, the sound gently vibrating in the air. Clutching a coconut shell filled with dried beans, she closes her eyes and flicks her wrists, shaking the rattle in a circle around the tub. I remember Collette using that same rattle to accompany her sister as she played the piano. Despite the combined efforts of Ellen and Marie, Collette has yet to relax and lean back into the water.

I stand awkwardly in a corner, a mere observer awaiting guidance. Uncertain of my role, I watch attentively, hoping for a cue or instruction that will allow me to contribute or participate in this ritual.

Marie starts humming the French lullaby that Collette sang to her beloved sister. Finally, Collette relaxes and leans back into the inviting embrace of the copper tub. Ellen, sensing the gravity of the moment, stands and circles the tub again, shaking her rattle to create an invisible shield of protection around Collette.

Marie turns to me and points to a large dried sea sponge hanging from the wall on off-white twine. I rush over and grab it, a bit overexcited to be included in the ritual. Taking a moment to collect myself, I inhale deeply, steadying my breath, and approach the tub with measured steps. Collette looks up at me and smiles. I freeze, and my heart seems to jump. This is her first hint of emotion since last night.

Marie gently lowers Collette's head beneath the water's surface. The lavender ripples caress her features, as if washing away any remnants of the curse. With a graceful motion, Marie raises Collette back up and reaches for a small towel meticulously folded at the edge of the tub. Tenderly, Marie dabs away the beads of water that glisten on Collette's cheeks. Then, lathering the sponge with fragrant soap, she cleanses Collette's entire body, paying careful attention to every curve and contour.

A pitcher of goat milk sits by Marie's feet in an elegantly decorated ceramic vessel. Ellen takes it and shakes the rattle in a circle around the milk, chanting a prayer. Marie squeezes out the sponge and motions for me to hang it back on the wall. I rush over and grab it, breaking the calm and controlled atmosphere in the room. Collette looks as if she is trying to hold back a laugh when we make eye contact.

As I turn to hang up the sponge, Ellen's rattle dances in the air, seemingly warding off any uninvited energies. Marie, still carefully attending to Collette's body, rinses away the soap, leaving her skin glistening like polished mahogany. Marie motions for me to come join them around the bath.

As I approach, I can feel an energy similar to what the handmaidens held me in, but now it's surrounding Collette. It is palpable. Almost physical. Ellen passes the pitcher of goat milk over the copper tub, and Marie gently holds it to her chest. With her free hand, she sprinkles a mix of herbs into it and walks over to Collette's feet. Whispering incantations, she begins to pour the milk into the bath. It cascades gently, swirling and mixing with the warm water, creating spiral patterns that dance upon the surface. Marie's movements are deliberate and elegant as she continues to pour, ensuring that every drop of the milk is carefully distributed.

Collette's eyes roll to the back of her head, and she dips deeper into the water.

"Kindly fetch Collette's clothes and towel from my bed," Marie says to me as she places the ceramic pitcher on the floor.

Like a faithful retriever, I hurry to the room and gather the garments, noticing a vat of coconut butter sitting next to the pile. I wonder if she means to share that with Collette. I know Marie is very particular about her body oils and butters. They can be very difficult to find in New Orleans, even for Marie. I was instructed to bring some for her when I came from Cuba. I scoop it up and carry everything into the bathroom, closing the door behind me with my foot.

Collette stands in the middle of the copper tub with Marie carefully giving her a final rinse with the bathwater in the ceramic pitcher. Ellen holds Collette's hand so she doesn't slip on the sleek metal as Marie fills the jug again and pours it over Collette's body. I place Collette's clothes on a high wooden stool and hand the towel to Marie.

With tender care, Ellen assists Collette out of the tub as Marie wraps the oversize towel around Collette's body, drying her supple skin and ensuring not a single droplet remains. Collette looks at me, and we can't help but laugh. Ellen and Marie smile, but their commitment to the sacred ritual remains unwavering. After they finish drying Collette's body, they take the towel and wrap it around her head. Marie's hands glide across Collette's limbs, anointing her with the creamy coconut butter. She carefully massages it into Collette's arms and legs, thoroughly rubbing her feet.

Meanwhile, Ellen picks up the pristine white cotton dress and drapes it over Collette's body, guiding it into place with utmost care. Marie unties the towel from Collette's head and tenderly dries her hair. Ellen gathers Collette's wild mane into a bun while Marie unfurls a large square of white fabric, skillfully transforming it into a headwrap. As if bestowing a crown upon a queen, Marie ties it snugly around Collette's head, the knot resting proudly above her forehead.

"Go cover your head, child, then we will be ready to go," Marie says to me as she straightens Collette's dress.

I walk back to my room feeling cleansed by the ritual as well. It was an experience unlike any I've had before. I've observed Marie caring for her patients, but this felt otherworldly, as if they reached up and snatched Collette's soul back from the brink. I wonder if the herbs that Marie used to restore my mind might not have worked on Collette, or if perhaps Marie believed that we couldn't afford the time for a slower healing process. The teas took weeks to properly work on me.

Suddenly, I hear someone retching and heaving outside. Pulling my curtains back, I see Marie regurgitating in the plot behind the garden. I watch as her fragile body constricts and contorts as she reaches for a nearby tree to hold on to. My door creaks open, and I jump away from the window.

Ellen walks in with a white headwrap and hands it to me. "I realized that you might not have one, so I brought you one of mine."

"Thank you," I say, then look back at the window. "Is she okay?"

"She doesn't do these types of healings anymore because it is so hard on her body."

I pause, considering, and ask tentatively, "What type of healing is that?"

"When Marie practices miraculous healing, instead of teaching a person how to heal themselves through herbs and such, she takes on the disease and alchemizes it in her system. It doesn't just disappear; she sucks it into her body and heals it for herself. I haven't seen her do this in years." Ellen walks to the window. "The twins are like granddaughters to her. She had quite a few children of her own, but she took to the twins like kin when she assisted their mother in birth."

I return to the window and see Marie leaning against a tree. Collette has brought her a glass of water. I watch as they talk beneath the flowered branches.

"Collette has been revived for now, but we must make haste in reversing the root. Poor child, I might've done just the same thing in her shoes, but we have seen too many misuse the power of this magic and pay major consequences. It is simply not worth it." Ellen stares out the window for a spell. "Come," she says, startling me out of our moment of silence. "Let me tie up your hair." She leads me to the edge of my bed and sits me down on the soft silken sheets. Ellen grabs my brush from the pink and white vanity and begins to collect my thick hair into a bun. "You know, this was Marie's daughter's room. Marie the second."

I'm scared to ask what has become of her. Ellen seems to intuit my trepidation. "She lives downtown. Doing work similar to her mama's. The gift passed on to her."

"How many children does Marie have?" I ask, curious to know why none of her family has visited since I arrived.

"Well, let's see. With her first husband, Jacques, she had two children who unfortunately died very young." Ellen pauses to think. I knew I'd felt that energy within Marie. A bereaved mother, just like me.

"So, there is François, the Maries, Célestin . . ." Ellen counts to herself. "She must've had at least seven with Christophe."

"Where are they? I have been here for months, and I have yet to meet them."

"Oh dear, I know Marie is very private about her life. Only the Maries survived to adulthood."

"Maries?" I ask.

"Yes, Marie-Helouïse and Marie-Philomène. There were actually four Maries. We lost Marie-Helouïse about ten years ago, so only Philomène is left."

I look toward the window, feeling a bit heavy. I had no idea that Marie had suffered such loss.

"They are not gone, child, Marie still talks to each and every one of them. Even the living one. I'm sure you will meet her soon. Marie has been quite protective of you. Your welcome ceremony was the only time she allowed the public to meet you."

As I contemplate, I realize that our only visitors have been Marie's patients. People on the street seem excited when we pass by, commenting on how they miss Marie's ceremonies. I begin to see what Ellen is talking about. Marie's morning Mass services might be her only outings. A surge of unease courses through me. *Is it really because of me?*

My heart pounds, palms sweaty, breath shaky. I feel a burst of wind rising from my belly, passing over my tongue. I walk to the window and blow it out through the trees. Marie looks up at me, her white skirt billowing in the breeze. Inhaling deeply, she seems to straighten her posture.

"Come, child," Ellen says as she folds the crisp white headwrap into a triangle shape. "There is work to be done."

I walk back over to Ellen, grinning, utterly amused by her complete lack of reaction to the sudden burst of wind that blew forth from me, as if she encounters these moments every day. I sit on the edge of the bed, and she places the base of the triangle at the crook of my neck and then wraps it securely around my head. She ties a grand knot just above my forehead, like Collette's, even though Ellen's and Marie's knots are at the back of their heads.

"Elders tie knots behind them to signify our wisdom," Ellen says to me. "Virgins tie theirs in the front to show that they are walking toward their experiences."

I chuckle. "Oh, I'm no virgin."

Ellen shakes her head, trying to hold in a laugh. "A virgin to many of life's experiences, child."

I laugh, but all of this makes me think about my baby, my Kitari. Perfection masked as a child. I remember how her silken black curls felt on my fingertips, and her smell, like lavender and chamomile mixed with a drop of vanilla. I can almost feel her weight in my arms.

Ellen's skirt flips over her head as the winds pick up in my room. I rush over to the window, and like the men slinging bags of leaves off Marie's lawn, I throw the wind outside. Sweat beads on my forehead as I walk back to Ellen. She straightens out her skirt and pats it into place.

"Are you ready for this, child? I wouldn't put you in this position if Collette didn't need you. Do you feel strong enough?"

*Do I feel strong enough?* What an interesting question. I feel stronger than ever before, but with the strength seems to come an increasing amount of sensitivity and compassion. I'm not swimming in the lake of emotions that plagued me when my daughter passed, but Cosette's death has definitely taken a toll.

# CHAPTER 8

The river harbor reeks of spoiled fish. A slight breeze flows through us, but not enough to blow away the stench. The wooden planks beneath our feet creak and groan as water splashes through the small gaps between them. It's a bustling scene as fishermen busy themselves, emptying their nets filled with catfish, bluegills, and bass. Among the catch are crawfish, their tiny claws waving as they're released from the nets. The catfish are the most curious to me, with their long goatees and smooth skin. Cosette explained to me some of the strange and new breeds of fish that live in fresh water. The bluegills, with their vibrant sapphire and green scales, shimmer like jewels as the smaller ones are released back into the water.

We are silent as the fishermen weave in and out around us, rarely even acknowledging our presence. Marie has a pouch that seems to be dripping some sort of liquid from the bottom. Collette squeezes my hand as we walk up to an empty spot on the dock.

"*E li sa?*" Marie asks.

Collette nods. Our white skirts flutter in the wind as Ellen and Marie stand on either side of Collette. I gently release her hand and turn away from the ladies, almost back-to-back with Collette, fulfilling my role as lookout and guard for this ceremony. Ellen ties a white rope around me and Collette so I can guide her home after the ritual. She has to walk backward, without turning around, in order to reverse the spell. I look toward the dock and see the men rushing around, barely batting an eye in our direction. Ellen and Marie begin to chant. My strict instructions were not to turn around, no matter what I heard. They too have to look toward the water, not at me, until the river is out of sight.

As their voices begin to swell, chanting words in an unfamiliar tongue, the fishermen take heed. I hold their gazes, their judgment, until my winds can no longer take it. Their boats begin to rock in the breeze, and the men grab their hats and secure their vessels. Buckets of their catch flip over, and the men have to tend to their duties. They seem to forget about us once again.

I hear Marie yell a phrase in Yoruba, the language my mama tried to teach me as a child. I believe she proclaimed something to the tune of: *Be gone!* She then throws something into the water. Perhaps the pouch she was holding. The rope around my waist begins to pull, and I plant my feet on the ground. *I will not turn around.*

I feel Collette behind me as she begins to shake uncontrollably; I can barely hold my ground. I widen my stance to withstand the pressure. I grab the rope and pull it slightly away from my stomach. I can feel the beginnings of a rope burn. It takes every bit of my willpower not to turn around and check on Collette. All the while, I keep the fishermen busy with the weather. I cannot risk them interrupting the ceremony and perhaps losing Collette altogether. I think Ellen and Marie hold Collette for a moment because the pressure subsides. But Collette has begun moaning and grunting as if she were giving birth. My hands shake as my walls of protection slowly erode. Collette screams in agony, and the gusts of wind pick up speed. The fishermen grab the last of their catch and run for cover. One yells out to me as he passes, "A hurricane is coming. Get yourself to safety!"

As the last man trips off the dock, I begin to take deep breaths. With each inhale, I feel my erratic beating heart calm down. The waters gradually settle, and Collette's wails soften into moans. The once bustling energy of the harbor gives way to a peaceful stillness, interrupted only by the occasional lapping of water against the hulls. The boats slowly rock back and forth, finding their balance.

My clothes stick to my body, drenched with river water. I wring the knot at the top of my headwrap, and water gushes onto the wooden planks below me. The sun peeks through the remnants of my clouds.

"Are you ready, Oya?" Marie asks.

I almost turn around to answer her, but luckily I catch myself. "I am."

I feel the pressure from the taut rope once again. They must've released Collette from their grasp. The rhythmic pulling from her deep breathing is a welcome reaction to her intense ceremony.

"I am going to start walking now," I say.

No one answers.

Slowly, I drag one foot forward, allowing Collette to find my pace and follow it. The fishermen are gradually returning; I don't want their stares, so I blow a gust of wind ahead of us to minimize the onlookers.

"Is everyone still with me?" I ask.

"Don't worry about me and Marie, we can do this with our eyes closed in the middle of the night. Collette is attached to you, so she will be fine. Just announce if you are going up or down steps," Ellen says.

The harbor is at the edge of town, so we walk only half a block before we hit the French Quarter. Ornate iron balconies are draped with lush greenery and vivid flowers. The facades are painted in an array of pastel hues—soft pinks, deep blues, and sunlit yellows. Decorative shutters in contrasting colors frame tall, arched windows. Elderly Creole and Negro ladies play cards outside a four-story building painted cornflower blue. They are all clad in their Sunday best, various brightly colored dresses with tight bodices and sizable skirts. Their chairs seem to shake under the weight of the fabric. Each woman sports an elaborately decorated hat to match her gown. One lady, holding an umbrella embellished by strings of beads and tassels, puts down her hand of cards and steals a glance my way. She taps the lady beside her, and everyone at the table turns. Without any questions, they place their cards down and rush over to us, surrounding our makeshift formation and standing guard, their oversize hats concealing Collette in the middle. I feel my nerves begin to soften and my breathing relax.

A group of children playing ball on the street stop and stare as we walk by. They run up and find places to fit in around us, helping cover Collette as she walks backward. One of them looks at me and smiles as we march. My throat begins to tighten as I try to hold back my emotions. It's too late. A whirlwind encapsulates us in the eye of her storm. We are not touched, but other people on the street are running for cover from the winds. I hear the children exclaiming in disbelief as the elders walk in confidence, as if they have seen it all before.

"Is Marie making this happen?" one of the children inquires.

"God is, child," an elder responds.

I smile to myself, feeling the love from this group of strangers. I control the squalls with my hands at my sides so no one notices. I throw the whirlwind high into the sky. As everyone is looking up in wonder, I break up the winds with my hands and send them off safely.

"Wow!" the children exclaim.

"Marie, we headed to your place?" an elder asks.

"Valerie, is that you?"

"Yes, ma'am."

"Yes, we are headed home. You know how to get there."

We walk in sacred silence the rest of the way home. The typically bustling streets are eerily deserted, likely from the erratic weather. Collette hasn't made a sound since the ceremony, but I sense her walking with me by the pull of the rope.

I see the house up in the distance. "We are almost there," I say to our protectors.

I know that Ellen, Marie, and Collette probably know exactly where we are. We stroll slowly down Marie's block. The colorful Creole cottages and elegant Victorian houses lining the streets seem to be brighter today; they remind me of Cuba. We pass under the canopy of my favorite willow. The dappling light filtering through her hanging branches paints a captivating pattern on the ground. Valerie, the elder, takes the lead and ushers us up to Marie's house. As I approach the porch, I say, "Four steps up."

The elders and the children peel away from our foundation as I lead Collette up the stairs. Marie and Ellen chant something in Yoruba once again. There is a glass jar full of water sitting next to a carton of eggs. Marie asks me to pass them to her. I grab the rope around my waist and show it to Marie.

"You can untie it now."

I struggle with the knot, and the young girl with the faded cap runs up and loosens it in no time. Her smile reminds me of my little sister Oshun's. Slightly crooked and full of mischief.

I hold the carton up to Marie, and she grabs an egg. Slowly, she passes it alongside Collette's body, rubbing it over the dips and curves, much like she did in the bathing ceremony. I notice that Collette's white headwrap is soaked, clinging to her hair, and water droplets trickle down the nape of her neck. I want to hold her, to wrap a towel around her, to comfort her. Marie nods at me to finish my task, and I quickly fetch the glass, careful not to spill the water. Marie cracks the egg into the cup, and she and Ellen stare at the tangled patterns and designs formed by the raw egg swimming in the liquid.

The ladies nod at each other.

"She is clear, Collette is free!" Ellen exclaims.

The crowd cheers, though they have no idea of the real reason for their jubilation. This is a secret that we will all take to our grave. At least that's what Marie told us. Collette falls to her knees and weeps openly on the porch. I rush up and embrace her. She smiles through her tears and wipes her eyes.

# CHAPTER 9

As I place a generous mix of herbs in the boiling pot, I notice Collette staring into the distance. After the ceremony, I'm especially attentive to her needs and state of mind. Her expression is distant, lost in thought, and I wonder what she's thinking. The aroma of the herbs fills the air almost instantly.

"What's on your mind?"

She turns to me and rubs her hands the way Cosette used to before she would play the piano. "I just wonder where my sister is. I haven't felt her since . . ." Collette pauses.

"I'm sure she is with your mom, somewhere happy."

Suddenly, Marie, Thomas, and Ellen burst into the kitchen, their voices brimming with lively conversation and infectious laughter. Collette quickly composes herself, discreetly wiping away a tear before it has a chance to escape her eye. I can't help but wonder why she continues to conceal her emotions from Marie; it's quite futile, considering Marie's abilities.

"I made enough tea for everyone," I say as I begin to pour the steaming liquid into the porcelain cups.

"Yes, please," Thomas says, and takes a seat at the long kitchen table. Ellen and Marie join him.

I arrange the cups on a silver serving tray, accompanied by a jar of honey, a pitcher of cream, and a small bowl of sugar. Collette springs into action, dashing to the cabinet to retrieve the sweet tea biscuits, which she places neatly on the tray. Thomas, ever the helpful soul, steps up behind me and offers to carry the tray to the table.

"Thank you," I reply as Thomas takes the platter, making his way over to the ladies.

I can't help being struck by how Thomas treats Ellen. It's a rare sight to encounter a white man who shows such genuine respect for a Negro. I've observed that New Orleans has a unique perspective, with French men here often valuing African, mulatto, and quadroon women as prizes to be won. They even host balls dedicated to white men finding their colored mates. While it's curious to me, I must admit I prefer it to the way whites treated us back in Cuba. Despite our efforts to establish a separate, somewhat free village there, much of the island remained under the tyranny of white men. Although the slave trade has legally ended, many Africans on the island are still owned by white families.

"Are you joining us?" Thomas asks, interrupting my reverie.

"Oh yes," I stammer as I pull out chairs for me and Collette.

I've committed to memory each person's way of taking their tea. Marie has hers straight, without cream or sweetener, while Collette likes hers with three spoonfuls of sugar, a habit she shared with Cosette. Thomas prefers honey, and Ellen, true to her versatile tastes, enjoys a bit of sugar, cream, and a dash of honey. Like clockwork, everyone absently prepares their tea exactly as I had anticipated.

Amid the laughter, Ellen's gaze falls on me as she shares her news: "I'll be departing in a week's time. I've extended my stay as long as I could, but Thomas and I need to return to our business."

I knew this moment was coming; Ellen couldn't stay with us forever. Yet I never would have predicted the ache in my heart upon hearing her plans. Marie, ever perceptive, seems to pick up on my unease. Nevertheless, I take a sip of my tea and offer a nod of understanding, all while noting that the weather remains unchanged.

"Are you staying for Mardi Gras?" Collette asks.

"Oh, we wouldn't miss it!" Thomas chimes in.

I had heard about Mardi Gras, had even seen announcements in the paper, but still don't quite understand what it is. Marie told me that she is going to have me and her daughter on the carriage float with her. I do have several questions on my mind, but it doesn't feel appropriate to bring them up right now.

"There are a few things I would like to do before my departure, and I would love for you and Collette to join me," Ellen says.

I look at Collette and smile. "It would be our pleasure."

"Great! It's settled—you will come with us to the prison."

"Wait, what?" I question.

The entire table erupts into laughter. I cautiously chuckle along with them, wondering if Ellen is joking.

"Marie's other responsibilities need some attention. She tends to the imprisoned souls. Praying for them and giving their last rites," Ellen says as she adds more honey to her oversweetened tea.

"Isn't that dangerous?" I ask Marie.

"It's actually my favorite way to give back," Ellen says as she sips her tea.

"Oya, not everyone has the support they need to make the right choices in life, and even when we do have support, people make mistakes. They don't all of a sudden become monsters once they break the law. What do you say to the man who stole the loaf of bread to feed his children?" Marie questions.

I come to a sobering realization that I might be more of a threat than the men behind bars, having potentially caused more harm than all of them put together. I halt my self-righteous thoughts and acknowledge that, without Marie's assistance, there's no telling where I'd be or the havoc I could have unleashed.

"I would be happy to help in any way I can."

"One of them will be getting their last meal. You can help me cook the gumbo," Marie says.

*Their last meal.* I can't imagine knowing my last meal. Would I even be able to eat?

"I will be braiding everyone's hair before we go. We want to keep it away from our faces when we are in the facility," Marie says as she reaches for a biscuit.

Ellen claps her hands. "Have you ever had your tresses done by the famous Marie? Hairdresser to the royals and aristocrats!"

"Oh, Ellen, hush your mouth."

"It's true, the young ones don't know how sought-after you were for balls and weddings. The white elite would book her months in advance for Mardi Gras. Why, I even saw two white women fight outside of Marie's hair salon for an appointment."

"Stop, Ellen," Marie says as she blushes.

"May I be struck down by lightning if I lie!"

Everyone stops and looks at me. Ellen covers her mouth and lets out a holler that the whole neighborhood could hear.

"Speaking of Mardi Gras, I need to pick up some trinkets to throw out to the crowd. We have official colors now," Marie says.

"What are they?" Ellen inquires, leaning over the table in anticipation.

"Purple, green, and gold. Purple for justice, green for faith, and gold for power."

"Nice! When did they decide that? I love it!" Ellen exclaims.

"Just last year. I'm having glass-bead necklaces made of the colors. Oya, you'll probably get to meet my daughter Marie there. She has taken over many of my events now."

I'm uncertain about Marie's feelings regarding these matters. It's unclear whether she has any strong emotions about Mardi Gras, the necklaces, her daughter, or the fact that she's taken on her legacy work. There is no excitement in her voice, but it doesn't convey any signs of upset either. It is as if she is simply stating facts. I've spent several months here without any family visitors, and I find myself quite eager to meet her daughter.

"Collette, can you and Oya pick up the bead necklaces from Mrs. Robinson's store? They should be ready by early afternoon."

"Yes, ma'am."

It's the first time in a while that Marie has directly asked something of Collette. Maybe she believes that Collette is ready to return to work, or that keeping her busy will offer her a distraction from her mourning.


The weather outside is splendid, a quintessential spring day in New Orleans. Though a subtle hint of humidity lingers, it's as if the sun has deftly dissipated most of the moisture. Collette and I leisurely walk down the very same street she and Cosette showed me on the night we attended Moses's speech.

"We should take the streetcar again," Collette remarks with a touch of uncertainty.

I haven't used the streetcar system much during my time here. Typically, when we need to travel a distance from our home, Marie provides us with her carriage. But I have fond memories of Cosette making me laugh on the crowded tram. I hide my giddiness inside, taking note of Collette's concern.

The steam-powered streetcar glides up; a fresh coat of paint accentuates each detail on the car. The number 127 is painted in white over a shiny green background. I can almost see a gold outline trimming the number. I peek around the train to see if the colored horse-drawn car is close behind. Collette grabs my arm and pulls me into the pristine trolly.

"But—"

Collette forces me through the doors before I can properly protest. The car is somewhat full, with a couple of free seats in various places. We begin to walk toward the available spots, and the white patrons move over and cover the seats with their bags.

"Please take a seat," the driver says, waiting to take off.

"This seat is taken," a woman says with her hand on her bag.

"You are holding everyone up!" a man shouts from behind us.

Collette grabs my hand and bolts down the aisle. She fixes herself to spit on one of the white women who blocked a seat, but I push her toward the exit. We run down the thin metal steps and jump from the car, cursing at the passengers as they drive away.

"If they only knew what I could do to them—what *we* could do to them!" Collette says as she shakes her head.

A surge of anger wells up in my gut, and my fists clench. Again, there is no change in the weather outside, but inside me it's a tempest. I look up toward the sky and exhale forcefully, releasing a massive gust of wind. The clouds above part as the squall ascends toward the heavens and vanishes into the distance.

"You should've blown them all away."

I wanted to, I really did, but I've learned about karma by watching Collette. I hope she has too.

"Cosette would've stopped me before I went on that streetcar. I'm still learning how to navigate without her guidance. I knew not to go on, but I forced us both."

The worn horse-drawn streetcar with a black star painted on the front glides to the rescue. While the stench of horse manure wafts past me, it's a familiar and even comforting smell compared to the sterile, unwelcoming ride of the whites-only tram. The rhythmic clatter of horse hooves echo on the cobblestone street as the skilled handler reins them in to a gentle halt. The driver's warm smile instantly settles me.

"Why, it's the most beautiful women in all of New Orleans!" he exclaims.

Collette blushes and offers a shy smile, her grip on my hand firm as she leads me in the car.

We shuffle into the pewlike wooden seats, collapsing into each other as the driver signals the horses to move forward, jerking us even closer together. Laughter bubbles up as we attempt to settle ourselves in the jostling tram. Collette stares out the trolley's window, still gripping my hand close to hers.

Unexpectedly, she asks, "Are you going to California?" The question catches me off guard. Why would she even think that? The idea of heading out west hadn't crossed my mind until this moment.

"No," I reply, my tone perhaps more forceful than I intended. I find myself reflecting on why her question elicited such a reaction in me.

Collette's eyes lock on mine with searching intensity. "When Ellen mentioned that she was leaving, there was an energy between you two that's hard to explain," she continues. "You have this way of gravitating toward her."

A deep ache settles in my heart as I recall that moment. It's true, I did feel a strange pull in my chest connected to Ellen, especially when she shared her travel plans, but I hadn't considered leaving New Orleans as an option. I'm silent for a moment, grappling with the realization.

"I just want you to know," Collette says, her voice gentle and reassuring, "that I will be fine. Don't stay just for me."

A lump forms at the base of my throat, rendering me speechless. All I can do is hold her close. I feel the wind begin to encircle us. I inhale deeply to regain control over the weather. Fortunately, the breezy gust from the trolley window conceals my personal storm. We both startle when the bell rings, abruptly signaling our stop.

"This is us," Collette declares as she pulls away. We try to wait for the horses to come to a halt before scrambling to our feet. The streetcar jerks to a stop as we make our exit amid the collective forward thrust of passengers.

# CHAPTER 10

The glass beads gleam brilliantly in the sunlight streaming into Mrs. Robinson's store. A crowd of onlookers is gathered around the window, transfixed by the display of faux jewels glistening in shades of purple, green, and gold. Marie has ordered hundreds of these dazzling trinkets to throw to the crowd at Mardi Gras.

Collette, enchanted by the purple necklace she holds up to the light, inquires, "Do you have a basket or a box we can use to carry these?"

Mrs. Robinson nods and scurries to the back. Her gray tresses, unruly and escaping her bun, are evidence of her bustling activity, likely spent stringing together the scores of necklaces for Marie's Mardi Gras order. Her diminutive frame darts in and out of sight as she searches for the baskets.

Collette bestows the glass jewels around my neck. She affirms, "Purple is your color."

I gently lift the necklace, the smooth beads rolling about my fingers. It truly deserves a spot in Marie's jewelry box among her treasured keepsakes.

Out of breath and a bit frazzled, Mrs. Robinson drops two large baskets on the counter. She exhales. "It seems like every krewe in New Orleans has ordered their trinkets from me, so I must get back to work. I hope Marie is pleased."

"She will be," I say, still holding the purple beads around my neck. "What's a krewe?" I whisper to Collette.

Collette answers as she and Mrs. Robinson place the necklaces, separated by color, into velvet pouches that match the hue of the corresponding jewels. "They are the different groups that host Mardi Gras events, like masquerade balls and floats in the parade. They each have a particular item that they throw to the crowd."

"And it seems like I'm making all of those items this year," Mrs. Robinson adds with a chuckle. "That should do it," she says as she places the last necklace in the pouch.

"*Mèsi*," I say as I gently put the velvet bags in the baskets, careful not to crack the glass beads.

"They are stronger than you think," Mrs. Robinson says as she witnesses my attentiveness. She continues, "By God, they will be thrown out to the mobs, they better be durable." She laughs to herself.

We attempt to pick up the baskets from the counter, but they are heavier than we think. Collette helps me readjust the handles so they can fit around my shoulder. Much better. I do the same for her and we are off, heaving the weighty baskets out of Mrs. Robinson's store.

As we start down the street, we both lean to the left, trying to compensate for the loads we are carrying on our opposite shoulders. I turn to Collette, searching for any uneasiness. The only sign of distress is her strain to lift the basket.

"Ladies! Ladies," a man hollers as he rushes over. "Let me take those for you. Where are you headed?"

Before we can protest, he swoops in and grabs our baskets with ease. He throws them around each of his shoulders and smiles. Both Collette and I freeze. He may be the most captivating man I have ever laid eyes on.

"Ladies?" he repeats.

His smile seems to twinkle with anticipation as he awaits our response. He stands at least a foot taller than I, and his smooth brown skin reminds me of my mother's and Obatala's. Small holes dot the sleeves of his shirt, revealing glimpses of the muscles beneath.

Collette giggles and doesn't say a word. I clear my throat. "Mister, we are headed for the tram to the French Quarter."

"I'll take you there. You new in town? I haven't seen you around," he says as we head toward the streetcar stop.

"Somewhat. I've been here a few months, but Madame Marie keeps a pretty close eye on me." For heaven's sake, why am I blurting out all of my business?

The gentleman looks at Collette and seems to recognize her. "Marie . . . Marie the voodoo queen?"

"Yes," Collette says.

"I didn't recognize you without your sister," he says to Collette, then looks like he wants to swallow the words he so haphazardly let escape his lips.

Collette is silent.

"I am so sorry," he says.

Collette forces a smile and turns away, still matching our strides.

"I am Shango. *Se yon plezi pou m fè konsans ou,*" he says in Creole as he readjusts the heavy baskets on his shoulders. "Oh, pardon, it's a pleasure to meet you," he repeats in English, seeing the confusion on my face.

A sudden, intense jolt courses through my soul, as if a lightning bolt of memories and emotions has struck me. I'm overwhelmed by thoughts of my baby and her father, Ogun. It's a sensation that I remember feeling when I first met him, a connection so powerful it felt like destiny. Strangely, since arriving here, I haven't thought of him once. It's like he never existed; like there's been a barrier, a block, preventing me from thinking of him. My hands begin to tremble, and I'm caught off guard by the intensity of the emotions flooding back.

In the midst of my inner turmoil, Collette rushes over and takes hold of my arm. I hadn't even realized that she was paying such close attention.

"This is Oya, she's staying with us for the time being," Collette says, rescuing me.

"Oya, what a beautiful name. What does it mean?"

My voice a little shaken, I answer, "I'm not certain. It came to my mother in a dream."

He flashes his twinkling smile again, and the lightning returns. "I'm sure Marie didn't mention it, but my father and I build her float for Mardi Gras every year. I've been helping since I was a child. If you want, I can come pick you up tomorrow and give you a sneak peek of the float."

"I'm not sure Marie would like that."

He stares into my eyes, and it's as if everything around us disappears. I gasp to catch my breath, and Collette moves in closer to steady me.

"I would love to see you again," he says, just above a whisper. Shango places the baskets down and turns toward the street. "If you like, I can wait and help bring the baskets into the streetcar."

"Why, thank you," I say with a slight Southern drawl. *Where that came from, Lord knows.*

Collette covers her mouth in an attempt to conceal her laughter. Simultaneously, with her other arm, she holds me in the same comforting way she used to during my flashbacks. I sense her sending me both energy and physical support. In that moment, it's as if I can almost feel Cosette on the other side of me as well.

I take a deep breath and try to communicate like a regular person. "Shango, what does the float look like?"

"I don't want to ruin the surprise. Please can I call for you?"

"I'm pretty sure we will have to do some chores to prepare for Mardi Gras again tomorrow. Maybe we can meet you then. Are you far from here?" I ask.

"I know where his workshop is," Collette interjects.

"Then it's a date," he says as he tries to conceal his excitement.

"I think if we say early afternoon, that would be the best prediction," Collette says, again with the same sneaky excitement that she had when we went to see Moses speak.

The trotting horses pull up with the black star trolly. Shango turns toward me and takes ahold of my wrist. I am startled by his forwardness. He leans in and kisses the top of my hand with such tenderness that I can feel tingles shimmy from all my extremities into my lower belly. I shift a little to shake them off.

"I have so much to say, but I'm too much of a coward to tell you now. Maybe I will have more courage tomorrow," he says with such confidence that I can't believe his claim of cowardice.

Shango swings the baskets over his shoulders and leads us to the door of the streetcar. Our trusty driver greets us with a wide smile.

"Good day, Monsieur Dougé," Shango greets the driver.

"And what a great day it is to have these ladies in my car once again," the driver says with a full belly laugh.

Shango walks in and places the large baskets on two empty seats in the front. "You are all set. I will see you tomorrow," he says as he backs down the metal steps.

My hands begin to shake so violently that Collette rushes me to our seat before I can say a proper goodbye. As we sit down, I realize that my legs and my arms are trembling as if my body were freezing. My breath quivers as I look at Collette in desperation. We hear the wind howling from afar, and the rain begins to pound on the tin roof of the streetcar.

"*One . . . two . . . three.*" I try to do my counting exercise to keep myself present, but my attempt is futile.

*N*

The warm sand covers my feet while I bathe in the sun at my favorite secret cove. My pregnant belly glistens in the sunlight as if I just rubbed coconut oil all over it. Ogun is in the water, splashing about like a child.

"Come in! The water is perfect."

My belly is so big that it's hard to figure out a way to get up. *I remember this now, I remember all of it.* Ogun rushes over and helps me up. He kisses my belly, my neck, my cheeks, then pulls me in for a peck on my lips. My stomach is like a huge wedge between us, and I can't help laughing.

"I hope she has your smile." Ogun always knew that Kitari was a girl.

He takes my hand and slowly guides me into the bright blue waters. *I want to stay here with him, when I thought my life was perfect.* He knew everything about me and loved me anyway. We float out to the tip of the rock that conceals my secret cove. My belly helps me float as he treads water beside me.

There is a weight hovering over me, a sense of anticipation for what's to come.

*This is when he tells me . . .*

"I have to go away," he says with such heaviness.

I am silent. I knew this was a possibility. Whenever there was a threat of war, the Spanish would call upon him. My stomach tightens a bit more intensely than usual. My arms freeze.

"Are you all right, my love?" Ogun swims closer to me and holds me up.

"Dear God!" I can barely yell from the mounting pain in my stomach.

The clouds gather above and unleash a burst of rain upon us. Ogun wraps his arm around my chest and quickly swims us back to shore. As we reach the sand, he lays me at the edge of the water, the rain continuing to pour down around us.

"This is all natural. Our baby is coming."

"It is not natural!" I yell. "You are leaving us."

It hurts too much to cry. The rain pours down on us as I squirm in pain. Suddenly, just as quickly as it started, the pain disappears. I take a deep breath while I can. The clouds dissipate a bit as I turn around to Ogun, who is holding me from the back.

"Let's get you to your mother," he says as he helps me to my feet.

We leave our soaked blanket and picnic basket and rush out of the cove before the pain returns. *I don't want to do this again!* We've almost reached the road before my next contraction hits. I double over in pain.

✗

"Quickly, get the drenched towel!" I hear Marie yell.

I gasp for air and sit up straight in my bed.

"She's back!" Collette shrieks as she wraps her arms around me.

Marie, Thomas, Ellen, and the handmaidens fix their gazes on me, frozen in their tasks. Ellen pours tea with a steady hand while Thomas holds a damp towel, poised for action. The two handmaidens stand at attention, ready to carry out any instructions.

"I thought this was over," I lament. "I thought I was healed."

I sink into Collette's arms and weep. I think she signals for everyone to leave, as I hear them shuffling across the floor. It sounds like Ellen places my tea on the bedside table, and then I flinch, feeling her hand touch my back. I cling tightly to Collette until the door closes. Gently, I pull away. "I can't believe this is happening again."

"You're okay," she says.

"I'm definitely not. My mind just took me back to the worst possible memory that I have. One I didn't even remember until now!"

"Maybe it's because you have healed so much that you are now ready for it."

I shake my head. "I don't know."

Collette reaches over and picks up the tea from the table. The familiar smell makes my stomach churn; I forgot how bitter it was. I take the tea and blow on the surface. The steam curls up, looking dangerously similar to the clouds in my flashback.

"How did you get me to the house? Did I cause a big storm?"

"A few kind people on the tram lent a hand, thank God. The rain stopped as soon as you blacked out. One man helped me with the baskets while another literally carried you home. I was hoping you wouldn't wake up in his arms!" Collette covers her mouth and giggles.

"That would've been a disaster." I join her in laughter. Taking a small sip of the rancid tea, I shake my head and ask, "Can I tell you something?"

"Anything," Collette responds as she scoots closer to me.

"I completely forgot about my first love in Cuba, Kitari's father. I had absolutely no recollection of him until I met Shango. I mean, we were set to get married, but he was called off to war. How could my mind do that?"

"We have countless ways to protect ourselves. You have been healing from some serious pain. Maybe you could handle only one heartbreak at once," Collette consoles.

"I can't believe that I'm right back where I started."

"No, that's not true. You are healing. I can feel it. Just be gentle with yourself."

I slowly take another sip of tea. While I don't feel as if I'm doing better right now, I understand what she is saying. My mind wanders, thinking of Shango's muscles as he lifted our baskets. "That Shango . . ."

Collette smiles. "He is something."

"I feel strange talking about him when I just recalled Ogun. But it's really only because of Shango that I remembered. Something in me awakened when Shango looked at me, the same way it did with Ogun." I pause. "I don't think I can see him tomorrow."

"You know what's best for you," Collette says, but I can feel her yearning for me to go, like she wants to live through my actions.

I notice that she is sitting directly under the large painting of the Black Madonna.

"Do you want to know something else?" I ask her.

"I want to know it all." Collette smiles as if she's about to hear the juiciest town gossip.

"My mama is like the Black Madonna."

"How?" she asks.

"Obatala was the only child conceived while my dad was alive. As my mom would tell it, my father visited her in her dreams. That's how my sister and I were conceived."

Collette's eyes widen.

"The town shunned her because they thought she was sleeping with their husbands when she was pregnant with me. No man was ever found coming or going from our property. Mama never brought another man into her bed. She swears that I was conceived in a dream. I thought she was crazy until I heard the story of the Madonna. People shunned her as well, but she gave birth to Jesus."

"So, are you saying you're—"

"Oh, I'm definitely not!" We laugh again.

I'm not sure how we turned this conversation into humor, but I have never shared that secret with anyone. I feel light. I feel welcomed and, for once, normal. I realize, in that moment, perhaps there isn't just one instant when we wake up healed. That each day is a journey toward it if we try. Some days I'm the midwife and other days I'm the one laboring. Just yesterday I was making Collette tea, and now here she is, helping me. I wrap my hands around the warm teacup and take a sip, careful not to swallow the loose bits of herbs.

Collette reaches over and gently removes the purple glass-bead necklace from my neck. "It is indeed durable," she says as she hangs it up on my vanity mirror, "just like you."

# CHAPTER 11

As anticipated, Marie beckons me and Collette to run errands for Mardi Gras. Curiously, she shows no hint of apprehension regarding my recent episode. Strangely, this lack of concern acts as a balm to my frayed nerves, encouraging me to return to the rhythm of daily life. Marie has prepared a batch of my tea for me to sip throughout the day, and my chores have been delegated among the staff.

"We need sugar, flour, powdered sugar, butter—what else?" Marie asks. "Ellen is making beignets for Mardi Gras, and we need to make the gumbo here before we go to the prison tomorrow. They only let me use the kitchen there to reheat, not cook. Collette, you know all of the ingredients for that?"

"Yes, ma'am," Collette says a little too eagerly.

Marie squints in her direction, then shrugs, seemingly brushing off suspicion because she doesn't have the time or energy to deal with it. I'm of the mind that Marie knows just about everything we are thinking. I scuttle over to Collette and grab one of the large baskets for the market.

"We have to cook the gumbo tonight, get moving. *Tout suite,*" Marie commands.

Collette and I trip over each other's feet as we hurry to the door. Marie never rushes us, so it feels urgent. We almost get stuck in the doorframe as we try to squeeze out together with the baskets. Collette's eyes are so big that I try to shut the door before Marie catches a glimpse.

As soon as we get outside, Collette bursts into laughter.

"You are completely horrible at this!" I say to her as we run away from the yard.

"I am, I totally am," she says with tears of laughter.

"You know that Marie definitely read your mind."

"She was young once, she doesn't care," Collette says with a smirk.

We look at each other and squeal in anticipation and excitement. However, deep within, I'm conflicted between feelings of guilt and the inexorable pull of destiny. My stomach begins to rumble. "I don't think I can do this."

"Don't be silly," Collette responds.

"It's all too much. Remembering Ogun. Now Shango!"

Collette turns me around and stares into my eyes. "You are here to live this life to the fullest. We don't know how much longer we get on earth. If you feel for him, go get him. He is obviously a mess over you!"

"You really think so?"

"He couldn't hide it!"

Collette grabs my hand and leads me toward the streetcar stop, the handles of our empty baskets around our shoulders. The black star tram pulls up to the corner down the block.

"Wait! Wait up!" Collette yells to the driver as she pulls me in tow.

We rush over to the streetcar with our baskets wavering in the wind. I place mine on my head the way my mother used to when we went to the market in Cuba. It slips right off as I walk up the rusty metal steps of the tram. I grab it before it hits the ground.

"Are you feeling all right today, ma'am?" the driver says with a bit of concern.

The last time he saw me, I was passed out and being carried away by a stranger. I can feel the heat rising from my neck to the top of my head. I want to disappear. Collette pushes me forward and greets the driver. "She's feeling fine, thank you for asking."

I rush past him and hold the basket on top of my head again. Collette follows suit because there is no room in the narrow seats to hold the baskets in front of us.

"I think we should go see Shango first," Collette blurts out.

The rushing blood in my face has no time to settle before it begins to rise again with talk of Shango. My upset stomach rumbles, this time loud enough for others to hear. I want to run away. I want to hide from this feeling and never deal with it again.

"Oui" is all I can muster.

Collette's lips curl into a smirk, perhaps because she hears the dance happening in my belly. As beads of sweat trickle down the sides of my face, Collette attempts to encourage me. "You are going to be just fine, Oya, perfectly fine."

I stare ahead. Taking in the verdant trees, graceful horses, and kaleidoscope of vibrant colors—all to keep myself present. I don't feel an episode coming on, but extreme emotion scares me. Rightfully so, I believe. Clutching my basket tightly, I lean closer to the open window, listening to the rhythmic trotting of horses and the steady squeak of the trolley wheels. Elegant women saunter by, resplendent in their Victorian attire, with puffed sleeves and high-necked dresses in hues matching their parasols.

*Ding! Ding! Ding!*

"This is our stop," Collette says to me as she adjusts her basket. We are just one stop after our street.

"Why did we take the streetcar? We are right by our house."

Collette laughs. "It was there."

This time we remain seated until the streetcar comes to a halt. We shimmy out of the narrow bench and say "Thank you" to our beloved driver.

I can feel my mind wandering to avoid thinking about Shango. Why am I so terrified? When Mama would talk about her love for my father, all I could do was fantasize about having a love of my own. Ogun was that. Ogun had my heart. How can I give it to another?

"Don't overthink this," Collette says as she stares at me. "He's just a gentleman caller. You will probably have plenty once Marie begins to send you to the balls."

"I am not interested in that. I can't imagine prancing around for a man to pick me." I laugh at the thought. He is not just a gentleman caller. I feel it. I know it. My stomach begins to churn again.

"Take a deep breath."

I inhale. Collette steps in front of me and places her basket on the ground. She grabs mine from my head and stacks it on top of hers. She takes hold of both of my hands and looks into my eyes. "I do not want you to rush into anything that you are not ready for. You have experienced the unthinkable, losing your child. I know that I have been pushing you, but it's because I saw the spark between you two. Plus, Cosette and I have always thought Shango was absolutely wonderful. I just got overexcited."

"No, you're right. I need to live for today. Shango, here we come!"

We burst into infectious laughter. People on the sidewalk give us ample room as they walk around us with a side-eye. The ladies in the poof dresses seem to let out a "humph" as they turn up their noses and carefully step onto the cobblestone streets to avoid us. I realize that I did not dress up in the slightest this morning. I didn't think twice. My hair is a mess, and I'm wearing my kitchen apron.

"Look at what I'm wearing," I cry.

Collette begins to laugh again. "What were you thinking?"

She has on Cosette's Saturday dress, the faded pink one with flowers. As I assess her outfit, I think she must be about my size. The look on my face must've tipped her off.

"Oh, no. No. No. No."

"Come on! Please!" I beg.

"Where would we change?"

"I don't know, the alleys are usually pretty empty. We could find a place there."

"You owe me big-time," she says, shaking her head.

We grab our baskets and run to a back street. It reminds me of the alley we walked down to see Moses speak. Wooden crates are stacked up to the side of a rusted green door. I stand behind the boxes and untie my apron. I hang it on the crates and pull off my plain cream dress. The tattered edges never have been so glaring; I even spot a few holes along the bottom. Collette always looks flawless, so I know this is a serious sacrifice for her. I hand her my mangled dress, and she passes her newly pressed pink frock to me. I smell a hint of rose petals on it as I slip it over my head.

The green metal door behind us begins to rattle as someone turns the knob. I grab my apron from the carts and accidentally knock them all down. Collette grabs our baskets with her dress halfway on. We run full speed to the other end of the alley, trying to adjust our dresses midstride.

"Hey, you! Hey!" We hear someone yell as we speed away. I turn around and see a man running after us. I send a gust of wind down the passageway, kicking up all the trash and wooden carts. He shields his face and runs for cover. We can't help but laugh with our undergarments out for him to see. At the end of the alley, we turn the corner and stop to pull our dresses down.

Collette drags me back to the main street and leads me to a beautiful green area with massive trees. I recognize it as the park a few blocks away from Marie's house. Were we walking in circles?

"This is Congo Square."

I gasp. "Is this where Marie used to lead ceremonies? I never knew it was this park."

"Used to? She still does. Sometimes Marie the second takes over. They look so much alike that people confuse them. Some even say that our Marie drinks babies' blood to stay young."

"That's absurd! They don't really believe that, do they?"

"Oh, people believe all sorts of rubbish. Especially about Marie and her cer-emonies. The Christian and Catholic folk think she's the devil."

"But she goes to Mass every day. She is Catholic."

"Yes, but she is also the voodoo queen who leads all the voodoo ceremonies and activities. Even though she is the woman many of the aristocrats go to for their problems and has been a trusted guide for folks over decades, she is hated for it." Collette leads me to a bench and sits me down. "Heck, I hated her too for most of my life."

"What are you doing?" I question.

"Your hair is a mess, I'm just going to braid it."

Collette proceeds to tell me about the rumors and vitriol that Marie has had to endure amid the massive reverence. While she has healed the sick and wounded and tended to prisoners, some still believe her to be an evil, supernatural force. I feel a twinge of fear for how people may react to my own abilities and decide, in that moment, that I will never let anyone else see my powers.

"Ouch!" I exclaim.

"Hush, I'm almost done," Collette says as she pulls my hair in multiple directions.

If I had not seen how beautifully she would braid Cosette's hair, I would think she has me here to torture me. "It's a bit tight," I cry.

"I said hush up," she snaps, spoken like a true granny. "Marie wouldn't change her experience for anything," Collette continues, "she told me that. Despite all the fear and hate, she loves what she does." Perhaps she is trying to distract me from the pain.

"There!" Collette exclaims, patting my hair down.

I trace the braids on my head with my fingers. The complicated designs seem to overlap, with twists and turns all over my scalp. Collette begins to pinch my cheeks. I slap her hands away.

"What are you doing?" I yell.

"Just bringing a bit of color to your face."

"That hurt," I complain.

Ignoring my cry once again, Collette pulls me to my feet. "Stand up. Let's see the final product." She adjusts the dress and straightens it out. "Why, don't you look like a morning rose."

As if on cue, a man walking across the street whistles in my direction. I feel the blood rush to my face.

"There's that color," Collette says as she caresses my blushing cheeks. "I think we are ready! Well, at least you are." She lifts the hem of my dress on her and examines the holes.

"Thank you," I whisper, feeling the weight of so many things in my heart.

The guilt surrounding my memories with Ogun throbs like an open wound. As we begin to walk toward Shango's workshop, I have to remind myself that Ogun left me for training and battle countless times. He is married to war and was absent frequently. Even when I was pregnant.

*Breathe. Stop. Take a breath.*

I halt in my tracks and inhale deeply. Collette and I gaze upward, witnessing a dark cloud forming in the heavens. Curious, I raise my hand and circle it, discovering that the cloud mirrors my motions. I throw it farther up in the sky until it disappears into the distance.

"Are you sure you want to do this?" Collette questions as she grips her basket to her chest.

"I'm not sure of anything right now."

"*Dames!* Ladies!" We hear Shango's voice in the distance.

He charges toward us, his bare chest revealing muscles that seem to dance with each powerful step on the cobblestones. His pants are tattered and embellished with a riot of colorful paint splatters. With a beaming smile that he can't seem to contain, the whites of his teeth gleam against his vibrant, untamed spirit. Breathing heavily, he utters, "I didn't think you would come."

He regains his breath, and his smile widens as he grabs our baskets, even though they are empty. My body vehemently reacts to his presence, completely and totally without my consent. If my cheeks were not red before, they are now—although I never thought it made a difference until Collette pinched them earlier. I involuntarily lick my lips, catching myself biting the corner of my mouth. I'm tongue-tied, imagining his last name, wondering what my new signature will look like.

He runs to stand beside Collette, protecting her from the side of the street. "I hope it wasn't too hard to find," he says, attempting small talk. "I can't wait for you to see the float."

We haven't said one word since we walked up. I look at Collette; I'm sure my eyes are bulging from their sockets. Collette mouths, "What?"

I clear my throat. "It wasn't hard, Collette remembered. We have to go to the market after and run some errands for Marie."

"Great, so it all worked out," he says, leaning back so he can see me around Collette.

I blush and look forward to avoid eye contact as we turn the corner. Standing in the middle of an empty lot is a magnificent float with clouds, a golden chariot with regal, thronelike chairs, and purple, yellow, and green stars littered about the cotton billows. An older gentleman hammers some nails into the fluffy floor.

"Father!" Shango yells as he runs up to the man. "This is Oya, and you know Collette."

Composing myself, I smooth down the fabric of the rose-scented dress, wondering how the frock still smells like Cosette. Despite my attempt to regain composure, my feet feel as heavy as bricks as I take hesitant steps forward, gathering the courage to introduce myself.

Shango's father pats his hands together, dispersing into the air what appears to be sawdust. He jumps off the float and makes his way toward me. "You don't remember me?" he questions.

"I'm sorry, sir, I don't," I say, bowing my head a bit.

"I was at your welcoming ceremony at Marie's. What a feast! I walked by your altar, but you seemed quite forlorn. I didn't want to disturb you. It is an honor to officially meet you. I'm Edwin."

"The honor is mine," I respond.

I don't remember much from the ceremony; it feels almost unreal. If Edwin hadn't mentioned it, I would've forgotten that it ever happened.

"And, Miss Collette, it is always a pleasure to see your face. My condolences. It's good to see you out and about."

"Thank you, Monsieur," Collette says.

"This float, it's simply divine. Has Marie set eyes on it yet?" I ask.

"Not yet," Edwin says.

"She is going to simply die!" Collette says a bit louder than I think she intended. She quickly covers her mouth.

We all walk up to the float, transfixed by the intricacies that went into every inch of the design. I even smell a sweet oil waft by as we approach the imitation clouds. "How on earth . . ." I say as I reach out to touch them.

"It's not quite dry yet," Edwin says as he rubs his hands together once more, seemingly admiring his work with us.

Caught in a moment of awe, I notice Shango's gaze fixed upon me. When our eyes meet, his lips curl into a knowing smile, devoid of shame or embarrassment. He boldly moves closer, bridging the distance between us. It feels as if the world around us dissolves.

I inhale deeply, holding on to my breath as if suspending time. There is a subtle shift in the air, and I observe the clouds on the float quivering in response to a gentle breeze. Collette, attuned to the change, glances my way as the wind brushes against her face. Sensing my need, she skips over and holds my hand. Simply with her presence, my breathing steadies and the winds subside.

"You good?" Collette whispers in my ear.

I nod. I think I am good. I think I am really good. The winds felt exhilarating, like they were igniting a fire inside me.

Collette seems to catch on. "Do you mind if I go buy the ingredients for the gumbo?"

She had it planned the whole time; she knew she was going to pull this trick. I start to challenge her but find myself at a loss.

Collette slips away and grabs the baskets; she's down the road before I can protest.

"Do you want to walk with me?" Shango asks.

"Sure," I reply.

Racing headlong into the moment, I keep my gaze fixed on Shango as he strides toward his father to tell him that he will return shortly. My cheeks ache from smiling so hard, but I can't seem to contain my elation.

"You seem happy," Shango says as he gently places his strong hand on my lower back.

I spin away, feeling the electricity course through my bones.

"I'm sorry. I feel like I have a lump in my throat every time I talk to you—like I have so much to say that it's getting caught in my chest. I have never felt like this before."

"I understand" is all I can muster.

Much like Shango, I feel my words ensnared in my throat, struggling to escape. A subtle aura of white light surrounds him, almost like the Black Madonna painting adorning my room. *Is it a halo?* I squint, briefly closing my eyes only to reopen them. The intensity of the light has diminished, yet a faint glow lingers.

"Can I touch your hand?" he asks.

I nod, a silent agreement to whatever unspoken connection seems to be weaving between us. As he reaches for me, his pinky softly brushes against my fingers, and the familiar surge of electricity courses through me once more. This time I resist the instinct to pull away, allowing the current to linger. My heart beats with such intensity that it feels as if he might hear it. He intertwines his fingers with mine, a firm yet gentle embrace. We draw closer until our foreheads touch. I giggle and turn away, feeling a bit dizzy from the rush of emotions.

"Tell me something about yourself," Shango says.

Caught off guard, I blurt out the first thing that comes to mind. "Well, I'm from Cuba."

Before I can continue, Shango interjects. *"Bienvenida a Nueva Orleans,"* he says, looking extremely proud of himself.

*"¿Hablas español también?"* I ask, but I'm pretty sure from his broken accent that saying "Welcome to New Orleans" is his only claim to Spanish.

"That's all I know," he says with a laugh.

I almost do not hear him as he speaks. His eyes, deep pools of darkness, reflect a profound knowingness, and I catch a glimpse of my own reflection within them. There's an inexplicable sense of familiarity, as if I recall him from a time before, a connection that seems impossible yet refuses to be dismissed. This haunting feeling lingers, casting a veil of mystery over our encounter that I find myself unable to shake.

We walk into Congo Square Park and head straight to a large oak standing stark against a row of willows dancing far behind it.

"Has Marie taken you here?" he asks.

Remnants of white wax are melted on the exposed roots of the tree. There are copper coins stuck in several crevices of its bark. Multicolored candies litter the soil around the tree, and I spot a bottle of gin snuggled in a crease between two roots. The mighty branches reach far across the square, providing ample shade in the Southern heat.

"This is the ancestor tree," Shango says with great reverence. "Do you know Papa Legba?"

"No, is he your friend?"

Shango laughs. "Sometimes," he says with a smirk. "Papa Legba is who we call upon to talk to our ancestors. He is the spirit who stands at the crossroads and gives us permission to speak to the other side."

I walk up and place my palm on the bark of the mighty oak. "Have you ever really spoken to your ancestors?" I ask.

Shango looks perplexed. "Of course I have."

I think of my father. How he lifted the veil of this world to create me and my sister. How Mama has called upon him countless times when she stares out at the ocean. I think about my Kitari: Would she even know me? And Cosette: Is she my ancestor if she is not kin?

"Do you commune with family past?" he asks me.

"I never have," I say, feeling somewhat ashamed.

"Marie has not led you in ceremony?"

"We have been in ceremony, but I don't think we communed with our ancestors. It was healing ceremonies," I say, hoping I have not revealed too much.

Shango moves in, holding both of my hands close to his chest. I breathe into his support, staring into his dark eyes. His voice breaks me out of the trance.

"You will never have to go through anything like that again."

"What do you mean?" I ask.

"I don't know what happened for you to have to do a healing ceremony with the most powerful voodoo queen in the world, but I know it must've been extremely difficult. I will do anything in my power to protect you from that hurt."

My legs feel like jelly, weak and unstable, yet he holds me up. I'm torn between wanting to tell him everything, to bare my soul to this stranger, and feeling like I can't say a single word. He leads me across the park to a long metal bench, and we sit down.

"Oya," he says.

"Yes?"

"I am just saying your name. Feeling it on my tongue. Feeling it in my soul."

I see his chest muscles tighten, I think on purpose. He seems to have remembered that he is shirtless. I almost laugh, but I don't want to make him feel self-conscious. Still, a smirk sneaks through.

"Tell me something about you," I say.

"I'm really just a simple man. I like to work with my hands." He looks up and thinks for a moment. "I am very protective. I try to keep those who I love safe."

I giggle. "Me too."

My smile falls a bit; I dread telling him who I really am. I can't sit here and let him think that he is safe pursuing me.

"I'm . . . I'm dangerous," I stammer.

"I know who you are, Oya, daughter of Yemaya. You are powerful."

I feel a flare of indignation, but I don't want to fight about how dangerous I am. How many lives I've taken. How many homes I've destroyed.

"I know who you are," he repeats.

I stare into his eyes, and I feel like I know him too. His steady gaze calms my incessant thoughts. He leans in and gently caresses his lips against mine. My entire body erupts into waves of goose bumps as he grabs the back of my head and pulls me deeper into his embrace. Our bodies move as if we are in a choreographed dance, each following the other's lead into boundless pleasure.

*Bam . . . bam.* A drum echoes throughout the park.

I jump back, remembering suddenly that we are in public. A whole drum circle has formed just across from our bench, under the ancestor tree. The other drums join in, banging out an infectious rhythm.

I notice a group of women in vibrant cotton skirts, grabbing the fabric and swaying to the beat. Encircling them, a crew of drummers pounds out a throbbing beat, guiding the flow of their movements. The women shake their hips and shimmy their shoulders to the music.

"Is it a performance?" I ask.

"No, it's a ceremony. All are welcome."

I feel like the drums are calling my name, the primal pull tugging at my very core like a fish caught on a line. My back arches and my chest rises, propelling me to my feet. As I approach, the circle of women opens up, inviting me in. Their skirts fan into billowing circles of color as they dance around me. I feel as if I am on a cloud, weightless, yet I'm pounding my feet on the compacted dirt below me.

The dancers turn and salute the drummers, touching their hearts and bowing. This seems to give the musicians a wave of energy. A muscular man with a ripped shirt, sweaty and breathing hard as he beats his drum, sings out a call-and-response. *Did he just say my name?*

"Oya, Oya, Oyyyyyyaaa," the woman sing in response.

Dizziness clouds my senses, yet my feet are propelled by the pulsating rhythms, dancing uncontrollably. Raindrops patter down on the drums, merging with the frenetic rhythm, amplifying its intensity. My body shakes as I see Shango walking up from behind the crowd. I hear the loud clack of thunder, and I think I fall to the ground. *Blackness.*

# CHAPTER 12

When I wake, I find myself in the tranquil confines of my room, greeted by the comforting aroma of herbal tea wafting from a steaming cup beside my bed. Wisps of vapor twirl above the dainty teacup. My body is sore, as if I were beaten from head to toe. I gently inspect my arms and legs for any signs of injury but find none. Frowning, I massage my stiff neck, wondering what could've happened to leave me in this state.

My door creaks, and I see one of Collette's eyes peeking through the crack. She hastily tiptoes to my bed. "Oh, good, you're awake," she whispers.

"What happened?" I ask.

"You don't remember?" she says with confusion.

"The last thing I remember was raindrops falling, and I think I was spinning in a circle."

"It rained all right! I was heading back to the park to get you, with two baskets full of ingredients for the gumbo, and the rain poured down!"

"Oh dear, was it a storm? Or worse?" I question with deep trepidation.

"It was just the rain, thank God. I ran toward the park to find you and Shango, but I couldn't see you anywhere. The drums seemed extra loud. I saw a crowd of people hovering in the middle of the circle, and lo and behold, you were in the center of that group. Shango was holding you up from behind, and you were going around the circle giving people advice. Your voice sounded different. Like really low and loud."

"How could this have happened?"

"It was merely a ritual possession," Collette says with no surprise.

"A what?" I ask, even though I heard her.

"A ritual possession. Surely you have seen one. Your mother has done it, I'm positive."

"My mother always kept me away from crowds, including ritual gatherings.

She would sometimes bring a small number of people to the house to bless it, or pray for me, but no possession."

"That is fascinating, with Yemaya as your mother," she says.

I can feel her judgment. "Get on with it, instead of shaming me," I snap back.

"I'm sorry, Oya, I didn't mean to shame you. Not in the least. I was just surprised. The ceremonies that Marie leads usually end with ritual possession. They start with the drums. The heartbeat of Mother Earth. Aligning us with the rhythm of the divine. Then Marie, or another priest or priestess, does an incantation."

"What is that?" I ask.

"It's like a series of words used to invoke the spirits or energies of the invisible realm. Sometimes the priests speak in tongues so it sounds nonsensical, but you can feel the power in the prayer. Then, if we are lucky, the Orisha will come down and mount someone."

"That sounds horrifying!" I exclaim.

"Was it?" she asks.

"What?"

"You were clearly mounted in ritual possession. You were relaying the messages of the divine."

"I don't remember it all, but the dancing felt pleasurable. Light. Almost familiar. It felt like home until I passed out," I say.

"You never passed out. After you were done, the rain stopped. Shango walked us home, carrying the baskets. He refused to let us help. I knew you weren't quite present because you had this peculiar smile as you followed us home. You just stared up at the birds and the trees. As soon as you got into the house, you went upstairs to your room and fell asleep. You wouldn't even let me help you change out of your street clothes."

I am stunned. How could I have done all of that without the slightest memory?

"I didn't tell Marie," Collette says in a reassuring tone. "How do you feel?"

"I feel good. Almost rejuvenated. My body is sore, though," I say.

"You would break out into deep dance trances, moving your body and contorting your limbs. Shango wouldn't let me stop you. He thought it might be dangerous to interrupt the possession."

"That explains it," I say as I massage my right shoulder.

Collette jumps as if she just remembered what she came in to say. "Ellen and Marie are making the gumbo downstairs. Do you want to help?"

"That sounds delightful, I've wanted to learn how to make it. That's why I was excited to go to the market with you," I say with wide accusatory eyes.

Collette smiles and grabs the teacup. "Do you want any?"

"I'm good. I don't think I need it."

"Let's go, then," Collette exclaims as she jumps up and grabs my hands.

"I'm sore, remember?" I protest.

"Oh yes, I'm sorry," she says as she rubs my arms, not helping my tenderness in the least.

I'm not sure how the sun is still out; I feel as though I've already lived through three days in one. Carefully treading down the stairs, I lean much of my weight on the handrail, hoping it is sturdy. Collette gracefully slips under my arm, offering her assistance as we descend the stairs together. Though it's challenging for me to accept help, I have had to learn the importance of others lending a hand when needed. As we approach the kitchen, Collette releases her grip.

We hear Ellen and Marie laughing behind the swinging door. I slowly push it forward so they can see that we are coming in.

"Good morning, sleepyhead!" Ellen exclaims as I walk into the room.

Okra, celery, onions, bell peppers, and parsley or coriander are all chopped on one side of the counter. Shrimp, chicken, and browned sausage are on a large cutting board on the opposite end. Marie is holding a glass jar full of white flour over a pot. "You're just in time!" she bellows, as if announcing it to a crowd. She holds the jar to her chest and looks at me. "Do you know the secret to my gumbo?"

I am silent. We don't have a dish like this in Cuba. Mama's specialty was ropa vieja, black beans and rice and the richest platanos one could ever hope for. My mouth begins to water.

"It's my roux," Marie says.

"It's her roux," Ellen repeats.

There are moments when their relationship reminds me of Collette and Cosette's: finishing each other's sentences, being awfully protective, and rooting for each other in every situation. The twins rarely argued; they always seemed to support each other, even in their small differences. Collette has taken on some of Cosette's idiosyncrasies, as if they have merged in her afterlife. Not only does she wear Cosette's clothes, but she's also adopted the habit of tucking her hair behind her ear when she is thinking. Collette used to tease Cosette about that, comparing it to tucking a cloud behind a tree because their hair was so thick and curly.

"Come, Oya, I want to show you," Marie says. She gives me the glass jar and leads me over to the pot on the stove. There is butter heating in the oversize pan. "Just sprinkle the flour in and stir at the same time. It's important for it to be smooth in the beginning so we don't end up with any lumps."

Marie lurks behind my shoulder, watching my every move. She tips the flour jar a bit so more powders out. "There you go. You have to stay over the pot and whisk it almost constantly. You don't want any black specks to appear; that would mean that you burned it and we'd have to start over."

"How long do I stir it?"

"A good twenty to thirty minutes will do."

"What?" I say in disbelief, like I was tricked into this position.

Everyone laughs and Ellen shouts out, "Do you have anything better to do?"

My arms ache, but I soldier through. I'm reluctant to share what happened at the park, anticipating that the news will reach Marie and Ellen soon enough. Despite the soreness, I take on the task, feeling honored that Marie entrusted me with the delicate process. I know it was hard for her to hand over the reins. Pouring in the last of the flour, I swiftly stir, focusing on the task at hand.

"You don't have to go so fast," Marie says as she walks over to the chopped vegetables. She continues, "And check if you need more heat."

The cast-iron stove brooks no mistakes. Placing the roux on the back burner, I reach for the metal tongs to remove the cooking plate. The coals underneath glow a promising bright red, offering ample heat. Still, I seek confirmation from Marie. "Is this good?" I ask.

She wipes some excess herbs on her apron and hurries over. "It's perfect. Now get that roux back on the heat."

I drop the metal plate harder than I anticipated and grab the roux with my other hand, whipping it as soon as it hits the heat. In the process, I accidentally knock over a small glass bottle of white power on the side of the stove. I catch it before it hits the ground.

"I wish my reflexes were still that sharp," Ellen remarks, walking over to retrieve the bottle. She hands it to Marie, who examines it in the sunlight streaming through the window.

"Intact," Marie declares. She slips it into her apron pocket. I note that neither of the ladies are inviting conversation about the substance, but Collette stares at me almost as if to say, "Don't you worry, I will explain everything later."

I continue to stir the roux and notice that it is turning a light brown tint. "Is this right?" I call out to Marie.

She rushes over, her white locks frazzled and pulled into a loose bun. "You have the magic touch. It will keep getting darker, but we must make sure that there are no black specks." She looks in closely and says, "No clumps. Ellen, no clumps! I told you she could do it!"

Ellen shrugs. "It took me years to perfect my roux. That's what Marie is so rudely referring to."

They erupt into laughter again. I sense the difficulty they'll face in parting ways. Best friends living on opposite sides of the world, or at least that's what it feels like. I can't help but think of my own yearning for Mama's touch—she might as well be as far away as California. The chasm between Collette and Cosette feels even more profound. It strikes me that on the other side of every sincere connection lies the grief of separation.

"Can you guess what ingredient I put into all of my dishes?" Marie startles me with her whisper in my ear.

Ellen and Collette simultaneously say, "Love!"

The roux is beginning to resemble caramel in both color and texture. Memories flood back of Mama making sea salt caramels as gifts for our neighbors and friends. Learning to make the caramel was a family affair, as people would request it year after year. Even Obatala, when he went away to school, took a large batch with him. Now his friends demand it whenever he visits home.

"We have a busy week ahead. What with the prison tomorrow, Mardi Gras on Tuesday, and my train on Wednesday, I feel a bit overwhelmed," Ellen says, seemingly out of nowhere.

Ellen rarely reveals her vulnerability, usually appearing as strong as steel. However, in this moment, she seems to have let down her guard. Before she is able to continue, Thomas walks into the kitchen, seemingly guided by his nose.

"I hope some of this is for us!" he exclaims, his enthusiasm cutting through the somber fog of energy like a sword.

"Absolutely," Marie responds. "Ellen, you are taking a train? I didn't know that one goes all the way to San Francisco. You usually take the ship, do you not?"

Thomas answers for Ellen. "We do. But we are interested in investing in the railroad. The Southern Pacific Railroad can take us out to Texas, where we will meet with some of my associates. And then we will take the Santa Fe Railway the rest of the way. It might not be as smooth as the ship, but it will be worth our time."

"Is this a venture worth my efforts?" Marie asks as she gathers the chopped vegetables on a cutting board.

"We will investigate it and send you a certified letter if we think you should invest," Ellen says.

I still feel a pull toward Ellen as she speaks about her travels. Both Marie and Collette look at me. Is this the first time Marie is intuiting the energy? They don't say a word, but their stares catch the attention of Ellen and Thomas.

"Is the roux acting right?" Ellen asks.

"I don't think that's—" Thomas is interrupted by a shove from Ellen.

"The roux is just fine, I think. Just fine," I say.

"Oya, did you know that my mother was from Haiti?" Ellen asks. I can tell a wisdom story is coming. "She came from a long line of voodoo queens. My grandmother, my great-grandmother, and I assume all the women before that. I only got to have my mother for five years in this life. The one thing she told me every day was to trust my inner voice above all the other noise in the world. I can almost hear her saying it. She had a heavy Haitian accent, but she tried to speak only English with me."

*What is my inner voice saying? I don't hear anything.* Can she feel my pull to go with her too? I don't hear a voice but a sensation: a part of me that feels like the next natural step is to go out west. *But what about Collette? And Shango?* What about this connection that we are forging?

Everyone is staring at me, waiting for an answer. I continue to stir the roux, wanting to run, wanting to hide.

"I don't know if I have an inner voice," I say.

"You can't keep running from your power, Oya. Your mother sent you here to develop it. You have learned to control your winds, for the most part, but you do not give yourself enough credit. You have an inner voice, even if it is not speaking with words," Marie says, lovingly scolding me.

They are waiting; even Thomas seems to be at the edge of his seat.

"I have felt an inexplicable pull to go with you, Ellen. But I am not well. I am not cured. I am still learning and healing. I was just getting accustomed to being here. How would I tell my mother that I am even farther away from her? How could I leave Marie and Collette?" I cry.

*How could I leave Shango?*

"All of those things matter not in comparison to your inner guidance. That is your voice. As much as we want you here, that is not up to us. Furthermore, if you are alive, then you are healing in some way. It doesn't ever just end," Marie says in a softer tone.

Ellen can't seem to contain her excitement. "We have plenty of room in the mansion for you."

This is all moving too fast. I stir the roux absent-mindedly, overwhelmed by possibility and the fear of change, again.

"You don't have to make up your mind right now, just know that the invitation stands. We would be honored to have you in our home," Thomas says, bringing a sense of peace to the situation.

Collette has been silent during the whole exchange. She has already given me her blessing, but this won't be easy for her.

Marie walks over to the pot and looks into it. "It's perfection. On your first time!" she exclaims as she removes the pan from the hot plate and places it on the back burner. Next she pulls out her large gumbo pot from the cabinet beneath the counter and places it on the stove. We are all captivated by her every move. She takes what looks like some sort of broth in a large glass pitcher and pours it into the pot. "Collette, can you bring me the vegetables?"

Collette hurries to the cutting boards that hold the okra, celery, onions, bell peppers, and parsley—or is that coriander? Marie adds the vegetables to the pot.

"Is that parsley or coriander?" I ask as she scrapes the last of the vegetables off the wooden cutting board with a large knife.

"It's parsley, my dear. And the okra is optional, but I add okra to everything," Marie says with a chuckle.

A rich aroma has already taken over the kitchen, and Marie has barely started. She grabs the infamous roux and scoops it into the pot with the broth and vegetables and begins to mix the ingredients together.

"Come stir this for me, Oya," she demands.

I rush over and take the large wooden spoon from her.

"If you see foam—oh, like that." Marie grabs the spoon back and scrapes the foam from the top of the liquid and flicks it into the basin on the counter. She gives me the spoon again. "If you see any more foam, just remove it."

As I stir the pot, Marie sprinkles in a variety of spices and salts. The savory smell continues to intensify.

Thomas walks toward the door. "My mouth is watering so much right now that it almost seems offensive."

We all start laughing. Ellen walks him out the back door and turns around. "He needs to take a walk until we are done here."

I could've sworn that I saw her tap his buttocks as he left.

"Ellen, can you start the rice?" Marie asks.

Ellen rushes back, snatching the five-pound bag of rice from the food cabinet. She measures out a few cups and drags the bag back into the small pantry. Meanwhile, Marie takes the browned sausages from the counter and adds them to the mix. She pours in the chicken and shrimp, then takes the spoon from me and stirs everything together. Lifting the wooden ladle, she blows on the gumbo and steals a taste. She closes her eyes. "We need a little garlic and black pepper, then we are done."

Collette is prepared with chopped garlic in a clay bowl. "It's always more garlic, always," she says with a smile as she passes by.

I grab the pepper grinder from the table and stand guard behind Marie as she adds the garlic. The kitchen is thick with the dance of aromas swirling with each other. I'm almost full from just the smells.

"Pepper," Marie says, and holds her hand out behind her.

I pass it to her like a baton in a relay race. She grinds the pepper in. We all hold our breath while Marie goes for another taste from the wooden spoon. *"La perfection,"* she says as she licks her lips.

"Fit for a last meal," Ellen says, reminding us of the significance of this moment.

Marie prays over the gumbo, then covers it with a heavy iron plate. "We will let it simmer, let the flavors mature." She can sense our disappointment but doesn't waste her breath.

Ellen and Marie lock arms and stroll out the back door, into the rays of sun peeking through the grove of trees behind Marie's garden. How is it still shining? It must already be evening.

Collette looks at me, trying to hold her tongue, but, as usual, she can't. "Do you know how close you were to your own death?"

"What are you on about?" I ask.

"That bottle you almost crushed was poison!" Collette reveals with wide eyes. "Why in the world would Marie have that in her kitchen?"

"You mustn't let on to anyone. Not a soul," she demands.

"Cross my heart and hope to die," I say while drawing an X over my chest.

"This will truly be the man's last meal. If prisoners request this mercy from Marie, she grants it. It saves them from the fear and humiliation of a public death."

I gaze out into the backyard where Ellen and Marie sit on a bench surrounded by the bountiful garden. The more I learn about Marie, the more I'm in awe of her. She's not afraid to get her hands dirty, dedicating herself to caring for the forgotten children of the world. While I can't fathom her intentionally harming anyone, there's an undeniable sense that this situation is different.

"Oya," Collette says.

I turn to her.

"Will you visit?" she asks with tears welling up in her eyes.

Everyone seems to know something that I don't, or something that I'm avoiding. I truly haven't made any decision to go with Ellen to California.

"If I do end up going, I will write you a letter every week. And you must come visit me in San Francisco! Can you imagine that?"

"I heard the streets are paved with gold," she says with a wink.

This moment is golden. This moment I will never forget.

# CHAPTER 13

I wake to the vibrant crows of a rooster, its morning song echoing through the narrow streets of the French Quarter. The air carries a subtle chill, and I pull my quilted blanket snugly over my shoulders. I lie in bed, gazing up at the canopy, not quite ready for the day.

I turn my head and see a tiny black spider traversing a small crack in the wall next to me. The house, usually abuzz with activity at this hour, is oddly silent. Missing are the noises of the servants scurrying about the house preparing breakfast or readying Marie for Mass.

Sitting up straight, I think of the day's plan to visit the prison. As I move to get out of bed, a handwritten note catches my eye. I accidently swipe the letter with my sheets, and it flutters from my nightstand, gently falling to the ground. In my rush to grab the note, my outstretched arm nearly sends me tumbling. Instinctively, I grasp the sheets for stability, and to my surprise, they offer an unexpected support. With cautious steadiness, I reach for the note.

The words on the paper bear the unmistakable elegance of Marie's handwriting. "Dearest Oya," it begins. "As a result of your recent spell, we have decided that you need your rest. We went to the prison and will be back midafternoon. Enjoy your solitude. With deep love, Marie."

While I looked forward to helping them, I must admit that I feel a sense of relief. The thought of giving a last meal had terrified me, keeping me awake with unease. Grateful, I lie back in bed and sprawl my arms out. Thoughts of Shango flood my mind, and I feel as if I've been granted permission to follow my heart, if only for a day. I must tell him about the possibility of my departure for California. My chest tightens at the thought of breaking this news. The curtains beside me flutter, and I sense my winds beginning to grow. Without hesitation, I walk to the open window and release my squalls into the sky. I feel proud as I truly recognize my newfound ability to control my powers. What once sparked great anxiety and destruction now has a simple remedy. I am growing. I am healing. Just as Marie said.

Still, every day I think about my Kitari. There has not been a moment when she hasn't crossed my mind, though I've refrained from speaking about her. Words hold no power to bring her back. I wonder how healthy I really am, but Marie sees deeper than my facade, I'm sure of that. She sees into me. I can feel it.

The doorbell rings.

*Who could that be at this early hour?* I grab my heavy maroon robe and drape it over my flowery nightgown, which seems a bit transparent from the wear and tear. I hurry down the stairs, my bare feet picking up loose specks of dust from the hardwood floor.

I open the front door, and my heart nearly lunges out of my chest. Shango stands with a dozen purple lilies. *"Mademoiselle,"* he says as he hands me the blooms.

I attempt to fix my hair and fold my robe tighter over my chest. "I wasn't expecting you," I say, reaching for the flowers. The scent of the lilies wafts past me, settling my nerves. "Come in." I stand to the side and motion for him to enter.

I guide Shango into the kitchen, steering us past the living room, where I haven't stepped foot since Cosette's murder. There's a stain that lingers, more evident than the physical one. Ellen bought Marie a new carpet, woven in Egypt and brought in on a trade ship. It's exquisite, with minute details that play into the overall design. Still, I can't bring myself to go into that room.

"Oya." His deep voice rumbles through the kitchen.

I realize that I'm not used to such a masculine presence in this house. Thomas has been here, but his voice is much more subdued, just like his presence. Shango cannot be muted. He looks as if he dressed up for me; none of his clothes have paint on them. Cream linen pants with a light brown button-up shirt that fits tightly on his chest.

"I can't stop thinking about you," he confesses. "It feels like a sickness. I think I'm supposed to enjoy this process, but I feel a bit unsteady. I work on the float; I think of you. I eat my dinner; I think of you. I walk on the street; I think of you."

I can't help but giggle. The torture is evident on his face. He joins in, timid at first, and then relaxes into the joy.

"I have been considering you too," I say in a tone that's a bit more somber than his.

Shango looks up, reading into my energy or my words, I can't decipher, but he feels something.

"Considering me in what? A decision?" he asks with some defensiveness.

"I have been through some very difficult times. My mother sent me here to heal. To get better. Not to stay forever."

"But things change," Shango says as he leans in closer. Face to face.

I've forgotten my train of thought. Waves of passion and stimulation cascade through my body. My eyes close, and my chest arches forward. Shango steadies me with his strong hands on my head and lower back as my body responds to these sensations. He caresses my hair. "Can I kiss you?"

His words join an amalgamation of my emotions, and I hear my voice say "Yes."

As his lips press into mine, a bolt of electricity hits me from the top of my head down to my toes. I almost pull away because it feels so real, almost painful. I know good and well that lightning did not strike me as I stand in Marie's kitchen, but my body is shaking. Shango holds me up as he tenderly bites my lower lip.

*N*

I pull away from our kiss and gently open my eyes.

"Ogun!"

"Why are you so surprised?" Ogun questions.

"Ogun, is that truly you?"

"What has gotten into you, Oya?"

I look down and I see my extended belly; I must be about five months preg-nant.

"Ogun, do you trust me?"

"With all of my heart, you know that," he says as he caresses my face.

"Things are not going to turn out how we think," I whisper, placing my hand on my stomach, hoping to feel Kitari kick.

"What are you saying?"

I want to tell him everything, but I don't think I'm supposed to. I can see it in his eyes that he has no capacity for the tragedy that befalls our young lives just months away from now.

"Things aren't going to work out how we think, they are going to be better," I say, knowing it's far from the truth.

Ogun bends down and lifts up my cotton dress to reveal my bump. He kisses my stomach from the top to the bottom. A tear gently rolls down my cheek and falls on his locks. He has no idea of the heartache, the sheer horror, that awaits us.

"We will be together forever," he says as he rises and wipes the tears from my eyes.

He reaches in and presses his full lips against mine. My body softens, tingling sensations emanating from every touch. I forgot how heightened my senses were when I was pregnant.

Ogun lifts me up and takes me into our bedroom. He lays me on our starched cotton sheets and kisses my thighs. I don't want to stop him. *I don't want this to end.* I grab on to the sheets and hold on to the feeling for as long as I can.

*N*

I pull the blanket over my head. Soft kisses flutter on the back of my neck. I turn slowly, holding the sheets in place like a canopy. Shango gently outlines my face as if committing it to memory.

"Shango?"

I look down at my naked body. Marie's silken sheets hover above us in my bed. Shango slowly pulls the covers down, tickling my skin; goose bumps rise on my back. My mahogany skin glistens in the sunlight.

Our breathing becomes heavy as he pushes in closer to my body, firmly massaging me from my lower back to my thighs with his strong hands. Beads of sweat decorate our pores, and I know that I have already shared myself with him. My whole body shivers, and, without me saying a word, Shango knows that I want him again. He has no idea that I can't remember the first time.

We lock eyes and he slowly takes me. The room seems to disappear around us, and our bodies begin to glow like the light of the stars. I hold on to him, feeling the connection of lives past, knowing that we have been together before.

"I remember too," he whispers in my ear.

As he pulls away, our skin has the glow of the fireflies that light up the night air.

"What is happening to us?" I ask.

Shango flashes a knowing smile. "Whatever it is, it's divine."

I try to wipe the glow off his skin, in disbelief of what I'm seeing. Shango cradles my hand and brings it to his lips.

"I'm not sure when Marie will be back," I whisper.

I'm not even sure how long we have been under these covers. Shango kisses my cheek and jumps out of the bed. He rummages about the room and collects his clothing in haste. His pants stick to his sweaty skin, making it hard for him to pull them up. I reach over and help him.

"I have some last-minute adjustments to the float before tomorrow, so I can't come back tonight," he says, kissing my lips and sending my body into pleasure again.

Barely able to form words, I say, "Marie will be here anyway. I'll see you to-morrow."

I want to say "I love you," but I don't—and neither does he.

"You are perfection," he says, grabbing his shirt. "I will see you tomorrow."

He runs out of the room and down the stairs before I can even think of saying another word. Pools of tears blur my vision. I use my sheets to wipe them.

"I love you," I say, just above a whisper.

I know that he can't hear me. My throat constricts, and my heart jumps as he closes the downstairs door. Thinking of both Shango and Ogun, I hold my heart and lie back down. I take a deep breath, fully stepping into this present moment. My heart belongs to Shango. I can't go to California now.

# CHAPTER 14

A jester, clad in a vibrant green, purple, and yellow hat with bells swaying from the tips, leaps in front of my face and lets out a hearty laugh. The scent of the alcohol on his breath is so thick that it nearly intoxicates me. Five different bands play second line music just on our corner alone. The streets teem with hundreds, perhaps thousands of people, transforming the neighborhood into chaotic merriment.

The float that Shango and his father crafted for Marie stands stark against the crawling mobs of onlookers. It is quite majestic, perched like a heavenly centerpiece in the middle of the drunken madness.

"Oya," Marie calls from the golden throne on the chariot, "come meet my daughter!"

Hastily, I clutch the hem of my cumbersome dress and weave through the buzzing crowd, heading toward the rear, where the metal stairs are positioned. The thoughtful placement of hanging lanterns throughout the float heightens the angelic atmosphere.

Ducking under one of the fiery lamps, I walk up the metal stairs and find myself behind Marie. She turns around, and to my surprise, she looks about thirty years younger and full of life. I think it must be from all the makeup or the excitement until I hear a voice from behind me say, "So, you've met."

I spin around, completely confused. They are identical in dress and appearance.

"It's the famous Oya, daughter of the beloved Yemaya. Mother has been keeping you on a tight leash," Marie II says with a wink. She sways her hips as she maneuvers around the clouds to the other golden chair. "Am I worthy enough to meet her now, Mama?"

"Meet Marie-Philomène, most people around here know her as Marie the second."

Resentment colors her snobbish smile, and she fans her petticoat around and lowers into her seat. The crowd roars at the sight of her, and she gifts them with a dainty wave, just rotating her wrist with her hand slightly cupped. Marie walks up behind her, her dress nearly ripping the makeshift clouds from the ground.

"Oya, you will sit in the chair behind us," Marie says.

Slightly elevated, and surrounded by lit lanterns, is a purple throne festooned with golden glitter. The craftsmanship is exquisite: Shango and his father even carved swirls of wind into the frame of my chair. I trace the designs as my heart begins to swell. One red rose lies diagonally on my seat. I pick it up and hold it to my heart, looking around the crowd for any sign of him. I jump, realizing that I've scratched my chest with a thorn. Wiping the blood before it drips on my dress, I press on the small wound with my finger, then place the rose in a vase fastened to the floor next to my chair.

Marie settles down beside her daughter, and a collective gasp ripples through the crowd. They whisper among each other, their wide eyes fixed on the mesmerizing pair of Maries. Collette mentioned to me that people often get the Maries mixed up; I wonder if this is the first time they are seeing the two together.

My dress, slightly less extravagant than theirs, bears the markings of French royalty. Like my chair, I am clad in different hues of purple. My waist is tightly encased in a whalebone corset. Even if I wanted to take in a deep breath, I wouldn't be able to. Before I left the house, Ellen swathed an exaggerated headwrap on my crown that is at least two feet high. I hold it in place as I climb the stairs to my throne, and the people's cheers crescendo into an overwhelming roar.

"They like you," Marie II says with a laugh. "Throw out the necklaces to them!"

"What?"

Marie II points to the basket next to me, and I see a large pile of the glass-bead necklaces from the shop. Before me, Shango runs to the front of the carriage float and pushes the crowd away from the two black stallions secured to the platform. I gasp, and my heart begins to thump even more intensely, with my corset pushing my breasts nearly up to my neck. My mouth opens to catch my erratic breath, but I have no room to hold it.

"Oya! Throw the beads!" Marie II shouts above the chaos.

I reach into the basket and grab a handful of the beautiful glass-bead necklaces. The mob begins to jump up and down to the second line music with tubas, trombones, and trumpets. They throw their hands in the air and start yelling at me. A young woman on my side of the float cups her hands around her mouth and hollers, "Over here!"

A group of people, dressed in colorful circus costumes with ceramic masks, rush toward the woman as soon as they see me poised to throw her a necklace. They reach their hands out, clamoring for the dazzling trinkets. Not far behind the crowd, a stream of fire blasts into the air. The streets are lined with performers— acrobats, jugglers, and fire-eaters—blowing flames out of their mouths! Vendors sell an array of treats from pralines and beignets to savory gumbo and jambalaya. Above the music, I hear the crowd screaming for me.

"Throw those necklaces out before they start raiding the float!" Marie II shouts.

Shango and his father hop onto the driver's bench and rile up the horses. Edwin pulls out a large conch shell just like the ones I used to collect in Cuba. He holds it to his lips and blows it, and a deep resonant sound hovers above the mix of cheering and brass music. The man riding the horse in front of us begins to blow his conch shell, seemingly signaling to the riders ahead to start the parade. Past where my vision can see, I hear the orchestra of conch shells communicating with each other until all the horses slowly begin to trot forward.

Marie and Marie II throw necklaces out to the crowd. Street corners and squares become impromptu dance floors where people twirl and gyrate with abandon. The sounds of drums, trumpets, and banjos echo through the neighborhood. Elaborate floats, adorned with vibrant decorations, flowers, and intricate papier-mâché figures, move slowly down the cobblestone roads. Masked riders in fantastical costumes throw beads, coins, and trinkets to the cheering crowds below.

Collette runs up to the side of the float and jumps onto the platform. Sitting with her feet hanging off the edge, she hands me a goblet with bright green liquid sloshing about. She attempts to hold it steady as we roll through the crowd.

"What is that?" I ask.

I think she says "absent," but I can barely hear her. I hold the goblet up, toasting Collette, and then I down the entire glass. It is not much, but it burns my throat as I swallow it. Almost instantly, I feel myself begin to float away. I hold on to the arms of my chair, trying to steady myself.

She is yelling something to me, but I can't seem to understand anything anymore. The masked men in the crowd begin to morph into the monstruous faces that they are wearing as costumes. The laughing women move their bodies like taffy being pulled on each end. I give Collette back the cup, and she jumps off the float in one fell swoop. Ellen and Thomas catch her; it's the first time that I'm seeing them. Collette laughs, like the other women on the streets, and disappears into the crowd.

Thomas covers his face with a golden comedy mask and grabs Ellen's hand. They jump up and down to the music playing in the streets. Ellen blows me kisses as my float trots away from them.

An array of hands reaches through the clouds beside me.

"The necklaces!" both Maries yell back at me.

The glass beads sparkle in the light of the firelit lamps hanging around my chair. My arms feel weightless as I fondle the many strands inside the basket. A group of wily youngsters begins to rock the float on my side. Marie II balls up a green necklace and pitches it to them like a fastball. They duck and miss her assault, but they scurry for the necklace. I begin to throw the beads their way too. They laugh and pick up the trinkets from the cobblestone road.

I take a deep breath, and it seems as though I suddenly have room for the air. I check my dress to see if there is a rip, but everything is intact. A smile grows on my face as I stare at the back of Shango's head, bobbing up and down with the rhythm of the horses trotting.

A young mulatto woman climbs on the side of the float, her dress soiled and ripped from the mayhem. Makeup is smeared down her face, and her eyes are bloodshot. She looks as if she is in need of my help, but I am now melting into my purple chair. I stare at her as she steals into my basket and pulls out a handful of necklaces. She then reaches her arms out to the sides and falls backward into the crowd. They catch her and hold her up to the heavens.

Marie looks back at me, concerned. "Are you okay?"

Everything swirls into a kaleidoscope of colors. I touch my face to make sure I'm still here. My cheeks are numb. I pull on my lips, stretching them farther than I think they can go. I blink my eyes hard and open them once more. I see the back of Shango's head again, but this time there is a woman hugging him. I rub my eyes to try to see straight. It looks like she is kissing him on his neck.

The fire in my belly fuels my winds before I can think. Marie grabs the top of her elaborate hairstyle, shielding herself from my squalls. "Oya!" she yells, maneuvering around her chair to get to me.

The woman kissing Shango looks in my direction, and she has no face. *What is happening?* Marie rushes up and checks my head the way one would for a fever. My winds subside, and I can barely keep my eyes open.

"Did you take something?" Marie asks.

I try to answer her, but my lips are rubber, bouncing together as I blow fish lips instead of speaking words. I lean my head back on the sturdy throne and allow Marie's voice and the rocking of the float to lull me to sleep.

# CHAPTER 15

I wake up hurling over the side of my bed. It seems as through someone predicted this reaction, because there is a rusted pail with a carved wooden handle up against my bedframe. Unfortunately, every bit of my bright green spew misses the mark. My dainty purple-flowered carpet has been rolled up and propped on my vanity chair. The hardwood floor bubbles with memories of yesterday's indulgences.

I sigh as I fall back in bed. My head is pounding from the inside. It feels as if it might explode. There is a timid knock at the door.

"No!" I moan as I cover my face with the thick down pillow.

The door slowly creaks open. Unhurried, methodical steps approach my bed. I can tell it's Collette; she is the only one who tries to be cautious of my rest. I hear the clack of a dish being placed on the side table. I can't think about food right now. She rushes out without shutting the door.

I peek from under the blanket and see a steaming bowl of gumbo on my bedside table. My stomach rolls and releases a rasping growl. Am I hungry? Collette shuffles back in with a soapy towel. "You just rest now, I got this," she affirms.

Collette wipes up my vomit and throws the towel in the empty bucket. She carries it to the door and places it right outside my room. A loud bang causes me to jolt up in bed. Collette hauls in a heavy deep green trunk with dark brown leather straps buckled around it.

"I packed up your belongings while you were sleeping," Collette boasts.

"You did what?" I'm almost offended.

"Ellen and Thomas leave in a few hours, and I know you are supposed to take that journey. Of course, you can always stay. I just wanted to make sure you were ready should you choose to go."

I look around the room, and every personal item of mine is gone. How did she do that without making a peep? The painting of the Black Madonna stares at me, similar to Marie's all-knowing eyes. Anxiety explodes from my stomach out to the tips of my fingers and toes. Thoughts of the woman kissing Shango flood my mind.

"I'll go!" I blurt out.

"Really?" Collette looks physically hurt.

"You are nearly kicking me out," I retort.

"I still didn't think you would actually leave."

"I have to get out of here," I say under my breath. Knowing that I need to be as far away from Shango as possible. My aching stomach stops me from jumping out of the bed.

"That absinthe didn't sit well with you," Collette says. "Eat the gumbo, it will help."

Reluctantly, I sit up in bed and lean against the wall. Looking into Collette's eyes turns on the faucet of my emotions. Her bottom lip begins to quiver and pulse in and out of a frown. Trying to hold back her emotions, Collette walks over and picks up the bowl of gumbo. Steam curls from the top, carrying the delectable aroma throughout the room. I wipe my eyes as Collette sits next to me. She dips the spoon in the gumbo and digs out a generous heap. Circling the food in front of me, she says mockingly, "Open wide."

I let her feed me. It feels almost cathartic. The spices and flavors dance in my mouth and seem to settle my stomach. It occurs to me that anytime I felt sick as a child, I would cause a storm, nothing too consequential, but a change in weather nonetheless. As I sit here, sick, unhappy, and anticipating a huge change, my winds are silent. I lift my hand and send a slight breeze to cool off my next spoonful of gumbo just to make sure I still have my powers.

Collette smiles. "I'm going to miss you."

"Come with us," I say as I take the next bite.

"I will never leave Cosette. I know she lives on in my heart, but her bones are here. What's left of her is here."

I sense that she's suppressing her emotions, perhaps to avoid crumbling under the weight of her grief. I know that she will have to deal with another layer of loss without me here filling in some of Cosette's roles. Yet, through it all, Marie will take good care of her.

"I will miss you," I say.

"So it's final? And what about Shango?"

I swallow hard, trying to ignore the lump forming in my throat. "We are done."

"What? What happened?" Collette questions.

"We are not right for each other."

Collette doesn't seem convinced. She knows that I am hiding something, but she doesn't pry. She puts another spoonful of gumbo in my mouth. It almost feels as if she is trying to shut me up. With my mouth full, I mumble, "No more."

Marie knocks on the open door. "Shall we pen a letter to your mother giving her the news?" She sits on the large trunk and rubs the top of it. "This was my luggage when I was in my twenties. I didn't travel much, but I wanted to make sure that I was prepared. I had big dreams."

"Is this really happening?" I accidently say out loud.

"Only if you want it to. You are welcome to stay with me as long as you desire. But when intuition calls, when that voice inside you speaks, you mustn't ignore it."

"Your clothes are laid out at the foot of the bed," Collette says, placing the gumbo bowl back on my side table.

A muted, plain cream dress with a tattered brown apron and thick auburn tights are strewn across the bottom of my bed. A gray sweater hangs on the side of my purple canopy. Surely this outfit is not for me. Heavy leather boots sit on the hardwood floor at the base of my bed.

"Your other clothes are in your trunk. Ellen prefers to travel dressed as a servant. It is safer," Marie imparts.

*What am I getting myself into?*

"Is the journey dangerous?" I ask.

"Not as dangerous as you."

# PART 2

# RAIN DANCE

# CHAPTER 16

The ground vibrates as we hear the train in the distance, the whistle blowing louder than any other sound for miles. Crowds of people, including travelers and weeping onlookers seeing off their loved ones, strain their necks to see the over-size locomotive clunk its way down the tracks. A young white girl, dressed in a pink and flowered frock similar to Cosette's, runs out to the tracks. The crowd gasps, but no one stops her. She places a shiny copper penny on the metal road-way and hurries back to her family.

Although the station is in New Orleans, the people here are different. They hail from all around the world, with various accents and attitudes. Most think nothing of me and Ellen, disregarding us as Thomas's help. Many are traveling with chickens in small wooden cages or goats and pigs on makeshift leashes. We walk by a man, wrists and ankles handcuffed, with four armed security guards surrounding him. I catch his eye accidentally, and he smirks slightly, not seeming at all bothered by his cumbersome chains. I stay transfixed in his gaze until we pass out of his sight.

"You know who that was?" Thomas asks without turning toward us. "That there was Jesse. I heard he might be on our train being transferred to Texas."

I can't shake the image of Jesse's cold blue eyes following me as we passed. I almost don't want to hear the rest of his story, feeling my nightmares already forming.

"I'm ashamed to say that I feel a bit starstruck," Thomas says as he twists and turns to find him.

"Now, don't be silly," Ellen says under her breath. "He would take your riches in a heartbeat."

Although Ellen sports the dull drapings of a pauper, her air and posture give away her regal status. I know she wants to grab Thomas, turn him around, and slap some sense into him. But she doesn't dare. Ellen is playing the role of a servant, hiding who she really is. Her voice is meek and almost an octave higher. I see her bow her head slightly and keep her sight line to the ground. She has slipped into this position quite effortlessly, almost making herself invisible. Though I know she has ample reason to do so, it breaks my heart that she has to pretend in order to be safe—that we have to disguise who we are so we don't make others uncomfortable.

The train approaches the station, assaulting our senses with its screeching, thumping, whistling, and smoking. I wish Marie and Collette had come to see us off, but neither is a fan of goodbyes. Ellen holds me close and covers my ears as the train pulls to a halt. Images of Shango attack my mind as the overload of sounds and smells roll in with our train.

*I am running away.* There is no question about it.

I can feel the quivering of Ellen's hand on my head. My aching heart won't allow me to fully register that Ellen feels uneasy, perhaps even terrified. This is her first time taking the train to San Francisco, but I am a passenger on her trip; I'm leaning on her to lead me.

"Now, don't you worry," she whispers in my ear.

A uniformed man jumps from the steps that connect the first two train cars. Declaring over the whistling of the train and the clamoring of the crowd, he shouts, "Niggers, animals, and luggage in the last carts!"

My stomach tightens, and sweat beads form on my forehead and armpits. As the man points to us, trying to usher us to the back, my rage feels louder than all of the happenings around me. The weather stays the same; my wrath doesn't send him flying up into the heavens and crash him down atop of his precious locomotive.

I see Thomas stammering as he tries to explain that Ellen and I have to stay with him. "I bought three first-class tickets." His voice is drowned out in the crowd as the man pushes us back.

"Sir, your help cannot travel with you, they will be perfectly fine in the back."

Ellen pulls out a handkerchief and wipes off my forehead; she knows exactly what I'm holding back. Should I release my winds, everyone would suffer.

"He's not worth it," Ellen whispers to me.

Without a formal goodbye to Thomas, we are led back past Jesse. This time people are crowded around him, some trying to board the train and others attempting to get a look at him. Time seems to stand still again as he finds me through a break in the crowd. The sun has peeked through the clouds, illuminating his piercing blue eyes as I pass.

I want to turn away. I want to hide my face. Why is he staring at me? There are tens of people surrounding him as he strains to follow me with his gaze. I trip on the back of Ellen's boots, waking myself from his hypnotizing glare.

"Keep going," the uniformed man commands.

I don't know why he has decided to personally escort us to our car; perhaps he doesn't want us running off, since he promised Thomas that we would be fine. The crowd lessens as we pass by the luggage car. Different uniformed men haul in various trunks, suitcases, and bags. The wind carries in the funk of a hundred beasts. Walking toward the smell, we weave through the farm animals waiting to be loaded into their car.

"We don't have many niggers," the man says, guiding us through the maze of cages. Behind the animal section, a handful of Negroes stand with luggage and newspapers.

The uniformed man scoffs as he opens the door for us to get on. "Have your tickets out," he commands.

The small crowd searches their bodies for their tickets.

"Sir," Ellen says, "our boss has our tickets. Should I go fetch them?"

"Head on in, I'll get them from him when I go back."

Ellen and I walk up the metal stairway. A cloud of mildew wafts by us and smothers us in its stench. Small puddles of water lay stagnant on the floor, with wooden crates ordered against the walls. Minuscule windows line the top of the traincar letting in the only light.

"Is this anything like your fancy boat?" I ask, breaking the silence.

"I have seen worse, believe me," Ellen says, walking to a cart at the back of the car and sitting down.

She pats the seat beside her as people begin to file into the car. While our luggage is with the rest of the passengers', it seems as though the other Negroes have carried their own bags. A man walks in with what looks like a tuba in a large fitted case. The wooden carts lining the walls begin to fill up. There are more passengers than there appeared to be standing outside the train. I scoot in closer to Ellen to create some space on the other side of the cart for another passenger.

A mother with twin boys, no older than five, squeezes in next to me. She directs the boys to sit at her feet. Although their clothes look worn and slightly torn, they match. Striped brown and white button-up shirts with tan corduroy vests and identical caps. Suspenders hold up their oversize pants, which almost cover their thick leather boots. I know the cost of a train ticket is more than most people's annual income; at least, that's what Thomas told me. I imagine the tickets back here are a bit cheaper but an investment nonetheless.

I wonder if they are running too.

As the people file in, so do their stories. We are packing into one train car with a mixture of reasons and destinations. The air is thick with mold and the scent of sweat and nerves. While the door is ajar, I muster up a gentle breeze to dry the train car floor and wash out the stench. The passengers feel the wind, but no one seems suspicious. The puddles on the floor slowly evaporate, leaving white rings on the wooden panels. The door slams shut, followed by the clanking of what sounds like a massive lock.

I look at Ellen with wide eyes. She reaches over and holds my hand, not a bit concerned about out boxcar prison. In the distance we hear a man holler, "All aboard!"

The train whistle blows as the engines begin to rev. The passengers run to one side of the train and wave out of the tiny windows. Ellen wraps her arm around me, gently comforting me as the chorus of voices sings their farewells.

A bump on the tracks jerks me out of my slumber. I jump awake and sit up on the rickety wooden cart. Ellen is alert, seemingly having stood guard as I slept.

"How long was I out?"

"I have no way of keeping time, but if I were to guess, I would say about six hours."

I look at Ellen's wrist, and the golden timepiece that she usually wears is nowhere in sight.

"It's best to travel without it in plain sight, dear," she whispers.

My stomach rumbles, and I'm feeling quite queasy. "How long is the journey?"

"It will take about two days to Texas, where we have accommodations for a week. Then another two or three days to San Francisco."

"It's so quick," I say in wonder.

"That is why we plan on investing. We are approaching a four-day travel time across the entire country. When you really think about it, the covered wagons took at least six months to make that trek, and stagecoaches are now at about a month. Everyone is going to travel by train eventually. Even my boat ride isn't less than two weeks."

Ellen keeps her voice at a whisper, but I can see her calculating opportunities in her head.

"Did we bring any food?" I ask.

"Of course," Ellen says, reaching into her burlap bag and pulling out an apple and a small loaf of bread.

I bite into the apple; the flavors explode in my mouth. My stomach begins to feel better almost instantly. As I chew the delectable fruit, the entire crew of passengers stare in my direction. With my mouth open and going in for the next bite, I look at Ellen.

"Red apples are quite a rare find around these parts," Ellen says with a bit of regret.

I bite into the next piece and slowly swirl it around in my mouth, thinking of ways to remedy the situation. Before I swallow the morsel, I turn to Ellen and ask, "Did you pack the tin of roasted nuts that Marie gave me?"

Ellen reaches into her bag and pulls out the large can of nuts. "What are you going to do?"

"I'm going to offer them to the people. Perhaps they forgot to pack some food."

With a slight look of disapproval, Ellen hands me the nuts. "That is very kind of you."

I hand my apple to Ellen and lock my finger in the tin key on top of the can and peel the cover off. Everyone is still staring at me; even the two boys sitting at their mother's feet have turned around.

"May I?" I ask their mother.

"Oh, don't be silly. We are fine," she says, not so convincingly.

"Please, Mommy," one of the boys pleads.

"Are you sure it's no trouble?"

"None at all," I say, pouring a handful for both the boys, and I insist that the mother takes some too.

Walking around the boxcar, I nearly force-feed each and every passenger. The silent voyage has been injected with a jolt of life. The man with the tuba unlocks it from his case and blows out a couple of tunes. The wooden carts make for great drums, and the mother beside me has a beautiful singing voice.

"Rena," she yells over the music, "my name is Rena. And this here is Lee and Charlton."

The boys are dancing in the middle of the train car. The occasional bump on the track sends them flying into each other, but it's no bother. They just get up and start dancing again. A woman from the other side of the car pulls out a basket of hush puppies wrapped in a red-and-white-plaid napkin. She passes them around, encouraging people to take their fill. Ellen is laughing with the older gentleman sitting on her other side, who had not muttered two words before this jubilee.

A sudden thrust followed by the screeching of the train's brakes sends the boys flying and a few of us tumbling off our carts. The violent vibrations ripple through the floor as the train struggles to come to a halt. The sensation lingers for what feels like an eternity. In these harrowing moments, it seems as though we're teetering on the brink of derailment.

Amid the chaos, Rena clings tightly to her boys, shielding them from harm. Meanwhile, the tuba player swiftly stows his instrument in its case, his movements fueled by urgency. Ellen rushes to the aid of the elderly man, helping him back onto his wooden cart.

"We can't be there yet, can we?" I ask Ellen.

"No, dear, something is amiss," she answers, wiping her dress with her palms.

As the scent of smoke gradually infiltrates our train car, I hasten to the exit, hoping to find an escape route. My suspicions are confirmed as I discover the door firmly locked, trapping us inside. A few men carry a wooden cart to the front, using it as a makeshift battering ram against the door. The cart shatters into splinters while the door stubbornly holds its ground. Meanwhile, the train continues its deceleration, emitting unsettling squeaks and screeches as it clings to the tracks.

Ellen tends to the passengers in the rear as I walk back up to the door. I discreetly touch the handle, silently channeling the power of the storm into my hands, obscured by the tumultuous shaking and bumping of the train. With a surge of energy, I unleash a mighty gust of wind, causing the door to burst open and sail away just as the train, at long last, grinds to a halt.

The whinny and gallop of horses pounding on the unclaimed earth echo outside. I peek my head through the door to see what's going on. The flash of Jesse's eyes hits me as a forceful blow to the back of my head sends me reeling into darkness.

# CHAPTER 17

". . . Yemaya . . ."

The fog of a white light slowly awakens me. I blink my eyes open, and a Native woman with two long plaits is inches from my face.

"Yemaya, is it really you?"

I rub the back of my head; there is a lump the size of an egg. I moan in pain.

"Relax, relax."

The last moment I recall was staring into Jesse's eyes. I jump up, searching for him.

"He won't be bothering you anymore," the woman assures me.

I slowly sit back down on the ground, which feels like bundles of hay layered on dehydrated dirt. The air is so dry and dusty that my throat and nostrils feel sore.

"You called me Yemaya?"

"I did," she says with a smile. "You remind me of someone dear to my heart."

"Yemaya is my mother," I say.

For the first time, I notice the group of people encircling us. A large fire burns in the middle, and I am sitting on a pile of dried grass and leaves.

"The Great Spirit has answered our prayers," a voice hollers from the crowd.

The fire glistens in the woman's eyes, and I see a tear fall down her cheek. She grabs a tattered leather pouch that is hanging around her neck and holds it tight in her palm.

"I never thought this day would come. Is Yemaya—" She pauses.

"My mother is alive and well. Living in Cuba."

"Oh, Great Spirit, good . . . good. I have so many questions, we all do. But I'm sure you are famished. Shall we commence with the feast?" the woman says, turning to the crowd.

They all begin hooting and making guttural noises in the backs of their throats. As they move closer to the fire, I see they are dressed in ceremonial garb. Large feather headpieces and beaded skirts, multiple bracelets climbing up their arms, and white paint decorating their faces. With each step, they pound the ground with their leather-clad feet, creating a rhythmic cadence that reverberates through the air. The drums feel similar to what Marie had at my welcome ceremony, yet slightly different from the rhythms on Congo Square.

I am flooded with questions as the woman approaches me bearing a soothing balm that looks like aloe vera, which she gently applies to my wound. As she wraps a piece of red fabric around my head, she assures me, "It will help keep the swelling down."

The pressure sends a wave of dizziness coursing through me, and I instinctively roll my eyes back, seeking relief. All I want to do is fall asleep. The splintery hay suddenly feels quite welcome.

"It is important for you to stay awake for a while. The people will help you."

Each member of the group approaches me holding a small gift as a token of celebration. A clay bowl, an ear of corn, a beaded necklace, a piece of dried meat—each offering carries a significance known only to them. Gratefully, I accept the gifts, savoring the food and basking in the festivities. I'm in too much pain to get up and dance, but I do feel the stirring within me to join.

An elder approaches and flattens out the hay beside me. "It's truly uncanny," she murmurs, her voice laced with a sense of wonder, "how much you resemble her." Her words hang in the air as she scans every part of me with her gaze.

I know that she is talking about my mother. I wish I knew more about her life. Mama had such a difficult time training me, learning my powers, raising me—she spent all of her time on me and saved no room to tell stories about herself.

"So they say," I answer.

I want to ask who this elder is, as well as the woman who spoke with me earlier. But the time just doesn't feel right. *What happened to me? Where is Ellen? And Thomas?* A subtle sensation draws my attention to a scab on my chest. I gently trace it, remembering the single red rose from Shango. Memories of him linger; I can't seem to stop thinking about him.

"I'm Amitola, Ozata's mother. She is the woman who spoke to you first. We can explain more tomorrow after you have gotten some rest."

She stands up without using her arms for support, rising like a string is pulling her from the heavens. The night feels long. I strain to keep my eyes open for what feels like hours. I can no longer take it.

Blackness.

�᷎

I wake up to the ocean lapping at my feet. A child's laughter in the distance draws my attention. Is it Oshun? I know that I am dreaming. I can feel it. I am at the waters in Cuba. A young child, no older that three, skips in the sand toward me.

"Kitari, slow down!" Mama says from behind me.

Kitari? I don't even turn around to see Mama, for fear that Kitari will disappear. She runs into my arms and laughs in my ear. I can feel her breath tickle my cheeks. I hold her hard. Taking in her smell, like chamomile and lavender. Her hair is freshly braided, with speckles of sand dancing on the ends.

"Mommy, look what I found." Kitari holds up a small purple shell. The inside shines like mother-of-pearl. Just as I'm about to compliment her find, the sand begins to swallow my feet.

"Mama!" I turn for the first time to try to find my mother. I can't pull my legs out of the sand. "Take her, Mommy!" I yell, desperate to save Kitari.

The quicksand wastes no time, enveloping me in its coarse abyss. Mama rushes over and grabs Kitari. She tries to reach for me with her other hand, but it's too late. My fingers slip through her grasp as the sand pulls me under.

�᷎

I gasp for air and jump up out of my slumber. Rain pours down on the outside of my tent. It pounds on the leather like drums. I swirl my hands around to see if it's my storm. The rain dances about in a circle, simulating a miniature whirlwind. It's mine, all right. I let it pour, thinking of my dear Kitari. I hold my stomach and lie back down on what seems like an animal skin rug. The darkness is absolute; I cannot see anything other than the faint outline of the pointed ceiling. The rain continues as I drift off to sleep.

# CHAPTER 18

I awaken to the sounds of celebration echoing through the air. Groggily rubbing the sleep from my eyes, I make my way to the entrance of the tent. The rain has ceased, though I'm unsure how long I let it pour. I hope I didn't cause too much damage. Flipping open the door flap, I see a mixture of mud and moist hay surrounding the perimeter. The sludge oozes between my toes as I step outside.

Children frolic, leaping through puddles and delighting in the aftermath of the rain. Nearby, one tent stands adorned with multiple pots set outside, brimming with water. There is a large piece of tree bark placed by my tent with yet more gifts. Unlike the sodden earth around it, these offerings remain dry.

Among the presents, a large shell catches my eye, its interior gleaming with exquisite mother-of-pearl. I think of Kitari and the shell she found in my dream. Beside it lies an intricately woven basket, vibrant with colors and designs, containing a folded animal skin rug. Bowls overflowing with berries and nuts encircle the basket. Why are they being so generous with me? I don't have any of my belongings to share with them. I can't even give them a red apple.

The woman from last night, I think her mom told me her name but I can't remember it, rushes up to me with a smile. "The council would like to see you," she says, out of breath.

She seizes my hand, pulling me along as we navigate through the village. Mud splatters in all directions as we zigzag around tents and other structures. Struggling to keep pace, I marvel at her seemingly effortless grace, as if she's gliding above the mire with each step. Her thin frame is surprisingly muscular. She flashes a peek at me, perhaps to make sure that I am keeping up. Two braids whip across her high cheekbones as she turns back to the path. Her dark, angular eyes seem to take in every detail, every obstacle, every moment. Ahead, looming in the distance, stands a grand structure decorated with intricate paintings and smoke spiraling from the top.

Suddenly, I stumble, nearly tumbling headfirst into a muddy puddle. She catches me in the nick of time. "Are you okay?" she inquires, walking backward as she asks.

I trail behind her, noticing that she has eased her grip on my arm, allowing me to keep pace more comfortably. Despite her initial urgency, she now seems mindful of my ability to keep up. I can't help but wonder why she is in such a hurry. As we reach the towering formation, she comes to an abrupt stop, taking a moment to collect herself. She is quite ageless; I can't tell how old she is. Last night, her wisdom made her seem perhaps around thirty, but her demeanor now feels closer to my age.

She attempts to straighten out my travel dress. "Did we leave you a change of clothes in your room?"

"I'm not certain," I reply, feeling nerves grow in my stomach.

"It's no problem," she says, moving the flap to the side and dipping into the entrance. She holds it open for me from the inside. "Ozata, my name is Ozata," she whispers.

"I'm Oya," I respond, tentatively tiptoeing in.

A council of elders sits in a circle around a small fire that consists mostly of glowing coals. The red light emanating from the blushing embers casts a crimson glimmer on the entire room. A smile creeps its way across the wrinkles of a petite woman with gray plaits down to her waist. She nods and motions for me to join the circle. As I sit down, I look back at Ozata. She leans in and says, "I'll be waiting outside for you."

I think she sees the concern in my eyes. "Don't worry, they will take care of you. And my mom is just across the way," she says, pointing to Amitola.

As soon as Ozata settles me in, she hurries out of the leather-framed door.

"Daughter of the Ocean Mother, Yemaya. Please state your name," Amitola begins.

"I am Oya," I say, carefully choosing my words.

"You have brought the rains," she says without changing her tone.

I made a promise to myself not to let anyone else know of my powers.

"I don't know what you are taking about," I say, playing ignorant.

The entire council stares directly at me. I can tell that they are not buying my story.

"Oya, daughter of Yemaya. Our story has been a tragic one. We have been killed and torn from our lands for generations. The threat of leaving this land due to drought was imminent. Our earth back home was luscious, abundant, healthy. We have been pushed out west, forced to live in barren country, forced to watch our children die. Yesterday a group of outlaws, perhaps five of them, built a large fire just over the hills. Ozata spotted the smoke and went to investigate. They were boasting about a train robbery and rescuing one of their friends. One said he stole his own personal slave. That's when Ozata saw you passed out, lying on the floor next to him. She knew that she had to do something right away, so she sneaked down to their horses and set them free, making sure they made enough noise for the outlaws to notice. She single-handedly rescued you from those brutes. During our rain dance ceremony, you finally woke up. We were certain that you were your mother—that the Great Spirit had delivered her to us once more. She never needed to hide who she was with us, and neither do you."

I fall silent, my mind drifting back to the few encounters I've had with Native women. They were boarders at Marie's house because no hotel would have them. They came to New Orleans to trade the bounty of their harvests. I recall one of them explaining that they seldom lingered in towns due to the diseases brought by white settlers, in addition to the hate they encountered.

"Thank you for the rains," a silver-haired man proclaims. "I am Chukwudubem, the eldest member of our people. Cora, your mother's teacher, was my oldest confidante. She returned to the earth and the Great Spirit only three years ago, leaving me as the senior member of our tribe. We have a proposition."

A proposition? I still do not know where Ellen and Thomas are. I am in no position to make a deal. Amitola must sense my unease. "Before we go into that, Oya, is there anything you need from us?"

"I was traveling with two people. We were headed to California. San Francisco, to be exact. I must find them to make sure they are alive."

"Ozata has already committed to that journey with you. Once she heard that those men kidnapped you from a train, she knew you would need to return. She is our strongest and most intelligent warrior," Amitola declares.

"We also want you to understand that this type of transactional conversation is not typical. We would support you even if we didn't need anything from you," Chukwudubem says.

I know this. I feel their hearts. They saved me and supported me before they knew I could bring rain.

"We will take you to your people. The drought has devastated our land and community. Can you bring the rains for seven days? On the eighth day, Ozata will have a plan ready to get you to San Francisco."

All eyes in the room fixate on me, their collective gaze bearing the weight of their hopes and fears. The fate of their people hangs in the balance, resting upon the tempests I wield. Yet I've never perceived my powers as instruments of creation or healing; I have never felt that my powers brought life. Slowly, reluctantly, I raise my hands, weaving them in a circular motion. Outside, the winds respond to my command, beginning to howl and swirl; I ensure that they rage high above the village, avoiding any further devastation.

In the crimson glow of the room, the elders rise slowly, their faces upturned to the heavens. The smoke flap atop the tent flutters violently as the rain pelts down, its torrents mingling with the hiss of hot coals.

Amitola rushes over to me, enveloping me in a tight embrace. I surrender to the warmth of her arms, sensing the depth of her affection for me and my mother. As she pulls away, tears glisten in her eyes. "There is no way that I can thank you enough," she cries.

Ozata bursts through the entrance, her hair wet and clinging to her back. "I knew it was you! As soon as I heard the winds, I put your offerings inside your house so they wouldn't get wet."

I'm still consumed by curiosity about Mama's role in all of this. It feels like a void, a missing piece in the puzzle of my life. Apart from the grim details surrounding my father's death, her story remains shrouded in mystery. It was difficult for her to tell us what happened to our father, but my brother insisted. We all felt like fatherless children. Yet I sense that Obatala, burdened by the weight of his absence, bore the brunt of the pain. Perhaps because he was a boy, or maybe because he was the only child born of his flesh. Oshun and I were born of his spirit. Mother said that he was always watching us, but his presence felt distant, elusive, leaving us yearning for a connection we could scarcely grasp.

My stomach churns uncomfortably. I think of the array of food laid out by my tent, but I'm uncertain of the dining customs here. Do they eat breakfast? Despite my eagerness to delve deeper into Mama's story, my hunger pangs betray me with an audible growl.

"Are you hungry?" Ozata asks with a smile, wringing her soaked braids out onto the floor.

"Starved," I say.

Ozata holds my hand and leads me out into the storm. As soon as the first raindrop hits her head, she begins to laugh. She holds both of my hands and spins me around in a circle. "How do you do it? I remember your mother becoming as strong as a bear when she touched water. What a great team you must be."

*A great team?* That would be hard to say. Mama devoted endless hours to keeping me safe, ensuring that I didn't cause harm to myself or others. Yet I witnessed her abilities firsthand. Mama's gift for healing was unique; she was capable of restoring health to people and animals alike. I watched in awe as she effortlessly returned stranded sea creatures to the water, her powers mending their ailments with ease. Her curative webs and strength kept people seeking her healing. Mama's compassion knew no bounds; she offered aid to all who sought her help.

"I want to know more about my mother," I say, a bit ashamed that I lived my whole life with her and might know less than Ozata. "Can you tell me anything that you remember?"

Ozata holds her hand above her forehead to shield her eyes from the rain. "I will tell you everything I know. It would be an honor."

I feel my heart expand and flutter in my chest, perhaps from excitement. My entire life, I have wanted to know Mama's story. Unlike the other children, I seemed to possess powers beyond my control. If I got upset or had a fit, I would unleash a hurricane on the island. Obatala always protected Mama and knew how to calm down anyone who had an issue with our family. And Oshun, sweet Oshun, no matter how sad I was, she could always put a smile on my face.

My stomach growls again. Ozata guides me toward a covered communal area, its roof fashioned from a mixture of sticks and leaves tightly woven with hay, offering shelter from the rains. In one corner, a woman tends to a large pot over an open flame, wisps of steam rise into the air. Beside her, a table displays a stack of frybread. As we draw closer, I see that the woman is cooking the dough next to the pot. It seems as though Mama did share something with me from this tribe. Frybread was my favorite breakfast as a child. I would put baked fish and avocado pear on it with a pinch of salt. It had to be perfect. If it wasn't, I would have a fit.

"Frybread was your mom's favorite," Ozata says.

"She used to make it for me every Sunday. I had no idea she learned it from you," I say in awe.

"Well, not me, exactly, but my grandmother, Cora. I was only seven when your mom came into my life. Actually, I was six, about to turn seven," she says, leading me over to the frybread.

I am hit by the delicious aroma of some sort of stew. It doesn't smell like Marie's gumbo, but I can feel that it is cooked with the same love. There are different spices used here than in New Orleans and Cuba. There is a heady, earthy smell to the food that is mesmerizing, pulling me in with its hypnotic blend. Ozata pours some stew in the bowl. I see beans, squash, corn, and some other vegetables.

"It's wild turkey stew, you'll like it." Ozata smiles, reaching for two frybreads.

It takes all of me not to pounce on Ozata and grab the food. I am famished. Why am I so hungry? We walk over to a large fallen tree, still covered by the stick roof, and sit down. I dip a piece of the frybread into the thick stew and scoop out a fair amount of turkey and vegetables. Before I gobble it down, I offer it to Ozata.

"I'm not hungry yet, I usually eat when the sun is high in the sky."

Before she even finishes her sentence, I take my first bite. With my mouth full, I mutter, "This is so good!"

"I'm glad you like it. It will be available all day. If you ever need food, or have any that you want to share, this is where you come. There is always something on the fire."

I am entirely grateful to hear that. What a beautiful practice. As my stomach settles, I turn to Ozata and ask, "How did you meet my mother?"

"I remember it like it was yesterday. Four strong warriors from the southern nations carried a large cocoon tied to a tree log into the village. We lived in what the white man calls South Carolina, by a river. Actually, there used to be a river here, just past those rocks," Ozata says, pointing in the distance.

"The stream helps us grow our food. Many people hunt and gather from the wild, but our ancestors taught us the secret of growing beans, corn, and squash. Some say I was born into the wrong people, because most of our tribe are peaceful. I came in with a warrior heart."

Something about that rings true for me. I want to tell her that I am a warrior too but I feel inadequate, having never been trained or deemed as one.

"As I said before," Ozata continues, "it was just days away from my seventh birthday when I met your mother. I had visions and dreams about her before she even arrived. I saw her swimming with the dolphins, weaving in and out of their paths with her powerful tail. I had never heard of a mer before that moment. I told my grandmother, Cora, about the dream, and she confirmed that she had received the same message. Your mother traveled underwater across the sea from Africa, following the ship that your father was on. He was kidnapped and sold into slavery, enduring the brutal ship voyage to Turtle Island. When they arrived, Yemaya had to cocoon herself for several days in order to turn into a human. Our brothers and sisters in the south would eventually find her cocoon and take the long journey to us. Just as Cora predicted, your mother came when the moon was full in the sky, right before the harvest."

I feel a giddiness rising from my belly into my heart. I am finally learning something about Mama.

"As soon as the warriors entered the village, we began preparations for a grand celebration. We knew the men would be hungry and tired from the journey, and we were all anxious to meet your mother! The warriors placed her cocoon in the middle of the village. People adorned the shell with so many different wildflowers. I was busy in my hut carving a small wooden replica of her as a gift. My visions were so clear that I knew exactly what she looked like."

Our feet begin to sink into the mud. The rains have been steady for a couple hours now. I lift my foot and place it out in the downpour, watching the dirt wash off.

"You have the power of vision?" I ask.

"Not by will, unfortunately. I don't know when the visions will come."

"I'm concerned about the excess mud; it might ruin the structures. Where did you say the river was?"

Ozata points to a clearing beyond the rocks. My gaze follows the river trail up to a mountain in the distance. "I'm going to give the village a break for a moment."

With Ozata staring at me, I summon the rains with the circular movement of my hands. I send the waters upriver, to the mountains, and concentrate the storm in the distance.

"Let's get that river flowing again," I say.

Ozata blushes and smiles. "You truly are a gift from the Great Spirit. You and your mother."

The sun starts to break through my dissipating clouds. "Should we tell the elders my plan?"

"They will figure it out. Actually, they probably knew about it before you did!"

"That is true," I say, slipping in the mud as I try to get up.

Ozata catches me, almost falling off the back of the log. We see children running in the distance, covered in the mud we just so desperately tried to avoid.

"Come," Ozata says, jumping up and running toward the riverbed.

I follow her, once again weaving through obstacles, jumping over rocks and around bushes. Does she ever walk anywhere?

"Hurry, the clay has been saturated." She breaks off a piece of what looks like white stone and beckons me to her. I feel an energy similar to when Cosette and Collette would hold me in prayer; I feel protected and covered. As I approach Ozata, she takes my hand and closes her eyes. I follow suit, inhaling deeply.

Her touch is cool and soothing against my skin as she begins to paint intricate designs across my face, neck, and shoulders. I stand still, holding my breath. Despite the dampness still hanging in the air from the rain, the clay begins to dry on my face, and I can feel it slightly tighten where she painted the designs.

The river has begun to flow slightly. I see a pool of water standing stagnant to the side, and I walk over to peek at my reflection. Startled to see that the clay drawings bear a striking resemblance to the Yoruba shapes that my mother would paint around the house, I touch my face in disbelief. Mama said it was the way she communicated with my father.

"How did you know?" I say in awe.

"The faces tell me the designs. I never know."

I stare back at my reflection, feeling both my mother and father with me. I never allowed myself to understand Mama. I've always loved her, yet I can't help but harbor some resentment for sending me away.

A torrent of emotion begins to well up inside me. I sniffle to try to hold back my tears, but I feel overwhelmed with nostalgia, for my mother, for Marie, the twins . . . The tears flow, morphing the clay into different shapes and smears. I fall to the ground, checking for a hurricane, before I allow myself to let go.

Ozata doesn't hesitate to join me in the mud, sitting beside me without a moment's pause. With a comforting gesture, she wraps her arm around me and allows me to cry. I feel the circle of energy protecting me. I rub my eyes, and the clay from my face paints my fingers. "I'm sorry, I messed up your masterpiece."

"This is what it was made for," Ozata says, holding me closer.

"I wasn't such an easy child to raise," I confess. "Mama spent so much time and energy protecting me and my siblings—actually, the whole island—from my destructive storms. If I got sad or angry, we had to deal with a hurricane. I always thought Mama was against me, but now that it has been so long since I've seen her, I see how much she loved me. How much she sacrificed."

"I am sure that you are your mother's pride and joy. When she was here, she was determined to find your father. So he made it to Cuba as well?"

My eyes well up with tears again. "I never met my dad. He died years before I was born."

"But how? How is that possible?"

"My father was killed at the plantation. At least, his body was. Mama was pregnant with Obatala already, so he was made with my father still alive. But after that, she communed with his spirit in her dreams and conceived both me and Oshun," I say, confident that Ozata will understand.

"Of course she did," Ozata says, smiling. "The love she had for Obatala was stronger than the confines of this world."

"Tell me more about her," I plead.

We have settled into our mud couch, and it has conformed to our shapes. Supported and literally held by the earth, Ozata continues. "Where did I leave off—oh yes! The cocoon was in the middle of the village. I had learned wood carving from my grandfather. He showed me how to carve a flute. But once I learned the technique, I was obsessed with carving little dolls. I had them lined up along the inside of our house, protecting me. I remember working on my carving of your mother for days. I wanted it to be perfect. I wouldn't even take a break to eat. I vaguely remember my own mother feeding me frybread as I concentrated," she says with a laugh.

"Is it your favorite, too?" I ask.

"By far! I'm almost certain your mother liked it so much because of me."

I look back at the covered area with the woman frying the dough and stirring the wild turkey stew. More people have arrived now, taking their fill. A man, similar to the height and size of Shango, stands to the side and lets an elder woman go in front of him. *Shango.* My heart begins to flutter, and I think about my cowardice. Would I ever get the chance to tell him that I love him? Why did I have to run away? My heart begins to ache.

Ozata places a hand on my back. "That night, the same day the men walked into the village with the cocoon, we saw a tiny crack in the shell. The elders wouldn't allow us to help because chickens and butterflies need the process of emerging from their shells and cocoons by themselves in order to develop properly. We waited patiently. One tiny little crack at a time until, finally, a huge push. The entire cocoon fell to the ground, and your mother stood there, naked."

I place my hand on my heart, thinking about how terrified Mama must've been, emerging from her cocoon in front of complete strangers.

"Her legs were shaking, so I knew she was scared. I ran up and gave her my doll. I wanted her to know that we knew who she was—that she didn't have to hide. I felt like she was my best friend. She was around seventeen, and I was six, the odd couple."

Ozata went on to tell me the adventures they faced and how the tribe was forced to move out west, how my mother came into a fortune during her search for my father and gave Cora the funds to buy this land, as much as the elders were against the idea. They believed that land could never be owned. Ozata is sure that's why she feels so connected to this particular place. Mama is a part of it. I look over yonder toward the mountains. The rain is still falling.

We will need to move from our comfortable mud seats soon. The river is beginning to have a robust flow. Our little safe heaven will be submerged before too long. I scoop some water into my hands and splash my face, washing away the remnants of the clay. Ozata uses her shirt to help me dry my face. "Do you want me to paint another design?" she asks.

Honestly, I am not sure. She most definitely is blessed with healing hands, but I'm doubtful I can handle it again.

"I will paint the markings of a warrior. I can tell you are one of us."

# CHAPTER 19

The day feels endless, with my rains still cascading down the mountain. Learning about my mother at my age weighs heavily on me, stirring a mix of emotions that I struggle to contain. It takes all of me not to fall into guilt. I feel like my mother worked her entire life to build something up, and I came along and knocked it down with my storms. Lost in thought, I absent-mindedly begin picking at the nuts and berries left for me.

"Can I come in?" a voice asks from outside.

"Yes," I answer.

Amitola enters with a change of clothes folded in her arms. She hands them to me and sits down.

"Thank you," I say, holding the clothes up.

"It is the least we can do. Ozata said that she told you stories about your mother. How are you feeling?"

I take a moment to check in with myself. My stomach rolls uneasily, a sensation that has been with me since leaving New Orleans. I can't seem to shake it. "I feel like she's a stranger to me."

"I was afraid you were going to say that. Mothers have the delicate responsibility of trying to do what we think is best for our children. For some reason, Yemaya did not think you were ready to hear her whole story."

"I think I can understand that now. Raising a child who can create a deadly hurricane with every tantrum is quite the task. I'm just trying to take it all in," I say.

"We just wanted to thank you again for the rain. Some elders foresaw that your rains will trigger nature into her normal cycle," Amitola says with a smile.

"I had some concerns about my rain eroding the lands; should I give it a break?"

"I think if you continue to concentrate on the river in the mountains, it should be fine. We will let you know if it becomes too much."

"I will bring some rains tonight to the village and the crops, then return it to the mountains when people wake."

"Thank you, Oya. Thank you," Amitola says, bowing as she backs out of my circular house.

Someone has left a few lit coals in my firepit, casting a faint red glow that offers just enough warmth for the night. Nearby sits a clay plate holding three pieces of frybread. As I reach for one, my thoughts drift to Mama and the stories Ozata shared about her. I ponder Mama's bravery in following my father. Here I am, running away from my love. My stomach twists uncomfortably at the memory of Shango. I thought I could leave him behind, but I'm haunted by the way he makes me feel. How Collette said he held me during the Congo Square ceremony, and the electricity between us every time we touched. It doesn't make any sense, but love rarely does. I hastily consume the frybread in hopes of settling the upset. But the discomfort continues, intensifying until I'm forced to rush outside, emptying my stomach at the entrance to my roundhouse. With sweat beading on my forehead, I return to the coals. I can't tell if I'm hot or cold. The regurgitation certainly didn't make me feel better. What is wrong with me? I take a few breaths to try and calm myself.

"Oya?" I hear a voice say outside my tent.

"Watch out for the mess right there!" I yell.

"I see it," Ozata says, walking around the contents of my stomach to get to me. "Do you need anything?"

"I have felt sick ever since I left New Orleans. I drank something called absinthe, and it didn't fare well with me."

"Your color looks a little off. Let's take you to the medicine woman."

Ozata slowly helps me up, and we navigate around the sickness at the door. This might be the first time I've seen Ozata move slowly. Much of the village is still out and about, sitting by fires and singing songs. Children are laughing and running. Sparks from the fires dance in the air while the adults sit drinking a steaming liquid. As I pass, people stare in concern. The laughter ceases, but no one intrudes on my space.

We step into the expansive dwelling from earlier, and a sudden chill washes over me, leaving me shivering. Hurriedly, I make my way to the glowing coals, seeking their warmth. Nearby, Ozata is engaged in conversation with an elder woman, her long gray braids cascading down her back. Together, they approach me, the elder holding a rolled-up mat in her hands. With a gentle motion, she unfurls it onto the floor, revealing an intricate design of vibrant hues.

"I am cold," I say, warming my hands on the coals.

"I know, my child, but can you lie down for a moment? Ozata, go fetch her a blanket."

My bones feel brittle as I crawl over to the blanket. My stomach is still feeling ill, but I try to keep it in. I hear the rains begin to beat on the leather covering. I'm too weak to send them back up to the mountains. The elder woman bends down and rubs my head. "My dear, my name is Chatavia. I met you this morning."

"I recall," I say, worried about the rains. I pray that they will not develop into something more forceful. I won't be the tribe's hero anymore.

Chatavia has a cup full of steaming liquid by my head. It smells like eucalyptus and perhaps mint. Mama told me that mint was my father's favorite tea. Chatavia waves the vapors over my face, motioning me to breathe in deeply. My stomach begins to settle.

"Before I can give you something for the sickness, I need to check one thing," she says, placing both hands on my belly.

Chatavia closes her eyes, and Ozata walks up behind her, placing a fur blanket over my shivering legs. As the elder lays her hands on me, I already feel better. I see a smile creep through Chatavia's wrinkles.

She opens her eyes. "You are not sick," she says.

Ozata and I look at her, confused.

"You are pregnant."

# CHAPTER 20

My belly is flat. I can see my heartbeat pulsating by my navel. Fear claws at me, threatening to unravel my resolve. Another loss would be unbearable. Is this the message Kitari tried to tell me with her purple shell? My stomach rises and falls with each breath. Shango is here; the best of him is within me. Yet a part of me recoils from the thought of his presence. Why? I yearn to prove my resilience, to demonstrate that I can endure. I gently rest my hand on my belly, grappling with the weight of uncertainty. If this child is not meant to survive, why subject Shango to the anguish?

As I look around my empty room, my gaze falls upon a collection of miniature wooden toys lining the interior wall. One catches my eye. I slowly approach the carved figurines and cradle a delicate representation of a pregnant woman, her curls cascading like clouds around her. She looks just like me! Ozata knew this entire time. Gently, I trace the contours of the wooden belly, seeking reassurance, craving certainty. It feels like torture having to go through all of this again without knowing if my baby will survive.

A tear rolls down my cheek. I use my hands to direct the rains up high in the sky. I think it's time for a rest. The river seems to be running again, more than just my storms. I wonder if there was some sort of block or dam stopping it? Whatever it was, it's gone now. I can hear the babbling from here. Clutching the wooden figurine close to my heart, I nestle into bed.

*N*

The icy grip of the river numbs my feet, yet I find myself transfixed by the dance of currents. My legs seem to morph into fins under the streaming water. Suddenly, a feeling of being watched pricks at my senses. I whip around, but no one is there. Turning back to the river, I spot a black panther calmly lapping at the water's edge on the opposite bank.

I blink several times. Is this a dream? I pull my legs out of the river, and they morph from a mer tail back into my feet. I look up at the panther, and Shango is standing in her place. My heart freezes in my chest, breath caught in my throat. Shango gestures urgently from the other side of the river, but his words are lost in the distance, swallowed by the expanse of water between us.

"I can't hear you," I yell.

Shango attempts to cross the river, but every step he takes forward pulls him farther backward. The river picks up speed, and the raging rapids makes it even harder to understand him.

N

"What?" I yell, jumping out of my sleep.

My breath heaving in and out, sweat dripping from my forehead, my hands clenched into fists, I slowly roll off my deer hide bed. There is a clay cup filled with water sitting at the side of my mat. I am used to waking up with little gifts by my side here in the village. My stomach rumbles, feeling uneasy again. I reach for the water and take a large gulp.

Can Shango feel me? Can he feel his child? I wonder what he was saying across the river. My throat begins to tighten as I try to hold in my emotion. I'm tired of crying. I'm tired of feeling sorry for myself. I want this child to live. Gently caressing my flat stomach, I wonder how small she is. Another girl. I can feel her.

*Bang!*

The sharp crack of a gunshot pierces the air, sending a shiver down my spine. Chaos erupts around me as screams mingle with the frantic patter of fleeing feet. I rush out of my tent and push through the panicked crowd, my heart pounding with each step. The distant whinnying of horses draws me forward.

My cloud of rain still pours water at the top of the mountain. I see it behind the dancing horses and the smoke billowing from their guns. It's Jesse and his men. I can't tell if they have injured or killed anyone. The fire in my belly starts to boil, and I feel the storm beginning to grow in my arms. Suddenly, I'm swooped up by the large man who reminded me of Shango.

"Put me down!" I yell.

"I'm sorry, orders from Ozata," he says, zigzagging back through the trees by the river.

I look over his shoulder and see several warriors with their bows trained on the men on horseback. Flashes of Cosette being shot by the men in New Orleans assault my mind. I have to do something. I raise my arms to send my storm toward the men, but the warrior flips me around midstride.

"Your winds will disturb the path of their arrows. The most important thing right now is to hide you. If, by chance, they get past our warriors, they must not find you." He puts me down by the bank of the river. "Follow the stream down, and you will find a cave. The women and children will be there waiting for you," he says before he turns and runs back to battle.

*But I am a warrior!* I want to yell it out to him. I want them to know that I can take out all of those men without an issue. Then I hear Marie's voice saying, "Not murder, Oya, all of your deaths were accidents."

I slowly walk down the river, kicking stones into the water. The gunshots die out, but I still hear the guttural war cries of the tribe. Every instinct I have wants to turn back. My body constricts as my stomach rolls. A wave of nausea trundles up my body, and I release the contents of my dinner on a nearby stone.

My rage subsides as I hold my belly. I reach down and rinse off the stone with water from the river, thinking of Mama again. She followed my father to this strange land. How did she find these allies? It seems as though many of them found her. What are the odds that Ozata would discover me by the smoking campfire? Perhaps my father really is watching over me.

The walk is longer than I anticipate. Every crack, rustle, or footstep I hear, I scurry behind a tree. Although it's very different from Cuba, the landscape reminds me of a cove I used to go to when I needed to be alone. Mama would let me explore and wander when other people were not around. She always knew where I was. It's like she had some sense that connected her to me.

My emotions rush up through my body, sending me shaking. I don't want to do this alone. I want Shango. I can no longer run from my feelings. My throat constricts, each breath coming harder than the last as I struggle to contain the storm raging within me. I want to feel his strong hand on my lower back. I want to hear his deep baritone voice that is incapable of whispering.

My fingers trace over my chest, seeking the scab where his rose grazed me, but it's vanished, leaving only smooth skin in its wake. Yet, as my hand drifts lower to my belly, I find solace in the undeniable proof of his presence—the life growing within me.

"Father, protect me!" I yell up into the heavens.

I'm dumbfounded by the outcry, covering my mouth in shame. How far am I from the cave? Did someone hear me? What if Jesse got away and heard my echo in the woods? My tears dry from the fear, and I run along the bank of the river, ducking low as I make my way closer to the cave.

In the distance, a mountain rises majestically, its peak obscured by the shifting clouds. The river, like a silver ribbon, winds its way through the mountain, carving a V-shaped cavern. I wonder if the cave is nearby. All around me is serene silence, broken only by the melodic chirping of birds soaring overhead.

My eyes catch the sight of a small moccasin on the ground. I pick it up and wonder if the children are nearby. Most of the young ones running in the village were barefoot. Marveling at the intricate beadwork, I take a deeper look and see a black panther rendered in shimmering beads, framed by the backdrop of a yellow and orange sun.

The faint sound of a flute lures me closer to the mountains. The notes dance up and down, seemingly tripping over each other in the most melodic way. A steady drumbeat accompanies them, mimicking a heartbeat. Although the sounds are soft, I don't think they are far. They seem to be keeping the music low so the attackers don't hear.

I have been walking for so long that my feet are weary and my throat is parched. I bend down by the river and drink of the waters. How long have I been on this trail? The warrior told me it was just up the river. I continue toward the mountains, following the flute.

As I approach the rocky terrain, the path becomes narrow. A bird whistles as I near a large stone wall. In the distance, distorted by the waves of heat in the air, a tribeswoman signals in my direction. I realize that she is the one whistling. Her long, thick black hair stands in stark contrast to the sandy-colored rocks. She ducks behind a sizable boulder after I acknowledge her.

I hurry through the rocky river, careful not to slip on the stones. The cloudiness of the water here shows me that the riverbed has been dry for quite some time. The silt and sand have yet to settle into their new element. There is no evidence of life in the river: The fish, snakes, and frogs have yet to discover her waters.

I pick up a stone that reminds me of Oshun. She always loved the flat ones that she could skip on the waters. I almost forget that I am in a hurry to find cover. I skip the stone down the stream, and it bounces seven times. Seven times! I wish I could tell my sister that; she would be so happy. Rivers have always been her favorite place. Mama would say that the river waters were sweet and the ocean salty. According to her, the spirits would play where the sweet and salty waters mix. She often went where the river met the sea to commune with Father.

I hear the whistle again, but the woman is nowhere in sight. I hurry toward the boulder.

"Oya," someone whispers from the mountains to the left of me.

It's the woman! Somehow she crossed over without me noticing. With a beckoning gesture, she motions for me to follow her. Moving at a deliberate pace, not as swift as Ozata, she leads me toward a large stone. As I trail behind, I realize that the mountain is hollowed out, concealing a vast cavern within. The cave stretches high, almost reaching the summit of the mountain. In the center, a small rock pool collects water, perhaps fed by my rains.

The women and children gather around the cave, their eyes fixed on me in solemn silence. They stop playing the drums and flute as we walk deeper into the hollow. Guilt tugs at my heart: I can't shake the feeling that I'm somehow responsible for their displacement. As I glance around, my attention is drawn to the walls decorated with elaborate paintings: herds of majestic buffalo, the sleek form of the black panther, brave warriors, and women carrying children in baskets on their backs. It looks as though they have recorded their history here. Despite the village being relatively new, these paintings appear ancient, layers upon layers of pigment telling stories of generations past. One wall is adorned with countless outlines of handprints, each one unique in size and shape.

"This way, Oya," the young woman says, guiding me to a fire.

They are making frybread. I feel the water in my mouth as we approach the elder preparing the food. I can practically taste the warm, crispy dough, and I find myself swallowing in anticipation of the savory treat.

"We know it is your favorite. You should continue to eat so you don't get sick," the young woman says, rubbing her stomach.

Does everyone already know that I am with child? The news travels fast in these parts. A young boy walks up with a clay cup filled with water. "It is from your rains," he says, handing me the water.

I am still parched, and my feet are swollen. I sit on a multicolored blanket the size of a shawl, reminiscent of a rainbow. Each woven line sports a different color.

"She's been working on that blanket for weeks, but last night, when she found out that you were pregnant, she decided to give it to you. She finished up right before you arrived. It's to protect you and your child," the young woman tells me of the elder making the frybread.

My fingers trace the intricate patterns of the woven cover, feeling the textures of each color as if they were crafted from different materials. I glance up at the elder, who watches me with a patient gaze as I admire my gift. Meanwhile, she continues to tend to the frying dough, expertly flipping it in the pan. Beside her, a stack of frybread awaits, tempting me with its warm golden-brown surface. With a gentle gesture, she offers me the plate, encouraging me to partake. I reach for the top piece.

"More," she insists.

I grab one more, noticing that the children are gathering around.

"She wanted to make sure that you had your fill before the rest of the group took theirs," the young woman says, translating all of the elder's actions.

The frybread melts in my mouth as the children run up and gather pieces to bring back to their families. It doesn't feel like we are in hiding except for the whispering. Even the children are running about in silence.

As I finish the last bite of my second frybread, my belly rumbles. I don't think it's asking for more. I slow down for a moment, seeing if I need to run out to release it. But my stomach settles. I pull the rainbow blanket from underneath me and wrap it around my body. The weight of the fabric drapes over my shoulders, offering a sense of security and warmth. It's as if the colors and textures merge to cocoon me.

In the distance, we hear the call of the conch shell. I'm taken back to Mardi Gras and Cuba. Where did they get the conch shell? I haven't seen an ocean anywhere nearby. As more villagers notice the distant sound, they begin to slowly pack up their belongings. I turn to the young woman who has been helping me and ask, "What is happening?"

"There is a victory, we can head back to the village."

From the somber faces, I never would have guessed that the sound signaled triumph. "Why is everyone sad?" I ask.

"We believe in the sanctity of life. Of everyone's life. We pray for our enemies as if they are our mothers, fathers, sisters, or brothers. We hope this ended with minimal damage."

I watch as the children care for their parents, gathering their belongings and placing them into baskets. I can tell they prepared for at least three days of hiding. This was not their first time. Ozata said that they purchased the land, against their belief in the earth not belonging to anyone. Their purchase doesn't keep trouble away. I imagine there is always someone trying to steal it from them. With the river and the waters back, their land is more "valuable" than ever. *Father, please protect these kind souls.* I know he is with me, my father. As he protects me, so shall he protect the ones I love.

I muster up a small cloud over the stone pool in the middle of the cave and let the rains pour into the miniature lake. The children yell, "Oya's waters are magical!"

They run to get cups, bowls, and buckets to catch the water. The adults join them with every vessel they can find. The waters seem to have washed away their concerns, at least for the moment. I keep the cloud there for a spell, until everyone has filled their containers.

# CHAPTER 21

As we step into the heart of the village, our eyes sweep over the aftermath of the chaos. Burned tents stand with their charred frames and singed leather curling away like black scrolls. The smell of blood and seared flesh assaults us all. Wisps of smoke spiral upward from the earth, lingering like ghostly whispers of the turmoil that unfolded here.

I call forth the rains, a gentle cascade that washes over the land, soothing the scorched earth and quelling any lingering embers. With each droplet, the smoke begins to dissipate, vanishing into the cool mist that now envelops the village.

The warriors stand vigilantly around the captives. Ozata walks back and forth in front of the four outlaws, her bow and arrows slung around her shoulder. With a kind yet firm wave, I motion for the children trailing behind me to return to the safety of their homes, their curious gazes reluctantly shifting away from the tightly secured men. As they scamper off, I slowly walk toward the warriors. Even from a distance, I feel the weight of Jesse's gaze upon me. Despite his precarious position, a wry smile tugs at the corners of his lips.

I feel safe to approach him now. A part of me wants to wrap them up in a tornado and send them high into the sky. He endangered Ozata's village, my new family. My stomach stirs as I walk up to the men, but I keep going. Jesse's menacing smile widens as I stand in front of him.

"We finally get some alone time, dear," he says.

I am silent, not knowing how to respond, wondering if he even deserves an answer. After a moment, I say, "You should be happy that these people respect life. If it were up to me, you would be dead."

"You can whisper them words to me on our honeymoon," he cunningly hisses.

I've slapped him across the face before I even know that I reacted. I can feel my clouds forming behind me, waiting for the command. Ozata runs up and yells, "We are going to take these men in for the reward. Jesse here has a handsome bounty on his head. We get even more if he is alive."

I take a deep breath and the clouds disperse.

"Did you see that, boss?" one of the other men cries.

"She is a witch, of course you would fall for a witch!" another outlaw says, trying desperately to untie his ropes.

"Jesse, I am going to ask you a question, and it would be best to answer it honestly," I command.

"All I have is my word," he says with his wily smile.

I clear my throat. "Did you take anyone else from the train that day?"

"You're the lucky one, baby. All I need is you."

My clouds begin to rise. "He's not worth it," Ozata says from behind me.

"Did you do anything to the train?" I continue.

"It was a rescue mission, lady. Jesse, just tell her what she wants to hear before we all meet our maker," one of the men beside him answers.

"Look, my team saved me from the gallows. All they were going to do is rescue me. I'm the one that made them come for you."

"I hope it was worth it," I say, turning around.

"They can't hold me, nobody can," Jesse says as I walk up to Ozata.

She asks one of her warriors to stand guard as we go discuss the next moves.

"You must be exhausted. How are you feeling?" Ozata asks.

The rage within me refuses to settle. What did he do to me when I was passed out? My clouds follow me as we walk toward my tent. No rain flows forth, but I let the men see my power.

"Do you think he was telling the truth?" I ask.

"I don't think that you should trouble yourself with him."

"My friends were on that train. I have to find them," I cry.

Ozata puts her arm around me and says, "And I will help you. We will take these men to town and then begin our search. Do you know where the train was heading?"

"Texas," I say.

"Well, you are in luck, because this is Texas. But this here is one of the biggest states in the union. We will inquire about where the train ended up when we bring the men into town."

Ozata leads me to my tent, which was not touched by the fires, and opens the flap. "Get some rest. Tomorrow is a big day. Now that the river is flowing and water has returned to the land, we can go find your friends. As much as we want you to stay, we know that you must go start your family."

That hit me like a boulder to my chest. For a moment, I forgot that I was pregnant. Clutching the protective rainbow tapestry around my shoulders, I am now acutely aware of the life within me. I cannot go find Shango until I know this baby has survived. The memory of my first loss looms heavy in my mind. Ozata closes the flap, and I hear her footsteps scurrying back to the prisoners.

Unfurling my rainbow blanket on the bed, I lie with my head toward the middle of the room. I stare up at the pointed ceiling of my tent and think about the confidence in Jesse's voice when he told us that no one can hold him. The nonchalant conviction chills me to the bone. I don't think I'll be able to sleep a wink with him out there.

They started a fire for the outlaws; I can hear the crackling. I think one of the elders went to go feed them. The thought of them devouring the frybread ignites a fiery rage within me. Why is it so difficult to let go of this resentment? I can sense Ozata's concern for my unborn child. She doesn't think it's good for my baby when I get upset. I wonder if that really makes a difference. Drawing in a deep, steadying breath, I make a silent vow to myself. I will do whatever it takes to maintain a sense of calm, to shield my unborn child from this chaos.

My mind drifts a bit. I am grateful that no villagers were hurt in the raid; I was convinced that there would be casualties. The reek of burning flesh we smelled was the scorched animal skins from the tents and blankets within. The thought of the villagers hurt or even killed by the outlaws is crushing. I wonder how I would've held back my fury if that had been the case. As I continue to stare into the tip of the tepee, I begin to see double, and I doze off.


The hollowed alarm of the conch shell wakes me up from my slumber. It is still dark outside. I trip over to the opening of my tent and slowly step out. There is a small piece of leather at my door. I can see it only because half of the villagers have ignited torches in their hands.

Ozata runs up holding a burning stick and grabs my shoulder. "You are here! I was so worried!" she yells.

"What happened?"

"The men got away. I thought Jesse would come for you."

I pick up the piece of leather at my door. There is writing that looks like chicken scratch on it. I hold it up toward the light and read it: "My love, our story is not over. I don't want you to hate me. I'll be back. J.J."

Chills travel up my spine.

"He wouldn't dare come back, but, just in case, I'm going to stay with you tonight," Ozata says reassuringly.

I chuckle quietly to myself, perhaps because of nerves. I think about what a kick Thomas would get out of this story, envisioning the scene as I entertain him with the ridiculousness of it all. His reaction, with that unmistakable twinkle in his eye and the puff of cigar smoke swirling around him, would be priceless. Despite everything, Thomas seems to hold Jesse in some strange regard.

But why? Jesse is nothing more than a deceitful outlaw, a villain whose criminal record seems to grow longer with each passing day. Liar, thief, perhaps murderer, and, with this latest incident, kidnapper as well. The absurdity of it all is not lost on me, and the thought of Thomas's reaction only adds to my amusement.

"Thank you," I say with relief.

Ozata looks around and plants her torch right outside my door. The flickering flame reflects red waves of light into my tent. The commotion outside becomes my lullaby, with children running and laughing, dodging the flames, and the serious tone of the elders wondering how the men got away with warriors standing guard. Nocturnal animals and insects crescendo louder than the tribesmen with their cricket calls and bullfrog croaks. Ozata tucks me into the rainbow blanket and tiptoes outside.

# CHAPTER 22

We decide to start with the authorities in the nearest town. I find myself traveling with little more than the rainbow shawl and the wooden figurine that Ozata made of me. Amitola gave me an outfit to travel in: a long beaded leather skirt paired with a simple button-up white top, clearly acquired through trade with settlers. My large leather boots feel cumbersome after running barefoot for the past week. The clothes I wore on the train, ripped and tattered from the ordeal, have been left with the elders to fix up and mend for trade.

The river is powerfully flowing as Ozata and I walk away from the village. We pack plenty of frybread and dried meat to last us throughout the journey. Ozata has on a cotton dress, cream-colored, with pleats folded and pressed down the front below the belt. It looks like a shirt and skirt, but it is one piece. Her hair is pulled back into a bun, and she has leather sandals tied up her ankles.

"I dress like the white man when I go into town. They are less threatened by me," Ozata says.

I look down at my beaded skirt and mismatched outfit. We both erupt into laughter.

"There is no style of dress that would make the white man more comfortable with me. My skin cannot deny my roots. I am not trying to be a part of his sick game, anyway," I say.

Ozata contemplates for a moment, then runs back to the village. We have only crossed the river and passed a few trees, so the tepees are still in sight. It is always a wonder to see how fast Ozata runs and navigates through the forest. She leaps over the wide river in one bound, her pleated skirt flipping over her head.

I walk carefully back to the stream, getting accustomed to the thick boots once again. I can't feel the shape of the earth beneath me, but the sharp stones are no issue. I jump on a pile of prickly thorns just because I can. The babbling river calls to me; I can hear it rushing from the mountains. The earth around the village has already adapted to the water. Tiny green sprouts decorate the banks of the waterway with the promise of new life.

I'm startled by a husky war cry. I look up, and Ozata is running full speed toward me in full Native garb. She has even painted her face with the white chalk from the river. With limited effort, Ozata flies over the stream and lands by my side.

"Thank you, Oya," she says, breathless.

"For what?"

"Reminding me to be myself regardless of who I'm around."

As we venture once more into the embrace of the forest, our matching beaded skirts dance in the wind. The bottoms are fringed, the leather cut about half an inch apart, a technique that seems to be a common feature on many of their garments.

"How far is the town?"

"Half a day's walk, which is why we had to start so early," Ozata says.

"We definitely have enough frybread," I say, chuckling.

The woodland is peaceful as we create paths through the overgrown forest floor. Other than the occasional chirping bird, it is overwhelmingly quiet. I blow some wind through the trees just to hear the leaves rustle. Ozata and I have surrendered to the stillness of the journey, for the most part. I feel almost awkward breaking the silence.

"How far are you taking me?" I whisper.

"All the way," she responds in her normal tone.

"All the way to San Francisco?" I question.

"All the way to San Francisco," Ozata repeats. She chuckles to herself. "I'm imagining Yemaya's face if I said to her, 'I rescued your daughter from the hands of a kidnapper, and I sent her off on a train by herself to San Francisco!'"

We both laugh. "I know this is not an easy journey. I am indebted to you."

"Your mother saved my life, and you saved my people, so let's call it even. Do you have any other questions about her?" Ozata asks, kicking a stone into a bush.

She has already told me so much. I feel grateful. "What was she like, her personality?"

"She was hilarious when I knew her, you would've never known the difficulties that she'd endured. She always wanted everyone to have a good time. And she was curious and extremely smart. She learned our language and the English language in less than a week!"

"Unfortunately, that intelligence was not passed down to me." I giggle.

"But the humor was," Ozata says.

A whiff of an offensive stench blows by us. I instinctively use my winds to push it away.

"We are close to the town," Ozata says.

"What is that smell?"

"The sewage. There are many people in the town, and their outhouses line the perimeter of the land."

"Is that to keep enemies away?" I ask, waving my hand in front of my face.

"I honestly do not know. They probably want to keep the stink out," Ozata says.

There are fallen trees, empty bottles, and trash scattered about the edge of the pine forest. The landscape seems to drastically change into a desert with dry sand, much like what Ozata's village looked like before I came. Amid the stench of the sewage, I smell something familiar.

"Are we by the ocean?" I ask.

"Texas City is a port town; the ocean is on the other side."

Thoughts of Mama, Cuba, Obatala, and Oshun flood my mind. I haven't tasted the salty waters of the sea in so long. A wave of excitement hits me.

"I'll take you to the shore after we tell the authorities about Jesse and his gang. I wouldn't bother reporting him if he weren't after you. I try to stay out of white men's business," Ozata says, seemingly regretting her decision.

Ozata adjusts her skirt and takes a deep breath. I can tell that she is nervous. Before we get to the entrance of the town, we hear someone shout out, "It's them Black Indians again!"

"What Black Indians?" I ask.

"I think they are talking about us," Ozata says.

Before long, we are surrounded by four white men on horses.

"State your business, redskin," one man demands.

"I'm here to report a kidnapping," Ozata says.

"Is the one missing an Indian, like you? Or a white?" He emphasizes the "w" as if he's blowing out an oil lamp.

"Well . . ." Ozata stammers.

"Go on, spit it out!" he yells.

"The one missing is standing right next to me. I rescued her," she says.

"A nigger? Don't nobody care about a nigger gone missing." All of the men laugh.

"I wonder how Houston would feel if they found out Jesse and his gang of outlaws went through your territory undiscovered?" I ask.

The men stop laughing and settle their horses. "Jesse James?" they question.

"That's the one," I say.

Reluctantly, the main man, perhaps the sheriff, says, "Follow me."

They lead us into the town. Beaten dirt roads and weathered wooden buildings surround us. The stench of waste and fish intensifies as we venture deeper. Saloons hum with activity; their doors swing open, with locals staring in our direction. Horses trot down the streets, pulling wagons laden with goods, while cowboys on horseback herd cattle through the town.

I have yet to see the ocean. The last lawman on horseback turns around and spits on the ground beside us with contemptuous disregard. Ozata and I remain stoic, refusing to dignify his crude behavior with a reaction. But as the acrid scent fills my nostrils, my stomach churns uneasily. Without warning, I find myself retching in the middle of the road.

"Ain't nothing worse than a nigger but a sick nigger," the last man comments.

We sidestep the mess and leave it there without so much as covering it. Proceeding to what appears to be the town's police station, we're greeted by an unsettlingly large gathering of onlookers. Their eyes follow us as we're ushered inside by the reluctant lawmen.

Upon entering the building, a tall man with dark hair and a neatly trimmed goatee leans casually against a desk. Before we can fully process the scene unfolding before us, the four lawmen swiftly draw their guns, aiming them squarely at the well-dressed gentleman.

"Is that any way to greet a stranger?" he asks with the same confidence as Jesse.

"You a bounty hunter?" the sheriff asks.

"Sure am," he says, flipping a toothpick around his tongue.

"You looking for Jesse?" another man asks. The men put away their guns, clearly still suspicious.

"I wish I was, that's a handsome bounty. But I'm here for her," the man says, pointing at me.

Ozata jumps in between us, fully ready to defend me.

"Whoa, girl! I come in peace," the man says as he hands Ozata a folded paper.

She reads it. "Is your friend named Thomas?" Ozata asks me.

"Yes," I say.

"It looks as if Thomas hired a tracker to find you," Ozata says, handing the paper back to the man.

"I'm Roosevelt Smith, a pleasure to meet you," Roosevelt says, tipping his hat.

"Damn Yankees," the sheriff scoffs under his breath.

"How did you know I would be here?" I ask.

"Lucky guess. I have been visiting the towns surrounding Houston to ask questions. Thomas and Ellen had to head out to San Francisco. Ellen had a court date that she couldn't miss or else they would put her away. They're planning to come back to help with the search, but I found you."

"More like we found you," Ozata retorts.

"Is Ellen okay?" I ask.

"They hired me after her first day in court. It seemed to go in her favor. We'll send a message saying that I'm going to bring you home."

"Oh, I'll take her, sir," Ozata argues.

"Here," he says, handing Ozata what looks like a bag of coins.

"What's this?" Ozata asks.

"Reward money for finding Oya. Courtesy of Sir Thomas and Madame Ellen."

"Who would pay that amount for a nigger?" the sheriff bellows.

Roosevelt widens his eyes. "Seems like I arrived at the perfect time."

As if by clockwork, the men pull out their guns again. "You can't leave without paying your taxes," the sheriff yells.

"You don't want to do that," Roosevelt threatens. "If you put your weapons down now, you won't get hurt."

Outside, the dirt roads kick up dust from my winds, and Ozata grabs hold of her bow. The men refuse to put their weapons away. Before I have a chance to bring the storm, Roosevelt shoots three of the men, including the sheriff. A tall, lanky man remains with his gun shaking.

"Run!" Roosevelt yells at him.

He trips out of the building, looking at the squirming men holding their wounds. Roosevelt kicks their guns out of their hands and leads us to the door.

"You know, we really didn't need you to save us," Ozata says.

"Something tells me you're right about that."

We step out into a harsh gust of sand. Roosevelt tries to shield us with his dress coat. I subtly calm the winds with my hands without him noticing. The crowd has dispersed, perhaps because of the chaotic weather. The town square now lies deserted except for a few lingering souls scurrying for cover from the whipping sands.

"I am going to make sure Oya reaches Ellen and Thomas," Ozata says with a firm demeanor.

"Suit yourself. You have enough for a train ticket there and back three times over," Roosevelt responds.

"What's the plan?" I ask.

"We are going to ride up to Houston and take the train to San Francisco from there," Roosevelt says, untying one of the sheriff's horses and jumping on. "You coming?"

Ozata and I swiftly scale the lawmen's horses, seizing the reins. With a gentle nudge of our heels, we guide our mounts toward Roosevelt. I send a final gust of wind behind us, discouraging any potential pursuers.

Dusty streets weave through the heart of the city, lined with a mix of wooden buildings and sturdy brick structures. Despite my winds, the air is thick with the scents of horse sweat, leather, and a hint of fresh bread from a nearby bakery. Shops and establishments populate the streets, their wooden facades decked with hand-painted signs advertising goods and services.

We gallop toward the shore, the vast ocean spreads for miles behind the buildings.

"Where are we headed?" Roosevelt shouts from his horse behind us.

"To the beach," Ozata hollers back.

"Don't you think we ought to get out of town?" he asks when he catches up to us.

"We aren't staying long," I say.

As we get closer to the water, townspeople begin to come out of their homes and general stores, their boots kicking up small clouds of dust. A blacksmith stares at us from his forge, his face aglow from the molten metal. My whirlwinds of dry sand have ceased, and people are emerging, suspicious of our presence. Roosevelt definitely has a point; we should make our way out of town.

"Oya," Ozata says in a cautious tone.

In front of us, Jesse and his gang burst out of a bank with bags full of coins. We slow down to a trot and realize that they have their pistols and rifles trained on us. Smoke begins to cloud out of the bank.

"Let me handle this, ladies," Roosevelt says, riding out in front of us.

Jesse yells out to me, "Fancy meeting you here." He throws his bag of coins over his shoulder and turns to Roosevelt. "Come to return my rightful property?"

"Boss, let's get out of here," one of his men shouts.

Jesse tosses his money to his crew and holds his hands up to show that he doesn't have a gun. "I'm just coming to talk," he yells from the edge of the road.

He walks up to Roosevelt, who remains on his horse, and the men commune in the middle of the dusty street. We can't hear what they are saying, but it seems as though Roosevelt is growing increasingly angry. Suddenly, Jesse grabs Roosevelt's foot and flips him off his horse.

Ozata pulls out her bow, targeting Jesse before he can get any closer to us. His gang begins shooting in the air as Roosevelt stumbles to his feet.

"Don't you dare move an inch closer," Ozata yells to Jesse.

My winds begin to pick up, and the townspeople, one by one, run for cover. Roosevelt and Jesse's men disappear in a cloud of debris. Jesse runs full speed ahead, and Ozata releases her arrow into his shoulder. He falls to the ground, writhing in pain.

Ozata rides straight into the chalky fog, reemerging with Roosevelt situating himself behind her in midstride. "Let's go!" Ozata yells.

Jesse's gang runs through the dust, guns blazing. Roosevelt ducks, trying to wipe the dirt from his eyes while holding tight to Ozata. I see Jesse struggling to get up as I turn my horse around. I clear a path through the circling dirt with my squalls and ride like the wind out of town.

# PART 3

# WINDS OF CHANGE

# CHAPTER 23

The shrill whistle of the train pierces the air, jolting me awake as we glide into the bustling San Francisco station. Ozata stirs beside me, roused from her slumber by the commotion, then settles back to sleep. We had to sit at the back of the train, though at least there were proper wooden benches arranged in rows this time. I nudge Ozata gently, letting her know that we have arrived.

Roosevelt rode at the front of the train, likely enjoying the comforts of the plush velvet seating and first-class dining that Thomas once described to me. Meanwhile, Ozata and I made do without such luxuries, grateful that we had brought along an ample supply of frybread to sustain us during the arduous three-day journey.

"We are here," I whisper in Ozata's ear.

As I look out at the beautiful city, I am reminded of New Orleans. While there are not as many Negroes, it is certainly diverse. There are streetcars, much like the whites-only ones in New Orleans. I see quite a few men with static black hair and white skin. From far away, I thought perhaps they were Indigenous, but as we pull in closer, I am certain they are from somewhere else. Ozata yawns and begins to gather her things.

"Did you ever think you would be in California?" I ask.

"I didn't even know what California was before I met you," she says, stretching her arms to the sky. "I don't ever need to see another piece of frybread for the rest of my life."

"Blasphemy! Don't say that!" I respond, laughing.

"Fine, but at least not for a year."

The train whistles again as we come to a final stop. I have my rainbow shawl that has been keeping us both warm during the train ride. Fortunately, I didn't get sick during our travel. I rub my stomach and take a deep breath to steady myself.

"I don't plan yet on telling Ellen and Thomas that I am pregnant," I whisper.

"I won't say a word." Ozata covers her mouth and widens her eyes.

"How long will you stay?" I ask.

"I will have to be getting back soon. Perhaps I'll stay for a night or two if Ellen allows. Then I must return. I pray to the Great Spirit that Jesse did not go back to my village," Ozata says, rubbing her hands.

Thoughts of Jesse faded on the journey. As a matter of fact, I didn't think of him once during the train ride. My thoughts were consumed with images of Shango, as if I could feel the lingering sting of his rose scratching my chest. But Ozata has to return to the roads that Jesse traveled, back to the hills where she found me by their campfire. What a different story I would be living if she never rescued me.

Our section of the train is packed. It isn't just Negroes; there are many white travelers occupying the narrow wooden seats in the back. Everyone seems a bit sluggish from the voyage, hungry and parched. We were able to share our fry-bread with a few grateful passengers, but most of us haven't had a proper meal in three days. We stand in line waiting for the door to open.

The lock unfurls like the inside of a clock, encircling the door handle. As it swings open, a uniformed man ushers us into a crowd of cheering people. Roosevelt sent a telegram to Ellen informing her of our travels. I wonder if she is here. We shuffle into the aisle, the line packed tightly with people anxious to de-board. My belly brushes against the person in front of me, and I attempt to slow my pace. But the press of the crowd behind me propels me back into the stranger.

By the time we get to the metal steps, Roosevelt is waiting by the door. "Wel-come to the land of milk and honey, where the streets are paved with gold!"

As soon as Ozata steps on the ground, I see her excitement growing. I am confused; I didn't think gold would have that effect on her.

"I feel the people, the original people," she says. "They are here somewhere, or they blessed this land. There is powerful earth beneath this nonsense."

That's more like her. We follow Roosevelt out of the station, darting through the crowds, trying to keep up. A large dark carriage drawn by two white horses stands regally on the street outside the train station. Cobblestone pathways weave through the heart of the city, worn by the countless footsteps and wagon wheels that have traversed them.

As the sun casts long shadows on the uneven streets, Victorian facades embellished with intricate details rise proudly, each building vying for attention in this bustling display. The air is filled with a cacophony of sounds—the rhythmic clattering of horse-drawn carriages, the chatter of vendors peddling their wares, and the indistinct murmur of conversations in a multitude of languages.

People of diverse backgrounds, including many of the men I saw from the train, rush through the streets. Women in sweeping skirts and corsets, their wide-brimmed hats shielding them from the sun, navigate the narrow walkways. Men dressed in well-tailored suits and bowler hats move with a confident stride.

Horse-drawn carriages, furnished with brass fittings and polished wood, traverse the thoroughfares. The air carries the tantalizing scents of street vendors selling roasted chestnuts, exotic spices, and freshly baked breads. My mouth waters as Roosevelt leads us closer to the burnished black carriage.

The door barely has time to open before Ellen jumps out of the cab.

"Oya!" she hollers with so much bravado that the streets seem to pause for a moment and take notice.

In Ellen's embrace, the floodgates of my emotions burst open. I hold on to her, finally feeling home. Not the city but Ellen. She is my sanctuary, my refuge, the true embodiment of home.

"Now, now, child. Thomas is waiting at the house. His impatience has almost got the best of him."

Ellen is clad in a deep maroon velvet dress with a corset and bulging sleeves. A miniature hat with black lace cascading over her face alludes to a state of mourning. I'm too scared to ask; I can't handle any bad news.

"This is Ozata, a good friend of my mother's and now of mine," I say.

"You are welcome at my house as long as you please. Any friend of Oya and Yemaya is a friend of mine," Ellen says, pulling Ozata in for a hug. "Roosevelt, you have done well. I hope you are free for a dinner at my place tonight to celebrate."

"Of course, Madame," Roosevelt says. He shakes our hands and disappears into the crowd of people.

"Come on, I know you both must be hungry. We've prepared a quiet meal for you so you can rest up for the celebration dinner tonight."

"My kind of people," Ozata says through a chuckle.

Ellen ushers us into her carriage. A white man, dressed in black, holds the door open for us. He bows, averting his gaze, as we enter. Velvet seats, much like the ones I imagined in the first-class section of the train, frame the inside of the carriage. There is a scent, perhaps lavender, dancing through the air. I remember Marie's garden and the lavender sprouting along the perimeter, blessing us with its fragrance. Marie would make small pillows filled with the herb for the new mothers who came to birth with her. She would instruct them to place it under the sheets to ensure a good night's rest.

Seated in the horse-drawn carriage, Ozata leans forward, hands resting on the windowsill, her fingers gently tapping in rhythm with the clip-clop of the horses' hooves against the cobblestone streets. As the carriage ascends the steep incline, the sounds of the bustling city below blend into a distant symphony.

The climb into the hills transforms the scenery. Narrow streets give way to broad avenues, and quaint buildings are replaced by imposing mansions. My eyes sweep across the grand residences, each one a symbol of opulence and wealth. The air changes, carrying a sense of privilege and prestige even more imposing than that of New Orleans.

The mansions, enhanced with intricate details and surrounded by lush gardens, stand proudly against the backdrop of rolling hills. The carriage winds through the affluent neighborhood until it comes to a stop.

A wrought-iron gate swings open, revealing a meticulously landscaped garden that frames the impressive facade. The mansion rises majestically with multiple stories, each adorned with ornate details. Carved moldings and cornices grace the edges of the building, while large bay windows show off the interior of the house.

The entrance to the mansion is marked by a grand double door, exquisitely carved and flanked by gas lamps that cast a warm glow even in the bright light of the sun. Ozata and I are speechless as we walk up to the building, which looks more like a cathedral than a home. As we step inside, we are greeted by a grand foyer decorated with a chandelier that sparkles with crystal brilliance. There is plush carpeting, Victorian furniture, and artwork hanging on the walls. A woman resembling the mulattoes in New Orleans rushes up and attempts to take our belongings. She soon realizes that Ozata and I have traveled light. "I will take your things to your room. Your trunk is already up there," she says, smiling.

"Oya!" Thomas yells from the top of the stairs. He rushes down, careful not to fall.

From where I stand, I see that the mansion boasts spacious rooms with high ceilings. An elaborate fireplace, richly decorated with marble and carved wood, stands in the living room. An Egyptian woven rug, just like the one Ellen bought for Marie, covers part of the mahogany hardwood floor. A white piano, much larger than the one Marie has, is displayed on the opposite side of the fireplace.

Thomas grabs my face and turns me around to check where I was struck. "You are all in one piece!" he says. I can see that his eyes are pooling with tears. "I won't keep you. Go freshen up and come feast!"

Ellen walks up. "This is Ozata, dear," she says.

*Dear?* She never referred to Thomas as "dear" in New Orleans.

"How rude of me," he says, taking Ozata's hand and kissing the top of it.

A white woman, small in stature, with delicate features and blond hair, walks up.

Ellen says, "This is one of my protégés, Teresa. She is becoming quite adept at reading the Comstock mining shares." I look at Ozata, and she seems as confused as I am. What is Comstock?

Teresa humbly smiles and reaches out her hand to greet both me and Ozata. "Can I help with anything?" she offers.

"We don't have much," Ozata says, then turns to me. "Can we share a room?"

"Nonsense, we have thirty rooms, you can have your own," Ellen insists. "I'll give you the one right next to Oya."

"Thank you," Ozata says.

The mulatto girl leads us up the grand stairway. Marie's entire house could fit in one of Ellen's rooms, and Marie's house was grand compared to our cottage in Cuba. My wildest imagination could never dream up such opulence. I look back at Ozata, who seems unimpressed. I reach out to hold her hand. I'm not ready for her to leave.

We trail closely behind the girl, mindful of the large interior of the mansion. Despite the warmth of the sun outside, the air in the hall feels chilly, sending a shiver down my spine as we tramp past the empty rooms.

"Here you are." The young woman leads us into a sizable room with a fireplace of its own. The outside of the hearth is shaped into an arch with bricks fanned out across the top. A pile of wood is stacked beside it. "My name is Bethany, if you need anything," she says.

"Thank you."

Bethany attempts to show Ozata to her quarters, but she says, "I'll stay here with Oya, there is plenty of room."

"As you wish," Bethany says, backing out the doorway.

"Is that good with you?" Ozata asks.

"Yes, it's what I prefer. I'm already dreading your departure," I say.

I shake my rainbow shawl open and spread it onto the oversize mattress. Its vibrant colors contrast the whites and creams used to decorate this room. Ozata walks around, contemplating some distant thought. I want to interrupt her, but I let her be. While scanning the room, I see my trunk in the corner. It is time to change out of these clothes; they feel like they are sticking to me.

At the far side of the room, a vanity mirror and stool catch my eye. I sink onto the chair, untying the laces of my boots. Glancing up, I catch a glimpse of myself in the mirror. Remnants of every part of my journey since the kidnapping are etched into my face. Running my hand over the back of my head, I search for any trace of the bump from Jesse's blow, but, miraculously, it's gone, erased by Ozata's healing ointment. Squinting at my reflection, I notice faint lines of the white clay that Ozata painted on my face. I am filthy.

I cannot dress in my clothes from New Orleans looking like this. I slip off my boots and make my way to what I think is a closet, only to find something far more extraordinary. Tile flooring reminiscent of ancient Greece leads to an ornate white bath with legs of gleaming gold. The room is bathed in light streaming through a large window. On a marble counter nearby, a porcelain bowl filled with warm water beckons, accompanied by four small towels, a bar of soap, a bottle of body oil, and a delicate vial of perfume.

There is a knock on my open door. Ozata answers, "Come in."

Teresa walks in with two bright white towels. I go into the bedroom to greet her.

"I hear that you will be rooming together. Here are your bath towels. You will find your rinse-off bowls are ready in your bathrooms. Ozata, your bowl, soap, and wash towels are in your original room across the hall. Feel free to freshen up there. There is a bell affixed to the wall by your door. Do not hesitate to ring it if you need anything. The cooks are almost finished preparing your meals."

We thank Teresa as she walks out.

"Come," I say to Ozata, and lead her to my trunk. "We must find something for us to wear."

"Will it be like the pleated dress?" Ozata questions.

"Not exactly. They are made by the finest Negro seamstresses in New Orleans."

"So, not the white man?"

"Not the white man," I assure her.

We open the trunk and pull out one fancy dress after another.

"Forgive me if I'm wrong, but these all look pretty white-man to me," Ozata says with a crooked smile.

"They do, don't they?"

"And this whole house makes me feel like Ellen is winning at the white man's game, but it is all suffocating Mother Earth beneath us. I can feel the land whispering to me. The people are still praying for her. Her heartbeat is strong underneath this." Ozata bends down and puts the palm of her hand on the floor.

"She has no connection to the land from which she came," I say in her defense.

"Who, Ellen? She is the connection. Her ancestors live inside her," Ozata says, tapping her heart.

Ellen walks into the room just as Ozata finishes speaking.

"I could feel your concern as you stepped foot into my home. This land has been blessed by the original people. I can tell you feel that. We help each other out in any way possible. If one of their daughters wants to assimilate into the city, she comes through me. I have been threatened, beaten, and cursed by the whites for practicing my religion. My religion that honors the earth. I am still connected, my dear, don't let all of this fool you."

Ozata looks directly into Ellen's eyes, not ashamed of speaking about her; I am quite sure she planned to tell Ellen later. "Thank you for informing me. I can feel the prayers placed on this land. My people are fighting so hard to keep the old ways. It just scares me."

"I have fear too, but we can't let it stop us. I'd rather be a corpse than a coward." Ellen reaches for the black lace hat and removes it. "I won't be needing this anymore, as we found you," she says to me.

I breathe in relief, since I hadn't known why she was mourning.

"If you are willing, I would love to learn more of your story over lunch," Ellen says to Ozata, walking back to the door. "I'm sure Oya has clothes for you to wear."

Ozata looks back at me and I say, laughing, "The white man's clothes!"

# CHAPTER 24

Our "quiet lunch" is everything but that. Ozata and I are dressed in the finest white man's clothing. Her dress, a resplendent blue satin creation with a daring neckline, is nothing like she has ever worn. Her hair, braided meticulously into twin plaits with ribbons woven in, hangs down her back. Beaded leather ornaments with feathers sway gently at the ends.

I was able to untangle my hair in the bowl of warm water. I found a jar of coconut oil in my room and used it to soften my curls; the smell, like always, reminds me of Cuba.

My dress, a delicate shade of lavender, has layers of lace and trimmings on its bodice. I was nervous about tightening my corset, wary of the constriction on my growing belly. Other than the fullness in my breasts, my body has not drastically changed. The persistent swelling in my feet is easy to conceal, and I'm relieved to find that the corset is looser than usual. I found matching satin gloves that Marie must've sneaked into my trunk as a parting gift. In fact, quite a few of these dresses were tailored for me as presents. I suspect Marie was preparing to introduce me into society. What a nightmare that would've been. I'll have to tell Ellen about my pregnancy soon, so she doesn't get any ideas.

I look around, and the entire table seems to be waiting for me to pick up my fork. As I do, everyone reaches for their first bite of the juicy salmon steak decorated with thinly cut lemon slices and herbs.

"Oya, I don't mean to sound insensitive, but what happened to you when you were taken?" Thomas asks, sitting at the edge of his seat.

I look around at Ellen, Teresa, Thomas, and Ozata. The memory of the kidnapping feels like a distant nightmare; a haunting that now seems almost unreal. I don't want to dredge it up, but I feel I owe them the story. I must admit, I'm rather eager to burst Thomas's bubble about Jesse.

Ozata and I tell them about her heroic rescue, laying on the drama and communicating the tiniest details with undying passion. I forget that Ozata is such a storyteller. I share what I learned about Mama and how Ozata first met her when she was turning seven. We go on to describe the attack by the outlaws and our journey to Texas City, where we met Roosevelt.

"Well, damn," Thomas belts out. "Ozata did all the work, and *then* you ran into Roosevelt?"

"That's the story," I say.

Thomas turns to Ellen. "Remind me to pay Ozata for her work."

"No need," Ozata says. "Roosevelt gave me the reward money, and Oya blessed our land with—"

I kick Ozata under the table. She pauses, staring at my wide eyes. I do not want Teresa to know of my abilities.

"With her *presence*," Ozata finishes.

"I insist, take it back for your people. You never know when you might need it," Thomas says.

"The white man's money," Ozata says under her breath.

Where Thomas is absent-minded, Ellen is attentive. I know that she heard Ozata's comment. Thomas, on the other hand, is savoring his first bite of salmon. The fish is beginning to make me feel queasy. I slide the plate a bit farther away, but of course Ellen notices.

"Oya," Ellen says, "come help me with something in the living room."

I jump at her request, mostly to escape the overwhelming smells. I grab a piece of fresh mint from my lemonade and put it in my mouth. It cuts through the nausea almost immediately.

"Did you know that you were with child when you left New Orleans?" Ellen whispers loudly as I enter the room.

"No, ma'am."

"Have you missed your monthly?"

"Just barely," I say.

"Do you want to keep it?"

I stutter, "Keep . . . it?"

"If you are not ready for a child, you have many different options. We are in modern times, and we are modern women."

I hadn't thought that I had a choice. My stomach rumbles.

"Think about it, my dear. Only you can make that choice. Is the father Shango?"

*How did she know?*

"Honey, you were eyeing him the entire time you were on the float at Mardi Gras. It wasn't hard to figure out."

"But how did you know—"

Ellen cuts me off. "I know everything, child. Don't you worry about a thing. It is all going to turn out exactly as it should."

"I know we have to get back to lunch, but do you think I should tell him? Shango?"

Ellen stares at me in a way that makes me feel uneasy.

"I'm sure Marie told you, but I lost my first child. I don't want to get Shango's hopes up if this child is going to die too," I say. My emotion rises, tickling my nose and causing my eyes to water.

"Your words. Your words are your magic. The wind on your tongue as you speak your words rises into the sky and mixes with all the other words that have ever been said. When the time is right, those words return to you as actions and experiences. If you don't want something to happen, do not speak it into existence. Do you want this baby?"

"Yes."

"Then let us not speak of her demise. No matter how scared you might be, don't let the words out. I will light a candle and do some prayers for the fears you have already spoken. I am here to support you in any way you need."

I can tell that Ellen is upset. Perhaps she had other plans for me. I look around the room, dreading the fish smell that is slowly wafting in. I'm afraid I might get sick if I go back to the dining room.

"I think I should lie down," I say, holding my stomach.

"I'll send up some bread for you; you must eat."

Ellen turns, and her dress fans into a magnificent circle, revealing the colors hidden in the pleats of the skirt. She hurries back to her guests. I know Ozata might resent my departure, but she's more than capable of managing on her own. As I make my way toward the grand staircase, my attention is drawn to what appears to be a library.

The air carries the scent of aged leather and polished wood. Thankfully, it doesn't make me sick. The room is lined with dark mahogany bookcases, their shelves stretching from floor to ceiling, cradling volumes that whisper of worlds both real and imagined. Mama often brought books home for us to explore as a family. Obatala almost always volunteered to read, but when everyone went to bed, I would continue by candlelight.

Large arched windows invite the soft glimmer of natural light, filtered through heavy drapes that bear kingly patterns. The light dances upon the richly decorated Persian rug, which adds a touch of exoticism to the otherwise traditional space.

The centerpiece of the room is an imposing mahogany desk, with carefully arranged quills, inkwells, and a leather-bound ledger resting on the surface. A stunningly carved wooden chair stands on either side of the desk, perhaps the workspace for both Ellen and Thomas. Above the counter, an oil painting of Ellen gazes sternly upon the room. As I walk to the bookcase, it seems as though her eyes are following me.

My fingers graze the book titles; I'm waiting for something to catch my eye. My hand stops at *The Gilded Age: A Tale of To-day*. I slowly tip it out, careful not to disturb the other books. Mark Twain and Charles Dudley Warner. I tuck the book under my arm and quickly leave the library, running up the stairs with my dress fluttering behind me as though it's struggling to keep pace.

In my room, a daybed rests beneath a massive window. Beside it sits a small table holding a half-loaf of bread and a few squares of butter. It seems they brought it up while I was in the library. I tear off a small piece of the warm bread and eat it without the butter, feeling my stomach begin to settle.

Sunlight floods the room, bathing the walls in an orange hue, while the white and cream decorations reflect its brilliance. Dust motes dance in the rays, swirling around each other, seemingly clamoring for the spotlight. I recall Marie's words echoing in my mind: "You can read any element speaking to you in form. You can read water, stones, fire, smoke, clouds—everything in existence is trying to commune with you."

I collapse onto the bed, fully clothed. My bohemian-inspired dress is surprisingly more comfortable lying down. I grab my rainbow shawl and tuck it under my head, watching my stomach rise and fall with each breath. "I can't wait to meet you. I can't wait to play with you," I say out loud.

My words feel like lies. I'm scared. I don't want to imagine breastfeeding and crawling and swaddling only to be ripped of all my hopes again. I will not speak my fears. I will not give them life. Just like Ellen said to Ozata earlier: We do it even if we are scared.

I reach for the book. Bound in rich, dark leather, the cover is embossed with gold leaf, its designs tracing the contours of the title. I turn the page and see the authors: Mark Twain and Charles Dudley Warner. I'm not familiar with Warner's work, but I'm eager to begin. The parchment-thin pages are crisp and new. I breath in the smell of the inked paper, delighting in my odd obsession. Mama used to find me asleep with an open book straddling my face because I loved the smell of the pages so much. To my surprise, there are illustrations in the novel. I rest my head on the pillow and begin my journey.

I'm unsure how long I have been reading when Ozata and Ellen creak open the door and tiptoe in. It looks as though the sun has moved lower in the sky, not setting but close. When they see that I am awake, both ladies jump on the bed on either side of me.

"I wish I could stay longer." Ozata sighs.

"In the Black woman's house," Ellen adds, and they laugh.

"Ellen just gave me the most amazing reading—is that what it's called?"

"Yes, dear."

"I never realized how much my anger toward the white man consumed my life. Of course it was justified, but it was killing me on the inside. Not only was I hurt from the actual damage he did, my thoughts and hate took up almost all the rest of my time. Ellen showed me how to get in touch with my ancestors, who were not concerned with such things. Not just the human ancestors: Grandfather Sun, who shines on anyone no matter what they've done; Mother Ocean, who judges no one yet commands respect—who else?"

"So many came through for you. But I believe your maternal grandmother, Cora, was the most present."

"Great Spirit, yes! Cora is the one who loved your mom so much!"

Cora—what a beautiful name. I think that's my baby's name. My stomach turns in agreement. I know she is not old enough to kick, but I feel her. My sweet Cora.

Both Ozata and Ellen stare at me lovingly.

"Do you think you will be able to come down for the party later?" Ozata asks.

"As long as they are not cooking fish!"

"It will be mostly wine and cheese. A few other hors d'oeuvres. I've instructed the staff to keep pungent smells away from you," Ellen says.

I chuckle at the thought. Just a few days ago, I was dodging bullets, running barefoot in the mud; now pungent foods will be kept away from me.

"Oya, your knowledge of your history is limited, perhaps because your mother was tasked with the difficult job of raising you and keeping you alive. She didn't have time to tell you who you really are," Ellen says, as stern as her oil painting in the library. "There have been kingdoms and civilizations in Africa for longer than any of us can imagine. The way I'm living here is not as special or rare as the white man would like us to think." Ellen pauses, winking at Ozata, "Riches, gold, opulence, prestige, cleanliness, science, math, philosophy, writing, sewage systems, buildings, art, astronomy, astrology, temples . . ." Ellen takes a deep breath. "Shall I go on?" She stretches out on the bed, making space for a deeper inhale. She sighs. "This damn dress."

Ozata and I wait attentively for her to finish.

"All of the things that we think of as 'civilized' or 'the white man' are actually stolen from different parts of Africa. We are the mothers and fathers of these technologies. The Africans they brought over as slaves were architects, doctors, artists, agriculturists, teachers. The buildings you see on these streets all come from the great motherland. The Greeks and the Romans would study in Africa for years, and I mean to the tune of twenty or thirty years, then come home and be crowned the kings of philosophy or science. It is maddening knowing this truth and seeing it actively stripped from the Africans here." Ellen's eyes well up with tears. "You, my dear, are an Orisha incarnate. A divine energy in human form. I am honored to be in your presence."

I am silent, not knowing how to respond. I was able to take in all of Ellen's other wisdom, but it's hard to receive her praise. I bury my head in my pillow.

"Well, if she doesn't want to accept who she is, you can tell me that I'm the greatest warrior alive!" Ozata says in a singsong tone, sending us all into a fit of laughter.

Then a blanket of silence covers us. We stare at the ceiling, breathing in the calm.

"I leave tomorrow. Ellen took care of the entire trip. Including a chaperone back to my village, which I still think is unnecessary."

Ellen and I remain silent, staring at the ceiling. A tear rolls down the side of my cheek into my ear. I don't have the will to wipe it. I wish Ozata would stay.

# CHAPTER 25

A ragtime band fills the grand foyer with spirited music. Ellen, Ozata, and I are wearing our gowns from earlier, which seem even more extravagant amid the crowd, though everyone is dressed in their finest attire. Ellen has thoughtfully provided masquerade disguises for those who wish to partake, adding an air of mystery to the festivities.

The crowd falls into a hushed awe as the doors part to reveal perhaps the most elegant woman of the evening. Her frock is embroidered with sequined peacocks that climb gracefully up the side of her subtly curved figure. Tiny white pearls are skillfully woven into her slicked-back bun, contrasting beautifully with her hair, as black as tar. Her tight almond-shaped eyes, sharp and penetrating, look like those of the men I saw from the train. Her lips are painted a bold red, subtly pouted as if frozen in a perpetual kiss.

She glides in my direction. "Seems you are the lady of the hour," she says.

"I'm so glad you two are meeting!" Ellen boasts, locking arms with me. "Oya, this is Chantilly."

"The pleasure is mine," Chantilly says, reaching out her porcelain white hand to gently shake mine.

She smells like roses, not like the artificial scent in perfume but roses on the stem. I find myself captivated, as does everyone else in the room. All eyes track her movements as she graciously greets guests with an air of familiarity—smiles, hugs, laughter exchanged effortlessly. There's a mischievous twinkle in her eye as she playfully dances with a masked man, as though she holds a secret about some naughty deed he may have committed. I've never wanted to know something so badly.

Roosevelt walks in front of my gaze, interrupting the spell. "I hope you got some rest," he says.

His blue eyes, deeper in color than Jesse's, stand out against his olive skin and black hair. He puts a half-mask over his face and bows. "May I have this dance?"

"Certainly," I respond.

As he extends his hand, I place mine gently on top. Though I'm not familiar with the dances of this region, the twins taught me the steps of New Orleans, so I do my best to improvise. Sensing Cosette behind me, her hand at my waist, I allow her to guide me through the dance.

Roosevelt's strong hands lead me with grace. I surrender. We glide across the dance floor as if we choreographed the performance. The crowd seems to part, and I catch sight of Chantilly watching us intently. I'm momentarily distracted, almost tripping over my own feet in shock. She strides over to the band, standing tall, and then her voice fills the room with a soulful melody.

I feel Roosevelt's reassuring touch: He cups my cheeks and gently guides my face back to his gaze, locking eyes with me as we continue to dance to the intoxicating sound of Chantilly's voice.

"How are you holding up after being kidnapped by the most infamous outlaw?"

"Surprisingly well." I chuckle. "It feels almost like it was a lifetime ago. I suppose it could've been much worse."

"You are lucky; anything could've happened. That gang is vicious. So many people romanticize it all, but I have—*we* have—seen it up close and personal."

"Unfortunately," I say as Roosevelt spins me around.

Couples join on the dance floor, swaying, twirling, and embracing.

Ellen had quite a few eligible women show up early to the party. They gathered in the living room for a private meeting. They are now affixed to various well-to-do men. I noticed the women bringing second and third rounds of drinks to the partygoers, and now they are clearly seducing them.

It dawns on me that I haven't seen Ozata in some time. With a sense of urgency, I excuse myself from the dance floor and begin to search throughout the house. However, as I scour each room, a sinking feeling takes hold—where could she be? In the midst of my anxious search, Ellen passes by.

"Have you seen Ozata?" I holler out, hoping to catch her over the music.

Ellen turns and points to the backyard. A few masked guests have surrounded me, clearly wanting to engage. "Excuse me," I say, pushing through and running to the other end of the house.

In the garden out back, I find Ozata seated alongside an elder, engaged in conversation while sharing a pipe. As she exhales smoke in graceful circles, she passes the red clay pipe to the long-haired man beside her.

"Oya! There she is," she exclaims upon my arrival, a warm smile spreading across her face. "I was just talking about you."

Ozata and the man are sitting on a wooden bench with ornate iron armrests. I pull up a garden chair and take a seat.

"Oya, wind whisperer. Welcome," the elder says.

"This is Kaknu, a friend of Ellen's and one of the rightful people of the area," Ozata says proudly.

Kaknu attempts to pass me the pipe, but the smell is causing a reaction for me. I refuse the gesture, not wanting to offend him. Without any visual evidence of insult, he takes the pipe back.

"Kaknu has said that his people have been caretakers for the spirit of the land through all its transitions. The gold that people are extracting from the earth is a part of her veins, so they sing and dance to replenish her. I could feel that as soon as I stepped foot here. My people were forced out of our original land and pushed west. I remember my home, the trees, the animals, the plants. Everything was foreign as we moved." Ozata sighs.

"There has been much change and will be so much more change to come." Kaknu shakes his head as if he has something to share, but it's too painful. "Ozata, you are a warrior. Fight to keep the white man's poisons out of your people's bodies. I have had visions, and they are hard to share because our young ones want to be like this." He points to the people in the party.

Ozata and I stare at the merriment, the laughing, the drinking.

"I don't want to bring you down. Just know that the poisons don't mix well with us. They keep us disconnected from Mother Earth's heartbeat. We must hear her to thrive. We must feel her to truly be alive. Medicines, like alcohol, should be used only in ceremonies or else they become poisons," Kaknu pleads.

"I will tell my people of your wisdom and visions, Kaknu. Thank you," Ozata says, bowing her head.

Ellen opens the back door. "Oya, come, dear. I want to introduce you to a few people."

I turn to Kaknu. "It was a pleasure meeting you. I'm sure I will see you again," I say, struggling out of the seat in my king-size dress.

Ozata jumps up to help me. Once I stand, she puffs out my petticoat. "What a beautiful Black woman's dress," she says with a smile.

"We will have our time tonight," I say to her, my heart already aching from the thought of her absence.

I quickly follow Ellen, eager to meet more of her eccentric friends. As she leads me toward the library, a pungent odor assaults my senses; it's even more potent than the scent of the tobacco pipe. I instinctively breathe through my mouth, trying to avoid the smell, but I keep my lips only slightly parted so I don't give away my distress.

There is a sitting room adjacent to the library with a round table crafted from the same mahogany as the bookshelves and desk. Thomas, Roosevelt, and three other men sit around the table, smoking cigars. I should've recognized the smell because I loved running through the cigar factory in Cuba. The workers there knew me by name; I had a fondness for the aroma of fresh tobacco. Occasionally, the women even allowed me to help roll a few cigars; they said that I was very precise for my age. I could never stay long because my mother disapproved of me being there. Despite purchasing cigars for ceremonies, she never knew of my secret visits.

The smell is rancid now. This pregnancy is already more intense than my first. Ellen graciously pulls out a chair for me, and all the gentlemen stand. As I take my seat, one man steps behind me and carefully pushes the chair in. They all settle back into their places, and Ellen makes her way over to Thomas, sitting next to him.

"Oya, these are some of my colleagues. Alexander, Lew, Christopher, and you know Roosevelt," Thomas boasts.

Alexander is a Negro, perhaps in his twenties. He is dressed in military garb, and his face, though serious, is very handsome. His posture is erect as he slightly bows his head to me. Lew, the man who helped me with my chair, is of the same tribe as Chantilly and the men I saw from the train. Though he looks to be only my age, his hands are calloused and rough, as if he has been working for more years than he has been alive. Christopher is an older white man with a curled mustache. His suit is not the regular black or dark gray but a somewhat burnished inky maroon. He stares at me as I settle myself into the chair.

To my surprise, they are smoking cigars from the very factory I frequented as a child. How I wish I could enjoy the smell now.

"It is a pleasure to make your acquaintance," Christopher says to me.

"She is not one of the girls, Christopher. Keep your paws off her," Ellen snaps.

With a sly smile, Christopher blows smoke in Ellen's direction.

"These men think they can have whatever they want because they have some coins in their pockets now," Ellen says, chuckling.

"We dang near own the bank." Christopher laughs.

"Speaking of banks, Oya tell the boys about Jesse!" Thomas interjects.

"Thomas, don't make her repeat it again," Ellen says, trying to save me from reliving the story once more.

Lew looks at me and asks, "Is it really true that you were kidnapped by Jesse James?"

Apparently, Thomas already told them the story. Roosevelt sits silently, reserving his part of the adventure.

"In the flesh," I say.

Alexander chimes in, "Can you tell us one thing about him? And we will promise not to bother you again."

"Let's see—well, he would be overjoyed to be at this party to pickpocket each and every one of you," I say without a smile.

The men laugh.

"He's cold," I continue, my voice steady. "After he robs you, he'll take a bullet to each of your heads." With a swift motion, I form my fingers into a gun and mimic firing shots at each of them. The men are momentarily speechless. Then, with my fingers pointed at Alexander's head, I yell, "Bam!"

Belly laughter fills the sitting room. "Thank God he's not invited," Thomas says.

Lew opens the box of cigars and offers one to Ellen, then to me. I say, "No, thank you. But I have an interesting story about these."

"I like this girl," Christopher says.

Roosevelt gives him a side-eye.

"Hands off," Ellen barks.

Ignoring Christopher's comment, I go on to tell them how I would sneak into the factory and help hand-roll the cigars when I was a child. They are all impressed that I am from Cuba.

"You don't even have an accent," Lew says, with a slight accent himself.

"My mother learned English here in the States, so I sound a bit like the Northerners. Where are all of you from?" I ask, really curious about Lew.

"I live in Canada, but I grew up in San Francisco. I have investments here, so I come at least once every two years to check on them," Alexander says.

Christopher speaks up next. "I am from England, many moons ago. My accent has long since departed, but if you like, I can bring it back," he says, winking at me.

Roosevelt dang near cuts Christopher off, clearly annoyed by his advances toward me. "I'm from New York, a city boy who knows his way around the country."

Finally, Lew speaks. "I'm from China, but I've been here since I was thirteen. I'm resigned to the fact that this accent will stay with me. I like having that connection to my homeland and my people."

*China . . . where is that?* I make a note to ask Ellen later.

Christopher clears his throat. "May we speak freely here?"

"Yes," Ellen says. "Oya is my new protégé."

Christopher puts down his cigar in a large circular ashtray. "As Thomas can attest, the tensions have been high with many of the residents. They believe the Chinese immigrants are not helping the economy."

"That's a bloody lie," Lew says.

"I agree with you, Lew, I just want you to get your people ready if the mobs put some bite to their bark," Christopher says, rubbing his hands together.

"Listen, Negroes have been dealing with this for centuries. You must ignore the criticisms of the white men and concentrate on your business. Don't let them steer you off track," Alexander offers.

"Well—" Ellen says.

"We know what you are going to say: 'I funded the John Brown uprising,'" Christopher says, mocking Ellen's voice.

"It's true, you should be ready to protect yourself should the mob get violent. They are like caged animals," Ellen says.

"What is the trouble about?" I ask.

Thomas puts his cigar in the ashtray. "Many citizens—"

"Many white citizens," Ellen interrupts.

"Yes. Many of them have taken issue with the fact that our Chinese population have workmen jobs but are not spending their money back into the larger community. They are circulating it only among themselves," Thomas says.

I look at Lew. "Why is this a problem?"

"We are a threat if we keep our economic power. There are enough of us now to really make a difference." Lew blows smoke circles up into the air.

"I just hope nothing happens while I'm in town," Alexander says.

"It could happen at any time," Roosevelt declares.

"Sitting at this table, we have more money than all of the mob, over and over. Is there some solution we can come up with?" Thomas asks.

"They hate us," Ellen says, pointing to me, Lew, and Alexander. "Whatever we come up with, Christopher, Roosevelt, and Thomas would need to take it to the officials."

"I wonder . . ." Christopher pauses.

"What?" Ellen asks.

"The railroad strikes in the East have been a big deal. If we can get someone like James D'Arcy or Richard Dempsey to run the meeting, someone the crowd respects, perhaps we can steer their attention in a different direction. The strikers are fighting for things like eight-hour workdays," Christopher says.

"Are we trying to fuck ourselves?" Thomas asks.

I look up at him in surprise, not accustomed to Thomas using that type of language.

"The magician might be onto something," Alexander says. "We never wanted to be rich just to keep getting richer. We all pledged to give back in some way. If Richard or James can convince the crowd, this might be a good sacrifice to help keep the peace."

"I don't have a good feeling," Lew says, "but I don't have a better idea."

The band is still playing in the background as this group of comrades tries to solve the world's problems. I can feel the tension.

"I just got married," Lew says. We can all see that he is scared. If not for himself, then for his love. "I should get back home." He gathers his things.

"You never bring her," Ellen says.

"Not around this debauchery." He laughs, but I'm pretty sure he is serious. "Oya, I'll be seeing you around. How's this for an introductory conversation!"

"Be safe out there," I say.

"I'm not worried about me, so don't you dare," he says with a smile.

He goes around the table and shakes everyone's hands, thanking them. Ellen walks him to the front door. Christopher makes his way around the table and pulls out a chair near me.

"So, Ellen wants to keep you away from me. Why?" Christopher ponders.

Roosevelt unabashedly stares.

"I'm taken, if you really want to know," I say coldly.

"Such a pity. We would make a good team."

"A word of warning, that one has bite," Thomas says of me.

I stand. I'm not sure why, but I just don't like the way they are talking about me. Like I am a dog. I'm not angry, my winds are not waiting for my call, but I am annoyed. Thomas never treated me like this in New Orleans. I leave without excusing myself.

I hear Christopher's voice saying, "I think we've upset her."

The music in the foyer is a welcome distraction. I skip to the middle of the floor and spin around in a circle. I close my eyes and raise my head to the sky as I continue spinning, faster and faster. I get lost in the music until it suddenly stops.

I feel my winds encircling me as I slow down. A whirlwind has developed around me as everyone at the party stares in disbelief. I can barely see their faces through the surrounding storm. I send it out through the front door and hold my dress down so it doesn't flip up with the wind. I pretend that I am as shocked as they are.

I become the talk of the party. Some speculate it's an omen, a sign from God, while others rush to check outside for any impending storms. Surprisingly, not a single person suspects me of causing the disturbance, so I believe I'm in the clear—until I catch Chantilly's intense gaze fixed on me. With a beckoning gesture of her finger, she summons me over.

"I can always tell a bad acting job," she says.

"What do you mean?" I ask, trying to keep my cover.

"Walk with me," Chantilly says, turning away without confirming that I'm following.

I skip for a moment to keep up.

"I have seen things in this life. In China, they say the dragons are myths, but I saw one in my tree when I was young. It was floating, like a spirit. Everyone accused me of lying or having a big imagination, but I know what I saw. At that moment, I vowed never to forget there are things that exist beyond our comprehension as humans."

I pause, knowing that any excuse I make about my powers will be futile.

"Is this why Ellen is keeping you close? Does she know?" Chantilly asks.

I nod.

"Don't worry, I have many secrets about myself that I don't want surfacing. I don't have otherworldly powers, but I do have quite a few things that I wouldn't want coming out."

"I think it's only fair if you tell me at least one," I plead.

Chantilly is silent as she squints at me. "Chantilly is not my real name," she admits.

I wait for her to continue, but she just stares at me. "What is it?" I ask.

"Oh, honey, I will never tell." She laughs as she floats back to the band.

I'm mesmerized, just as I was when she first entered the room. Chantilly doesn't inquire about my powers or pry into my abilities. She doesn't make me feel different or turn me into a spectacle.

Ozata sneaks up behind me, wrapping me in a warm embrace. Startled for a moment, I quickly recognize Ozata's familiar hug, and we begin to sway to the music together. I grab her hand and take her out to the dance floor with Chantilly. We dance with abandon, but this time I keep my eyes open, making sure my winds don't crash the party.

# CHAPTER 26

My body heavy and weary, I thump down the steps, shielding my eyes from the morning light. I am not sick from the alcohol like my peers, but my body is recovering from the excessive dancing. I vaguely remember Ozata saying goodbye to me before the sun was up. She gave me one of her beaded leather hair ties. I cling to it in my sweaty hand.

I hear voices in the sitting room. Yawning, I slug over past the library and spy in, wiping the sleep from my eyes. All the women who came early yesterday are sitting around the mahogany table with Ellen and Teresa. "Michael said that the Comstock is going up this week, and gold is holding steady," a white woman with waist-length brown hair says.

"Lew said the same. Poor thing got so drunk before he said a word. He is so tight-lipped," a full-bodied Negro woman says, chuckling.

I recognize them from last night, but I was never formally introduced. Teresa is taking notes while Ellen begins to pace around the table. She spots me. "Oya, I hope your rest was suitable. Go get some breakfast, just let the cook know that you are ready."

I am still in my nightgown, lavender cotton with tiny white flowers. Ellen gave it to me in New Orleans. As I drag my feet to the kitchen, I hear Ellen's voice trailing off. "Did you all open your stocks?"

This pregnancy is making my mornings a bit slow. I've always been one to wake up with the sun and sometimes earlier. I don't even think I'm hungry, but I know I will get sick if I don't eat. When did those ladies sleep? I'm pretty sure I went up to bed when the party was in full swing.

I sit at the stretched dining room table; the chair screeches as I scoot in closer. The swinging door to the kitchen opens, and an older Black woman with a scarf on her head peeks through.

"Good morning, Miss Oya. What will you be having today?"

"Good morning . . ." I pause for her to tell me her name.

"Just call me Apple." She smiles.

*Apple, what an odd name, I wonder if she made it up, like Chantilly.* "Good morning, Apple, do you have some porridge or oatmeal? I don't think I can handle eggs today."

"We certainly do. Would you like some fresh-squeezed orange juice?"

"Yes, please," I say.

Thomas walks in behind me and pulls out a chair. Like the ladies in the sitting room, he looks like he has been up for hours. "Good morning," he says.

"Good morning," I reply.

He clears his throat. "I just want to apologize for any disrespect I caused you last night. I pride myself in really trying to learn how I can be a supportive person. I know this might sound ignorant, but do you remember what I said that offended you?"

I take a deep breath. I have honestly never been asked something like this before. "I don't remember what Christopher said, but when you said that I have bite—or something like that—I felt like you were talking about an animal. I didn't like it."

"I apologize, that will never happen again," Thomas says, placing his hand on my shoulder. The comfort from his touch makes me feel as if my father were here. I place my hand over his and say thank you. I was unaware that I needed that conversation. I was unaware that I needed that apology. I was unaware that I needed that love.

"I was up all night thinking about it. You are a guest in my house, and I want you to feel as welcome and comfortable as possible," he says.

"Technically, my house," Ellen says, walking in, laughing. "He was up all night worried about you. Did you work it out?"

Thomas looks at me to answer. "Yes, we figured it out. Thank you," I say.

"Good. The ladies want to know if you would like to join them tonight to go see Chantilly perform," Ellen asks.

I'm sure I perk up in my seat. I try not to seem too eager. "Yes, possibly. If I am up to it. Will you be going?"

"I have too much work to do. We are setting up the meeting that we were talking about last night. Thomas and I have a lot of planning. It might take a few months to get all the players we need."

Apple swings the door open with a steaming bowl of porridge and a glass of orange juice. My mouth begins to water. She places it on my table setting and smiles. "Now, you enjoy that, princess."

"Thank you," I say.

"We will let you eat in peace. Thomas, meet me in the library," Ellen orders.

"Duty calls," Thomas says with a smile, removing his hand from my shoulder. He will never know how much that touch means to me.

The dining room is silent. I rub Ozata's leather tie in my hand. I cannot hear the clanking of dishes in the kitchen or talking in the library. The porridge is like something out of a dream: just the right amount of sweet and salt, creamy and melting in my mouth. I think I taste vanilla essence. Mama used to put it in my porridge back home.

My last pregnancy, I craved everything I liked as a child. I was sucking on sugar-cane almost all day long. As I breathe into the silence, I hear the chirping of different birds. A crow caws in the distance, and a gaggle of geese sound like they are gossiping as they fly above. The peace always makes me think of Shango. I'm more weepy than usual, but I try to wipe the tears before they fall into my perfect porridge.

I close my eyes and see Shango standing at the door of Marie's house with a dozen purple lilies. I can almost feel him as he walks past me and into the kitchen. The smell of sawdust and musk whiffs by, intoxicating me. I want to do this over again. I want us.

N

I open my eyes and I am in an all-white room: no windows, no doors. This is not a memory. This is not a dream. I can't wake myself from it.

"Oya," I hear my mama's voice say.

"Mama?" I turn in circles, looking for her.

"It's me, baby. I'm sending you a message from the ocean. From where I used to commune with Daddy."

"How come I can't see you?" I ask.

"This is the way your spirit is interpreting my message. I just want you to know that I feel your baby girl. I feel her in you. Keep the colors of the rainbow beside you. I miss you, baby."

The lights turn off.

N

I wake up, and my porridge is spilled across the table and my orange juice is on the floor. Remnants of the whirlwind rattle the rings that hold the heavy drapes over the windows. Apple is staring through a crack in the kitchen door. Sweat drips down my face, and I am clenching the wooden table with my nails, Ozata's gift held captive under my palm.

Ellen and Thomas run in and rush to my side. "You are going to be okay, child," Ellen says, rocking me back and forth.

I release my grip on the table and see nail marks scratched into the wood. I don't think I was gone for long, but I could've really hurt someone. "Did Marie send some of my tea?" I ask, my voice shaking.

"Yes, dear. If you think you need it. She sent a whole box with us."

"I don't know if it's okay for the baby, but let's keep it close just in case this happens again."

Apple pushes the door open a little. "Can I come in, ma'am?"

"Yes," Ellen says as Apple hurries in with a broom to clean up my mess.

"No, I will do that," I say.

"Don't be silly, miss, I got it," Apple insists.

I settle back into Ellen's arms. "I think I need to write Shango a letter," I say.

"Is that what triggered the episode?"

I nod. I don't tell her what happened. Hearing voices in a room with no windows and no doors feels like the definition of insanity. I know it was really Mama, I can feel it.

"We have paper in the library, you can use that. Feel free to write at the desk," Ellen whispers in my ear.

I take the cloth napkin and wipe the sweat from my forehead. Apple sweeps up the shards of broken glass from my orange juice. Her hands are trembling as she hurries to clean. Slowly standing back up, she glances at me and drops the glass. She is scared. I don't have it in me to convince her otherwise. She sweeps up the glass again and hurries out of the dining room.

Ellen helps me up and stays by my side as we walk to the library. The smell of leather and old parchment pages is back. I take in a deep breath. It hits me that I probably should not tarry in the library. I imagine there are uncountable priceless books in here. A storm in this room would be devastating.

We head to the desk in the back, and Ellen gives me some stationery and a fountain pen. "A gift from a friend in Romania," Ellen says.

The ink is just in it. I don't have to dip it in the inkwell at all. That might need some getting used to. My brother taught me calligraphy when he was in grade school. I got so good at it that he would have me write his papers as he dictated. It was like an art form to me. It calmed me. But when I picked up this pen, there was no solace in sight.

"I'll leave you to it," Ellen says as she turns and walks out.

I sit with the pen to the paper for some time before I realize that the words are not coming out. I can't do it. I am overcome with a wave of exhaustion that will allow me only to submit. My head begins to nod, and though I try to fight it, my eyelids become heavy and the fountain pen slips from my fingers.

I wake up to the chatter of several women. Are they having another meeting? Night has fallen, and the library is blanketed in darkness. I see the flicker of several oil lamps in the hall heading to the foyer.

"Oya," one of the women calls out.

They are looking for me! I clear my throat. "I'm coming," I yell, fumbling to get up.

I wonder if Ellen knows that I slept here all day. Barefoot, I run on my tiptoes to the ladies' voices. Ellen's protégés are all dressed up again.

"Oh dear, she is still in her nightgown," a woman says as I approach.

"Did you want to go out with us tonight?" the heavyset Negro woman asks.

"I do," I say, more breathless than I intend.

The woman holds up the lantern. "Let's get you dressed, honey. It won't take us but a moment," she says, reaching for my hand. "I'm Candy, by the way."

Has everyone here made up their names? I grab her hand, grateful for the assistance. I don't want to miss Chantilly's performance. Candy has the uncanny ability to navigate the darkness, knowing exactly which room I'm in. She lights the lanterns in my quarters, opens the trunk, and selects a green frock trimmed with delicate lace. Without hesitation, she pulls the nightgown over my head and looks around the room. Seeing my undergarments in the bathroom, she hurries to fetch them.

"I used to work at the White House, dressing people." Candy chuckles. She always seems like she's laughing, even in the meeting earlier this morning.

"Did you meet the president?" I ask.

She laughs even harder, slapping her right thigh. "The White House, the department store, not the government. I don't even think we can step foot in there! Since Ellen has made it so most establishments here hire Negro help, I was able to get a job. Now I'm so rich, I only work for fun," Candy says proudly.

"From the job?"

"Oh, no, honey, from the stocks. Ellen taught us all how to invest."

I imagine Ellen has that on the list to teach me. "Are all the women like you?"

"Honey, nobody is like me." She laughs. "All of the ladies are at different levels, but everyone is striving toward financial independence. I'm not sure if you have been out much, but women are a rare commodity in San Francisco; there aren't very many of us. We stick together, not only to survive but to learn how to make our money grow."

Candy grabs the brush and coconut oil from the bathroom and whips my hair into a side-knot style in no time. She rubs my face with the left-over oil. I haven't had anyone do my hair since Collette. There is just something about having another Negro woman handle my tresses. It's like I can feel her love and power braiding through my hair.

She takes some lipstick and blush out of her purse and applies them to my face, carefully minding the curve of my lips. She smells like crushed vanilla beans and perfume, not a heavy scent that would make me feel sick, but light and clean. She pauses for a moment, admiring me like a work of art. "I am good!" she yells.

Candy guides me over to the mirror for the big reveal. My mahogany skin radiates a rich glow; it must be from the coconut oil she rubbed on my face. My lips, enhanced with the red hue, resemble the distinct Cupid's-bow shape I'd admired on Collette and Cosette. My hair, elegantly rolled and twisted on the left side of my head, echoes the elegance I observed on many of the women last night. I can hardly believe it's me staring back from the mirror as I turn my head from side to side, mesmerized, my eyes glued to the reflection.

"I'm obsessed with you too," Candy says. "Now let's get going!"

Eight of us squeeze into Ellen's spacious yet elegantly appointed carriage. As we settle in, there's a flurry of activity, adjusting skirts and tucking in elbows to make room. Luxurious upholstery cushions our seats. Conversation flows freely, accompanied by laughter and the rustle of fabric. Despite the close quarters, we fit in the seats, four on each side. I try to memorize everyone's names as we head into town. Candy I know. The rest yell out their names for me to repeat. I'm pretty sure they already started drinking before they came to fetch me.

"Sharon!" calls out a mulatto with a healthy batch of red curls.

"Sharon!" I respond.

"Nicole," says a Native woman close to Ozata's age. Where was she last night? Ozata would've loved to talk to her.

"Sharon and Nicole," I say. Pointing to each one.

"Yvonna," says a white woman with an accent I don't quite recognize. Her green eyes stand stark against her night-black hair.

*Shoot, I didn't catch her name.* "Can you repeat that?"

"E-von-a," she says, sounding out the syllables.

As the carriage hits a bump on the road, we collectively yelp, quickly followed by bursts of laughter.

"Candy, Sharon, Nicole, and Yvonna!" I say, trying to hold in my chuckle.

Everyone cheers.

"Michelle," a woman says in a thick French accent, "and my sister, Jatiana."

I repeat their names with a French flair. They look alike, with brown hair and sandy-colored eyes. I've never seen that hue before. I practice all the names in my head before the next girl speaks.

"Danielle, but call me Dani," she says timidly. She's a Negro, maybe sixteen or seventeen, with a Creole accent.

"I think I got it: Candy, Sharon, Nicole—"

"E-von-a!" everyone yells.

"Yes, Yvonna! Michelle, Jatiana, and Dani."

The ladies cheer as we endure the bumps of the cobblestone road. The moon hangs low in the velvety sky. The rhythmic clatter of hooves against the street echoes through the night as the carriage makes its approach to the illuminated facade of the city's most notorious nightclub, Chantilly's Corner.

The carriage, its polished wood gleaming in the lamplight, pulls to a halt in front of the entrance, the horses snorting softly as they come to a stop. As the footman opens the carriage door, we spill out, each woman more breathtaking than the last. Sharon's curls look like fire, illuminated by the many streetlamps and lanterns outside the nightclub. Michelle and Jatiana laugh as they jump out together in their matching gowns. They are not twins, I don't think, though they are close in age. Candy tips the carriage as she makes her way down the metal steps, her dress as flamboyant as her personality. Nicole helps me out and follows close behind. I think she might be new to the crew, perhaps one of the young people wanting to assimilate whom Kaknu described to me and Ozata. Yvonna glides out of the carriage with the grace of royalty, seemingly waiting for others to bow. Dani trips out behind her, and the coachman catches her before she hits the ground.

"Are you okay, miss?" he questions.

Dani composes herself and pats her dress into place. "Thank you," she responds.

As we make our way inside, the sounds of laughter and music spill out into the night, mingling with the clatter of carriages and the clip-clop of hooves. The nightclub pulsates with energy, its opulent interior bathed in candlelight and the shimmer of chandeliers.

A woman passes by in a glittery red dress with a cigarette in a long holder, but other than her, the rest of the people are men in tailored suits. Almost all white men. They part like the Red Sea as our crew flaunts by. A man tries to grab Candy's backside and she slaps his hand away, still laughing. I feel my storms awaiting my command. A few men bow to the ground as Sharon leads the way up to the front of the stage. There are two tables waiting for us with cards that say *Reserved* in calligraphy.

"Drinks on me tonight," Candy yells as she pops a bottle of champagne that was waiting at the table.

Men stare as if we are the entertainment. I whisper to Yvonna, "Is this how it always is?"

"Get used to being the star of the show, even if you're not performing," Yvonna remarks with a knowing smile.

Velvet red curtains drape low, concealing the stage from view. The pounding of drums, sweet keys from the piano, and a slew of horns bellow from behind the curtain. As the men settle into their seats at various tables and near the bar, the woman in the striking red dress approaches us bearing a tray of pink fruity cocktails. I politely decline and ask for a glass of water. "Are you sure, honey?" she yells over the music. I nod.

Silence. The music stops. The chattering ceases as the curtains drag open. Amid the garish surroundings, a hush falls over the room as the limelight illuminates the stage. The air is thick with anticipation as we wait eagerly for our curiosity to be quenched.

And then she appears.

A vision of elegance, her dress a masterpiece of intricate embroidery and vibrant colors. The fabric whispers softly with each movement. A delicate silk fan is clasped in her hand, its ornate design catching the light as she gestures gracefully to the audience.

But it is her beauty that truly captivates the room. Porcelain skin and almond-shaped eyes that sparkle in the green-tinted limelight. Her dark hair is decorated with red and gold ornaments, each one adding to her allure.

As she begins to sing, her voice fills the room with its haunting melody. A lullaby, perhaps, in her native tongue. Though I don't understand the words, I feel as though the whole room is holding their breath in fascination. Her eyes fill with tears, and I imagine she sings of a lost love. All of this has been a cappella, the band watching from the side of the stage, awaiting her cue.

Chantilly's voice crescendos into a vibrant belt while she raises one arm as if conducting herself. She whips her hand into a fist and abruptly stops the song. The audience erupts into applause. Chantilly looks down at our tables and winks. "It looks as though my girls made it out tonight," she announces.

The audience claps again, as we are surely part of the spectacle. She counts the band in, and the drums beat out the rhythm. Chantilly picks up a rattle from a tall table at the edge of the stage and begins to shake it to the beat. The piano joins in, and the horns follow suit. I recognize the players from last night at Ellen's. The drummer has his hair out and free, growing toward the stars. As he bops his head, his curls shake like a cloud around his face. He was lost in the music last night as well.

Chantilly serenades us through countless genres from the blues to opera. She even sings some folk. She ends with the French lullaby that Collette sang to Cosette. I shake my head in disbelief as my eyes well up with tears. A lump in my throat almost chokes me as I try to hold in my emotions. I do my counting exercise, trying anything to not cause a storm. *One . . . two . . . three . . . four . . . four . . . three . . . two . . . one . . .*

I make it. Everyone in the audience stands, clapping toward the sky. The men at the bar are hooting and hollering. I take in a deep breath of relief and stand with the rest of the crowd. People are throwing flowers and petals on the stage. A man hands Chantilly a dozen purple lilies, and my heart drops. She walks back to the middle of the stage and takes a bow. She looks at me and smiles.

Secretly, I send my winds up onstage, and all of the petals spin around her, encircling her in a flowery whirlwind. Whispers among the crowd wonder if this magic is a part of the show. Chantilly nods at me and "raises" the winds to the high ceilings and out through the front door, extinguishing some of the chandelier candles in their wake.

# CHAPTER 27

A loud knock echoes through the quiet of the night, penetrating my dreams as if woven into its fabric. *Bang! Bang! Bang!* reverberates from the hallway, disrupting the stillness. With a shiver, I pull a robe around me, feeling the chill that has crept into the air. Although the sun has yet to rise, the urgency of the knocking propels me from my slumber. It's not the door to my bedroom but, rather, the front entrance of the house. No one else seems to be awake; I'm the only one headed toward the door.

I feel my way down the stairs, grateful for a lamp in the foyer giving off some light. Silence. The knocking has ceased. I slowly walk up to the entryway, my storms poised and ready. Holding my breath, and tiptoeing barefoot on the mahogany wood floor, I summon the courage to move closer. My sweaty palms slip on the sleek metal of the knob as I attempt to turn it. I wipe my hands on my nightgown and try again. My heart pounds as I turn the handle and pull the grand front door open. No one is there. I cautiously walk out and see Chantilly lying unconscious in a bloody mess.

I run up to her, searching for any signs of life. I feel her faint breath. The iron smell of blood permeates the air. Her wounds are wet and swollen; newly inflicted. Whoever did this concentrated most of the beating on her face. I wish I had Mama's powers of healing right now. I wish Chantilly did not have to endure this.

But I know what herbs and medicines will help. I pick up Chantilly's unconscious body, and she is surprisingly light, even in deadweight. Blood stains my robe and nightgown as I carry her up the stairs. The first rays of dawn trickle in through the bay windows, casting us in patterned radiance. I push my bedroom door open with my hip and hurry into the bathroom. I gently lay Chantilly in the tub. Her clothes cling to the wounds on her body. With steady hands, I pour water from my basin over her, loosening the fabric and carefully removing her dress. Her undergarments are soaked in blood as well. I pour the rest of the soapy water I have left in my basin, which is not much, and go to fetch more.

The water from the well is a bit cold at this hour, but that might actually be good for the wounds. I rush back to the bathroom. Chantilly is still unconscious. I check her breathing again, and it feels a bit stronger. I grab a large sponge hanging on the back wall and dip it in the basin. I soak it with the cold water, squeeze it on her bloody undergarments, and gently peel them off.

To my surprise, Chantilly has the member of a man on her private area.

I take a breath to recalibrate and continue to squeeze water on her—or his— skin. My mind is jumping to many different scenarios, but I don't have time to entertain them if I'm going to save her life. She has made such an effort to be feminine, it seems wrong to say "him."

Once I have removed all of Chantilly's undergarments, I can properly wash her. Taking the wet sponge, I rub the bar of lavender soap to create a soothing lather. I am grateful that she remains unconscious, sparing her the pain. I gently scrub her body and wounds until she is clean, then use the rest of the water to rinse her off.

I place two large towels on my bed and lay Chantilly down. I cover her with another towel and rush downstairs. The house is slowly waking up. I notice Apple trying to avoid me as I run out the back door to find the herbs I need from Ellen's garden. I grab a bundle of leaves from the eucalyptus tree and search for other herbs in the patch. I remember seeing an aloe vera plant in the kitchen. I rush back inside and head straight through the swinging doors.

Without explanation, I ask Apple to boil the water for the eucalyptus leaves, grab the aloe plant, and rush upstairs. Chantilly still has not moved. I chew some of the herbs and place them directly on her wounds, covering them with pieces of aloe vera. I check her nose: still breathing. I get a clean robe and put it on her, covering her as she heals.

Ellen walks in as I check a gash on Chantilly's face. "My dear God in heaven!"

Chantilly slowly begins to stir, barely able to open her eyes. She moans.

"You have to take her to the doctor," Ellen insists.

"No," I say, thinking of Chantilly's secret and not knowing what the doctor would make of it. "No, these wounds are familiar. I can heal them with my eyes closed," I say.

"My dear Chantilly, who did this to you?" Ellen ponders out loud.

———

As the days pass, Chantilly's injuries gradually heal, much to our relief. We all take turns caring for her, ensuring she doesn't overexert herself during her recovery.

One afternoon, as I sit on my daybed engrossed in my book, I'm startled by the sound of movement from my bed. Glancing over, I see Chantilly stirring awake. She grabs the covers and pulls them up to her chest.

"You know my secret," she finally says.

"My lips are sealed," I reply.

Chantilly shudders with emotion. "You didn't tell anyone?" She seems so scared to ask.

"Not a soul. Did you tell anyone about me?" I ask, putting my book down and walking over to her.

Chantilly shakes her head. Her face is beginning to heal from the swelling.

"What happened?" I ask. She has not said a word about the attack since I discovered her.

"A man found out my secret. After my performance, he followed me home. He thought he could take advantage me, but he put his hands up my dress—" Chantilly breaks down into tears.

I'm careful not to hold Chantilly in comfort because of her wounds, but I sit beside her and cradle her hand.

"What if he tells everyone?" she asks.

"He won't, because then he would have to describe why he knows." Rage boils in the pit of my stomach.

I breathe, counting backward in my head, trying to stay calm for my baby. I squeeze Chantilly's hand lovingly, letting her know that I am here.

"Thank you for not sending me to the hospital."


In the following weeks, Chantilly and I grow remarkably close. She guides me around the city, showing me its hidden gems and procuring foods from her favorite Chinese market to satisfy my cravings. Children play in the streets of China-town, their laughter a bright contrast to the serious faces of shopkeepers and customers haggling over prices.

Ornate gateways give way to narrow winding streets lined with shops, markets, and laundry houses. The buildings, a mix of wood and brick, are plastered with red and gold signs. Vendors shout from their stalls, selling everything from fresh produce and foreign fruits to silk garments and handcrafted goods. Colorful lanterns hang above the streets, swaying gently in the breeze.

A group of elders sits outside a teahouse at a flimsy wooden table, clanking mah-jongg tiles on its surface. Chantilly has tried to explain the game to me several times, but I just don't understand. Incense smoke drifts out of a Buddhist temple, bathing us in the essence of sandalwood as we walk by. Down the street, we find shade under a large oak tree in a park and decide to picnic there.

As I spread out my rainbow blanket, Chantilly unpacks our treats from her basket: mooncakes, chicken dumplings, sweet-and-sour pork, and spring rolls. Ellen extended an invitation for Chantilly to reside at the house for her safety, so we have been connected at the hip. However, I have yet to tell Chantilly about my pregnancy, mostly because I'm uncertain about so many things. I thought I wanted a baby, but as the days pass, I'm more and more skeptical. Am I too young to do this, especially on my own?

"What's on your mind?" Chantilly asks as she hands me a flaky mooncake.

I pause for a moment, licking some of the red bean paste filling from my fingers. "I'm pregnant," I say. While I must be at least three months into my term, my body is still slim.

"How?" Chantilly responds, completely surprised.

"I have been this whole time; I've just been scared to say anything."

"Does Ellen know?"

"Yes."

"Do you want this?" Chantilly asks, seemingly searching my face for any sign of truth.

"I thought I did," I say, choking up.

"Listen, the ladies go through this often. We have many people who can help. Just say the word, and I can take you."

I've thought about this ever since Ellen said that I had a choice, but I've been too scared to ask again. I was so devastated when I lost Kitari, and my biggest fear is going through that loss again.

"How far along are you?"

"About three and a half months."

"Not to alarm you, but if you want to go to our doctor, you would need to do it quite soon," Chantilly says with a bit of concern. "Do you mind me asking who the father is?"

A wave of heat trundles down my body. While I have thought about Shango every single day since I've been here, I haven't conjured him with words. "Shango."

Chantilly is silent, waiting for more.

"I ran away . . ." is all I can say before the tears begin to fall.

Chantilly reaches for one of our cloth napkins to wipe my face.

"I'm no good at love," I say, sobbing.

"Don't be silly, you *are* love," Chantilly consoles.

"It's like I drown in my feelings as soon as I have them. Maybe because I was never really able to express my emotions. When I met Shango, I could barely form any words. My stomach was in knots, and my heart was beating out of my chest."

"Honey, that is normal!"

I manage to smile under my tears. "But then I ran away. I saw him with another woman, I think—then I ran away."

"What do you mean, you think?"

"We were at Mardi Gras, and I drank some absinthe, and it really didn't sit well with me. I don't think it makes you hallucinate, but I have no other way to explain what I saw."

"What did you see?" Chantilly leans forward.

"A woman was kissing Shango's neck, hanging all over him. But when she looked back at me, she had no face."

"Oh dear, that is terrifying! What did he say when you asked him?"

"I didn't. I just left. I ran away."

Chantilly's eyes blink rapidly. "What? You didn't even ask him?"

I shake my head in shame. She lifts my chin and cradles my face in her hands.

"No wonder you don't know what to do. When we get home, we are going to pen him a letter. How does that sound?"

I nod. I'm scared still, but I nod.

# CHAPTER 28

Though my stomach continues to swell with the growing life inside me, I still struggle to find the words to communicate with Shango. Chantilly and I have been trying to write this letter for months.

We sit with our feet dangling off the pier into the bay. The water has become one of our favorite outings, and Chantilly has shown me all the best places to get clam chowder. We splash our feet as I savor a spoonful of the creamy deliciousness.

"I have never seen anyone love food quite the same way you do," Chantilly says, laughing. While she revels in watching me eat, she rarely partakes. Mama always told me never to trust anyone who doesn't like food, but Chantilly has become one of my closest confidantes.

I try to get up, but my swollen belly makes it difficult to keep my balance. Chantilly rushes to help me. We hear the frantic quacks of a duck as Chantilly pulls me to my feet. Out in the water, we see a mother duck trying to wrangle her babies out of a strong current. A few ducklings are already several feet away from her. I summon my winds and tenderly blow the ducks to shore. They march out of the water single file and head to a nearby tree.

My stomach rolls as my baby kicks from within. I grab Chantilly's hand and place it on my belly. Cora kicks her. "I felt it!" Chantilly yells.

"My first baby died when she was born," I say, releasing Chantilly's hand.

Stunned into silence, Chantilly slowly envelops me in a lingering embrace. "I am so sorry, honey," she whispers softly.

For some reason, I find myself strangely disconnected from my usual flood of emotions. Perhaps I've cried all my tears, or maybe this numbness is allowing me to move through these uncertainties without succumbing to despair.

"My goddaughter is strong. I know she will survive," Chantilly says, rubbing my stomach.

"I'm ready."

I don't have to explain to Chantilly what I'm ready for. We hop into Ellen's obsidian carriage and head back home. I'm anxious as we navigate the twists and turns back up through the hills of San Francisco. The bay is a fair distance from Ellen's house, and I'm swiftly lulled to sleep on the ride.

The creak of the front gate wakes me from my slumber. We roll into Marie's driveway and Chantilly reaches over and grabs my hand. "Can you drop us off in the back?" Chantilly requests of our driver.

He maneuvers around the large eucalyptus trees and drops us off at the rear of the house. As we enter and make our way to the library, we hear Ellen talking to someone at the front door. I don't think much about it, but Chantilly can't help being meddlesome. "Let's go see who it is," she says.

Ellen's house is always bustling with guests, especially now, as the big meeting they've been meticulously planning approaches. I have been helping where I can. They have designated me as the notetaker, because apparently I have the only legible handwriting. I chuckle out loud, thinking about it.

Chantilly and I walk to the living room and hide behind a wall. We look stealthily around the corner, and I see a tall man talking to Ellen. His back is to us, but I think he might be the gardener. We are caught spying on their conversation when he turns. My heart drops into my belly. Shango!

My eyes begin to cross and see double. I grab onto Chantilly as I fall to the ground. Blackness.


"Oya," a deep, rumbling voice tries to whisper.

Am I in a dream? Chantilly stands behind Shango with a foolish smile. Ellen is at my head, just like she was with Marie when she fainted in New Orleans.

"Shango," I say, and all the emotions that I thought I used up come rolling in.

He holds my hand as he kneels on the floor, and I feel myself melting like the homemade ice cream that Ellen makes. Rum and raisin, her favorite. I finally find the words to say, "I was scared to tell you."

He places his pointer finger softly on my lips and then kisses them. My eyes roll to the back of my head in pleasure, and everything else seems to disappear. He pulls away. "I am here now."

Chantilly mouths behind him, "So handsome!"

"This is my friend Chantilly," I say in a weakened tone.

"I am the godmother," she brags, correcting me.

"Hello, Godmother," Shango says with a smile.

Ellen interjects, "Oya, how are you feeling?"

"Better," I say.

As I struggle to regain my footing, everyone reaches out to offer assistance, but it's Shango who guides me up with his strong arms. My heart races with a mix of emotions, but everything else seems to have slowed down.

"Why don't you show Shango to your room? He can freshen up before lunch." Ellen suggests.

Leaving Chantilly with Ellen, I walk Shango upstairs, observing the awe in his eyes as he takes in the grandeur of the mansion. It strikes me how quickly this opulence has become ordinary to me. Ellen has even set me up with stocks, providing me with enough financial stability to consider purchasing my own properties—something I never really thought about before.

"I worked so many odd jobs to get the money to travel here," he says.

We walk into my room. I realize that most of my interactions with Shango have been in my imagination. The flesh and blood, the real, feels so different. His smell of sawdust and musk is the same, yet even more intoxicating.

"I was scared too," he says.

I push him on the bed. What has gotten over me? He tries to hold in a smile as he lays himself down. I sit on top of him, my belly protruding over his. I place his hand on my stomach and Cora kicks him at once. Shango's eyes begin to water.

"I couldn't have imagined. I just knew that I had to be with you."

"What were you scared of?" I ask, suddenly feeling more secure than ever.

Shango slowly sits up, holding my back so I don't fall. "I was scared that you would not have me. I went to Marie's the day after Mardi Gras and she told me that you left."

"I'm so sorry," I say, kissing his face.

I want him to take me now. I want him to flip me onto the bed and seize me into his world. My nails dig into his back. His grip on my body becomes firm. My stomach, our baby, is between us.

Ellen's subtle knock on the open door jolts me out of my ecstasy. "The cook wants to know if you want chicken or fish. Oya, I'm pretty sure that your sickness has passed, but are you good with others having fish?"

"Yes, I'll have chicken, but I'm fine with others having fish."

"Are you certain? Do you have a problem with fish?" Shango asks.

"Not anymore, but it used to make me feel ill."

"I'll have fish, then. Thank you, Ellen," Shango says.

Ellen stands at the door for a moment. "There should be fresh water in the basin. Let the staff know if you need more. I can have a bath drawn up for you."

Shango laughs. "I don't think I would fit in the tub."

Ellen walks away. I stare into Shango's eyes. I have been waiting for this moment, dreaming about it for what seems like an eternity.

"My father thinks I'm crazy," he says, stroking my hair.

I kiss his lips again, still in shock that he is in front of me.

"Hell, I thought I was crazy," Shango says as we kiss. "I was ready for anything except this." He rubs my stomach. "I will find work with Ellen and Thomas to take care of us."

I don't tell him about my stocks and investments yet. None of that matters.

"Shall we get you washed up?" I say.

# CHAPTER 29

Our lunch unexpectedly turns into a work session as we delve into the final preparations for the labor meeting scheduled for tomorrow. Alexander came back in town from Canada for the event. Although Ellen, Lew, Alexander, and I cannot attend the meeting, we have been instrumental in its planning. The disdain for the Chinese immigrants has only worsened in the city, with even some white people voicing their grievances to me, whether it's a flippant racist remark at the market about the "strange Oriental" fruit, or random complaining about the Chinese stealing money out of their pockets. I wonder what they say about Negroes behind my back.

The crispy golden chicken is fried to perfection, and each bite delights my senses. Apple has brought all of her family recipes from the South; amid the spread is my favorite cornbread. Bowls of mashed potatoes, collard greens, creamed corn, and coleslaw are passed from hand to hand, filling the room with their delectable scents. Apple has slowly warmed up to me, but she still reaches for her cross necklace when I enter the room. I haven't had another episode in about six months now.

Shango squeezes my hand. I almost forgot that he was sitting next to me. I look at his plate, and he is already done with his fish. "Do you want more?"

"I would love seconds, *mon cherie amour*," he says.

Apple is standing against the wall. I motion for her to come over. Again she holds the crucifix around her neck as she walks up. "Can Shango have another plate?" I ask.

"Certainly," Apple says, smiling at Shango as she takes his dish.

Thomas, Christopher, Alexander, Lew, Roosevelt, Chantilly, and Ellen are arguing about some last-minute details regarding the meeting. "I just don't know if James has the charisma to sway the crowd if it gets out of hand," Thomas says.

"Well, it's a little late now to be thinking about that. Either way, he helped create a national Workingmen's Party, and the people trust him. He even turned down payment for the meeting," Christopher says.

Thankfully, he's given up pursuing me. Once they realized that I was pregnant, he and Roosevelt have been nothing but respectful.

Lew chimes in, "Thomas, Roosevelt, Christopher—will you be ready when the crowd yells out, 'What about the coolie man?'"

"What does 'coolie' mean?" Shango tries to whisper.

Everyone stares at him, seemingly forgetting that we were at the end of the table.

"It's an offensive word they use for Chinese people," Chantilly says.

I didn't know it was offensive. Everyone says it in town like it's normal. I know never to use it now.

"We are going to be in the crowd holding signs about eight-hour workdays, encouraging people to talk about that. I have a few men who will be spread throughout the gathering," Thomas says. "The people cannot know that the elite are behind this."

"Especially an elite Chinaman," Lew says.

"That's another one you don't want to say, Shango," Chantilly preaches.

"Noted," Shango says as Apple puts a new plate of food in front of him. "Thank you."

"So, the meeting will be at the corner of Grove and Larkin," Thomas says.

"Is that still a vacant lot?" Alexander asks.

"It is, we couldn't find a venue willing to host it. Except Chantilly's Corner, but that probably wouldn't work," Thomas says, attempting to make a joke.

"Why not? They are probably all paying customers," Chantilly says, laughing. "They hate our men but want to fuck our women. Typical."

"This all goes down tomorrow. We know the outcome could be some violence, but we have the police standing by. If we can get the men to focus on the railway strikes, we have done our job," Christopher says.

"Why exactly did I come back into town for this?" Alexander asks.

Everyone at the table laughs. "My compliments to the chef," Roosevelt yells to the kitchen.

Apple swings the door open and takes a bow.

———

The men gather in the sitting room for most of the day, planning. Shango joins them for a spell, but I want to take him into town if he's up to it. There is a street vendor who sells the best chicken dumplings. He might feel more at home when he sees that San Francisco is similar to New Orleans. The Negro population is not as robust, but the streetcars and even some buildings are almost identical.

I take a gander around the meeting. "Shango," I say, calling for him.

"You are being summoned, my brother," Alexander says. Shango hurries to me.

"Do you want to come into town? There are a few things I would like to show you," I say.

"I will follow you," he professes, kissing my hand.

The veins on his forearm seem to be lifted above his muscles. My body has thirsted for him for months, and now he is right in front of me. I want a week just to stare into his eyes. We don't need any words; we don't need anything. Only each other.

Our carriage glides through the bustling streets, which are pulsing with the rhythm of life. The sunlight dances on the facades of Victorian buildings, casting playful shadows on the cobblestone pathways below. Vendors line the sidewalks, their colorful stalls brimming with various fruits, fragrant flowers, and tantalizing treats. I see the dumpling cart and ask our driver to stop for a moment. It is a bit harder for me to get out of the carriage pregnant, but with Shango's help, I'm still agile. The air is alive with the sounds of commerce as merchants call out their wares and eager buyers haggle for the best deals.

I request two orders of chicken dumplings in Mandarin. Chantilly taught me a few phrases, and the vendors always get so excited when they hear me speak their language. "Xièxiè," I say, bowing my head and walking back to Shango. There are chopsticks, but the dumplings always taste better when I use my fingers. I take one out and hold it up to Shango's mouth. He swallows the whole dumpling in one bite, licking my fingers in the process. My entire body begins to tingle.

His full lips shimmer from the oil. With a delighted hum, he does a little dance similar to the jump-kicks the crowd was doing during Mardi Gras. "That there is something special!" he hollers.

People stare at me differently with Shango by my side. There is hatred rather than curiosity. I don't point it out to Shango because I want him to enjoy his first day here. But then some men saunter by, scratching their armpits and making monkey noises. My winds begin to blow my full head of curls into my face.

"It is not worth it, my love," Shango says.

The vendors grab their swinging wares and run after fruit that has blown off their carts. Trash and dirt slap the men in their faces as they wave their arms frantically to protect themselves. Why does everyone tell me that it's not worth it?

"Ouch." I bend over in pain as a small contraction takes me by surprise.

Shango rushes to my side. "Is it time?"

"No, it's too early. I have at least a month left. I probably just overexerted myself."

"Let's go back to the carriage. We can rest and eat in there," Shango says, leading me to the street.

The coachman helps me up as Shango holds my lower back. We climb onto the velvet seats, shielded from the judgmental eyes of the world. Shango picks up one of his dumplings and feeds it to me. I take a bite because I can't fit the whole thing in my mouth. I laugh as the oil rolls down my chin. "We can't make a mess in here," I mumble with a full mouth.

Shango pulls me in for a kiss. I try to down my food before he embraces me. There is a knock at our carriage window. The coachman is still standing there, staring. He yells, "Where to next, miss?"

Shango opens the door. I lean over him, pressing my body against his. "Can you take us to the pier, then back to the house?"

"Yes, miss," the driver says, then heads over to the horses.

We pull up to the majestic waterfront, greeted by the sight of towering ships anchored at the pier, sails billowing in the gentle breeze. Seagulls swoop and soar overhead, their cries mingling with the laughter of children playing on the sandy shores. The scent of salt water, mingled with the tang of freshly caught fish, carries on the sea breeze as it wafts through the open window.

"This is my favorite part of the city. On Sundays, they sell the best clam chowder," I whisper in Shango's ear.

"Not better than New Orleans."

"Ten times better." I chuckle.

Halfway paying attention to the time that has passed since my contraction, I try to reassure myself that everything will be okay. I don't want to worry Shango unnecessarily, but I also know I have to stay vigilant. If labor does start, I'll need time to call for my midwife. While I could probably birth her on my own if I had to, that would be my last resort. I try not to think of my labor because it brings up so many fears. Heeding Ellen's advice, I haven't voiced them, but they linger.

"You ready to go home?" I ask.

"I am," he says, knocking on the front window.

He gives a signal that the driver seems to understand, and we are off. On the way back to the house, the cobblestone roads rock Shango to sleep. The journey from New Orleans was long and taxing, I am sure of it. I didn't even ask him if he took the boat or train. I rub his head as dusk falls. The sounds of the city are muffled by the silence of the hills.

# CHAPTER 30

The house bustles with activity as people gather to prepare for tonight's Work-ingmen's Party meeting. The ladies, with sleeves rolled up and aprons tied se-curely around their waists, buzz about, making signs and carrying boxes. I've been tasked with outlining the messages and drawings on the posters, while the rest of the ladies fill them in with vibrant colors. Sharon, her fiery red hair pulled back into a ponytail, walks around making sure everyone has what they need.

Amid the flurry of activity, I can't help noticing that some of the women are in trousers! I have seen many things in my life, but never a lady in pants. I look up at Chantilly, in a flowing skirt and flowery blouse, and realize that perhaps the clothes we wear hold little importance in comparison to our character as humans.

With my pregnant belly making it challenging to bend over while on the floor, I settle at the dining room table to outline the multitude of picket signs. Mean-while, the ladies are gathered in the foyer, engrossed in coloring tasks spread out on the floor. Chantilly takes over Sharon's job and effortlessly assumes control of the room, delegating tasks and offering guidance. She is surprisingly good at getting everyone else to do the work for her.

Ellen brings a candle to the table. I look at her, wondering why she has a flame burning in the middle of the day. "Today won't go as planned, but it is nec-essary. I am burning this candle for our safety."

"What is necessary?"

"When a large number of people grow in anger, they have to get to their boil-ing point in order to cool off," Ellen says.

"And Thomas knows that?" I ask.

"He does."

"So the speaker, the location, are all a part of the plan?"

"Everyone knows it; the only thing we don't know is how bad it will get. That is why Thomas has notified law enforcement. You and Chantilly will be stationed safely at her apartment in Chinatown, so you are far enough from the fray. She hasn't been there for a while, so I'm glad you will be with her. We will all be at different locations; only our white counterparts will be at the meeting."

Ellen is echoing to me the plans that we decided upon months ago; she repeats herself when she feels anxious. Is she not telling me something? Through the window, my eye catches Shango carrying boxes to the driveway with a few of the men. I smile to myself. Ellen sees my reaction and turns around.

"He found you from across the world!"

"He did." I blush.

"Just keep the candle burning, I'll be back for it."

I continue to outline the pictures and words for the posters. I don't understand why we are doing something that we know is going to fail, but I trust Ellen and Thomas. There is a rumbling in the city that feels like it needs to erupt. I just don't know why we are in the middle of it.

Chantilly walks in and settles into the seat to my left. "Thank you for doing this for me," she says, leaning her head on my shoulder.

"You would do the same," I respond.

"And more," she says, leaning in. "How did it go with Shango? I want all of the details!"

"I am in love," I say, holding my breath.

"Well, I know that. What else?"

"I think he might ask me to marry him," I say.

Chantilly jumps up and down in her seat. "Making an honest woman out of you."

I hit Chantilly on the shoulder. "Stop!"

"What? I need someone to make an honest woman out of me, but—you know," she mumbles.

I hold Chantilly's face in my hands. "I love you so much," I say.

"Too bad you aren't my cup of tea." She chuckles.

Thomas comes to the table and sits down in front of us. He looks extremely serious. "It is almost time to start moving to our locations. Do you know where you will be?"

Chantilly says, "At my apartment downtown."

"Good. We will send a messenger to you with further instructions."

"Thank you," Chantilly says, holding Thomas's hand across the table.

Thomas and Chantilly help me gather all the posters and bring them to the ladies to color. Everyone seems a bit tense, as if we are walking headfirst into the winds of change. Christopher and Alexander pace around the foyer, reciting things that Christopher needs to tell their speaker, James D'Arcy. I have never met him, but they have said his name a good thousand times in the past few months.

Apple and the rest of the cooks pass around sandwiches to the participants. I think they are roast beef. My mouth waters as I hurry outside to make sure Shango received his. I find him sitting on a stone wall with his feet hanging over the side. He has already eaten half of his sandwich. "I just wanted to make sure you got some food," I yell up to him.

He waves the other half of his sandwich to show me. I smile and head back inside to eat with my stomach rumbling. The ladies are working diligently to finish the posters. Chantilly sits cross-legged to the side of them. She picks at her food like a bird, eating small bits of her sandwich. I get my plate and take it to the dining room.

My eyes are definitely bigger than my stomach. I'm barely able to finish half of the meal. Chantilly comes to the table and sits with me. "You sure you want to come tonight?"

"I will be there with you. I want to make sure we are around if Thomas needs anything. We will just be in your apartment."

"I haven't really stayed there since—"

"I know, that's another reason why I want to be there with you. Not because I think its unsafe but to comfort you."

Thomas yells out for all of us to meet him in the foyer. He opens the door and summons the people from outside as well. Shango walks in, shirtless, with sweat dripping down his chest. The women stare unasbashedly. I really can't blame them. Shango wipes his hands on a small towel and looks about the room. He spots me in the corner and heads my way through the small crowd. The ladies' eyes follow him until he gets to me, then their spell is broken.

"Put your shirt on, these ladies can't handle it," I whisper.

He reaches into his back pocket and pulls out a dirty shirt. I grab his hand and pull him closer to me. "Not yet," I beg.

"I think we are all here," Ellen says.

Ellen! I rush to the dining room and grab the candle. The flame has been blown out! I grab it anyway and bring it with me to the foyer. Ellen is talking. "We will dig for our courage tonight. If one of us is oppressed, then we all are."

Everyone cheers. Thomas walks over to Ellen. "We all know the plan. We have been going over it for a couple of months now. If we have everyone in place by four o'clock, everything should go smoothly."

Lew walks up to them. "My wife and I thank you from the bottom of our hearts for trying to neutralize the many threats and hatred. This group of people here, each and every one of you, stands for the world I want to live in. Heck, we already live in. Just . . ." He pauses. "Thank you."

Chantilly reaches for my arm and squeezes it. I hold the unlit candle in my other hand as Ellen slowly walks up. "What happened?"

"I'm not sure, I just went to go get it, and the fire was blown out. Can we light it again?"

"It's best if we leave it as such," Ellen says, taking the candle and trying to conceal her disappointment. She places the taper on a mantel that somehow I have never noticed. It seems to be built into the wall, and there are crystals, candles, herbs, and oils. She closes a ribbed silk curtain in front of it and walks over to Thomas.

"Let's go, we have carriages to take everyone to their designated places," Thomas commands.

I turn to Shango. "Where will you be?"

"I'm loading some of the equipment at the site and then heading to the pier with a few of the men."

"Be careful, my love," I say.

He gently places his lips on mine and kisses me.


Chantilly's apartment is not what I imagined it to be. It is very humble, above a Chinese laundry. As we enter, I see things thrown about the living room, I think from the struggle. The rest of her place is perfectly in order. She rushes to pick up the broken flowerpot and books from the floor. Drops of blood lead to the door.

I have my rainbow shawl around my shoulders. I remove it and place it across the cushions on the floor. There's still a basin of water in the kitchen. I take a small towel, dip it in the bowl, and lather it with soap. We took our shoes off at the door, so I tiptoe over to the front entrance and begin washing away the blood.

"Why do you live here? You can buy property anywhere you please," I ask.

Chantilly pauses for a moment, placing the broken pieces of ceramic in a basket. "I don't have to explain myself here. All the faces look like mine. And this is where I grew up. My father owns the laundry downstairs. He has basically disowned me, but he hasn't kicked me out."

Chantilly is so private about her life. I understand why. I'm grateful to be in her humble space. She continues, "My siblings never came with us to California. It was just me and my father. He wanted to bring his eldest son to help set up shop here and then send for the family. It didn't really go as planned." She says this with a half-smile.

"I guess it went exactly as it should," I say.

We continue to clean until there are no remnants of the struggle. Chantilly lights a stick of incense and walks around the room, circling the smoke in the air. The apartment is small but meticulously kept, every corner scrubbed clean and every surface polished to a gentle sheen. The walls are adorned with delicate scrolls and traditional artwork. A small shrine, sprinkled with offerings of old fruit and dried flowers, stands in one corner. Chantilly places the incense on the altar and removes the old fruit.

The main living space has a low wooden table surrounded by cushions for seating. A threadbare rug, worn with age, lies at its center. A single window overlooks the bustling street below, its panes framed with paper lanterns that cast a soft, diffused light into the room.

In one corner, a makeshift kitchenette boasts a small stove and a few pots and pans, their surfaces gleaming with careful use. A modest pantry, stocked with rice and dried herbs, fills one corner, while the basin I used stands on a small wooden table painted red.

The bedroom, tucked away behind a thin curtain, is easy to overlook. A modest wooden bed, its frame enhanced with carvings of flying dragons, takes center stage, and a single lantern hangs in the corner. A simple wardrobe stands against one wall. It's slightly open, revealing some of Chantilly's elaborate costumes.

A bell rings outside and I rush to the window. Just as I thought, the dumpling vendor! I grab my small purse and run to the door. "Do you want some?" I yell back to Chantilly.

"No, I'm still full from the sandwich."

I slow down as I approach the steps, remembering that I am pregnant. The rickety wooden staircase doesn't seem like it can handle my full weight. I cautiously creep down the stairs, realizing that I left my shoes in the apartment. The bell begins to ring farther in the distance, so I burst through the door barefoot, yelling, *"Děngdài!"*

I run down the packed dirt road, hollering for the vender to wait in Mandarin. Crowds of men come out of their homes and workplaces dressed in similar garb: a brown robe shirt, tied at the side, with a high collar. Most of them have short hair, but the ones with longer strands are staticky, with parts of their manes sticking up to the sky, straight and black. The vendor stops and recognizes me. *"Nǐ hǎo,"* he says, greeting me and pulling out his chicken dumplings. He already knows my order.

The other men stare as I gather the dumplings and begin to head back to Chantilly's place. No one says a word, but they keep their eyes on me. A man I'm assuming is Chantilly's father stands outside his laundry shop. He is carefully holding a pressed and cleaned white button-up dress shirt and staring at me. *"Nǐ hǎo,"* I say as I walk around him and hurry up the stairs.

The dumplings are even better today. I insist that Chantilly have at least one. She goes to the kitchen counter and gets two richly designed chopsticks and delicately picks up the dumpling, taking a small bite. I finish my whole bag before she's done with one.

"I hope the boys are all right," she says.

We sit in silence for a moment, feeling an impending doom that neither of us wants to voice. "Thomas and Christopher have it all planned out." I reach for my rainbow shawl and wrap it around me. The sun is beginning to set, and the cool night air is settling in. I look over at Chantilly's bookshelf. "Do you have any good books?"

"Many, but they're all in Mandarin." We both laugh.

*Bang!*

I grab Chantilly. A gunshot echoes, too close for comfort. We hear the chanting of a mob outside. They are yelling something that we can't understand. I run to the small window and open it. Hundreds of white men with blazing torches are running into the neighborhood, burning down buildings. "We have to go!" I yell back to Chantilly.

"Death to all coolies! Death to all coolies!" We hear them chant as we run down the stairs.

The stench of smoke and burned fabric swells in through the cracks in the wood. "Wait!" I yell as Chantilly grabs the door. "Is there a back entrance? I think the store is on fire."

*"Fùqīn!"* Chantilly screams. "Father!"

She kicks the door open and runs toward the store. I follow close behind. The building is full of curling black smoke. I blow it out with my winds, careful not to feed the fire. I bring some rains inside the store. Chantilly stands frozen at the back of the laundry. Her father's lifeless body lies on the wooden floor. A bullet straight through his skull.

*"Bàba!"* Chantilly shakes her head and falls onto him. "No!" She lets out a desperate scream and holds her father tight. *"Bàba,"* she says through her tears.

"Look what we have here, a nigger and a coolie!" two white men with torches say as they walk into the wet store.

I lift my hands and blow them hard against the smoky wall. Their fires are extinguished as they fall to the ground. They struggle to their feet and run out of what's left of the door.

"We have to go," I say to Chantilly.

Chantilly stumbles to her feet, her eyes red and puffy. I don't know what to say to her, but one thing is clear: We need to get out of here. Shango's words echo in my mind—he'll be waiting for us at the pier. We have to reach him. I grab Chantilly's hand and pull her out of the store. The chaos of the street unfolds before us. The night sky is ablaze. As I raise my hands, a torrential rain begins to fall, dousing some of the flames. Yet, amid the downpour, a bolt of lightning strikes dangerously close to the pier, sending a shiver down my spine. That was not from me. The air is thick with the scent of smoke and piercing screams. It's a nightmare unfolding before our eyes.

I run toward the water, avoiding any of the rioting men. They are filled with more than hatred; it's almost as if they are possessed. We look back, and several blocks are up in flames. It seems my rains are not making any difference. *Shango, where are you?*

Chantilly seems lifeless, only following my lead. We have to avoid the main streets. Although it looks like the men are not burning down the Victorian structures, I don't want them catching a glimpse of us. We hide behind a building.

"Are you okay?" I ask Chantilly, fastening my rainbow shawl tight around my shoulders.

Chantilly is silent, her eyes glossed over. She doesn't seem to hear or comprehend anything I'm saying to her.

"Coolie bitch!" a man shouts from in the darkness, and hits Chantilly on the head with an unopened can of food. She falls to the ground, blood spilling from her wound.

"No! No! No!" I yell.

I blow intense winds into the darkness, removing the threat of anyone else in the shadows. I take my rainbow shawl and wrap it around Chantilly's head tightly. I pick her up; it is much more laborious with my pregnant belly, but the mayhem has imbued me with strength.

The pier is not far ahead, but I have to cross a main street. The men are everywhere. I see the signs we created ripped and thrown about like confetti, littering the cobblestone streets. Thomas, Roosevelt, and Christopher are nowhere in sight.

"Father, help me," I plead.

A deafening explosion erupts in the distance, and all the men bolt toward it. I hurry across the street, struggling to keep Chantilly up. As we reach the edge of the bay, my heart sinks at the sight before me—the first pier is nearly engulfed in flames, its wooden structure consumed by the inferno. Panic rises within me as I realize I can't access my powers to quell the fire because I'm carrying Chantilly. I adjust her in my arms, desperately looking around. Scanning the bay, I see piers stretching out in both directions, their silhouettes stark against the backdrop of chaos. With uncertainty gnawing at me, I decide to move away from the explosion.

"Shango!" I yell into the night air.

The city is on fire. I drag my feet, barely able to hold Chantilly anymore. An intense contraction brings me to my knees. I place Chantilly on the ground next to me.

"Not right now, please!" I cry out loud.

"Die, Chinamen, die!" a group of men roar as they run by.

One spots me bent over Chantilly. He gathers his mob, and they walk toward us with their torches ablaze. The shadows on their faces distort their features, making them appear more like monsters. I gather all of my strength and lift them high into the air with my winds. They kick their feet and scream, dropping their torches on the street. My hands shake, holding their weight. I plunge them full speed back down to the earth.

"Not murder," I hear Marie whisper in my ear.

Before they hit the ground, I stop them. Suspending them in midair above the stone street that was poised to become their fate.

"Oya!" Shango yells from behind the men.

I drop them with the last of my strength. They scatter into the night as Shango runs to me. A violent contraction takes me back down. I yell up at the sky, tears streaming as I wallow in pain and look at Chantilly. I don't think she made it; she doesn't seem to be breathing. The contractions subside, and I take Shango's hands. "They got Chantilly," I cry.

Shango holds me to his chest. "We have to find shelter," he says.

"I can't leave her here," I say, weeping.

A contraction rolls in again, this time threatening a birth on the splintery pier. "She's coming," I say through my tears.

"Now?"

"Right now!" I yell. "I need my blanket." I point to Chantilly. Shango gently unties the rainbow shawl and lays her back on the ground. I can feel the baby's head crowning. "Mama!" I yell out into the waters.

I get into a squat position and direct Shango to place the blanket underneath me. He is shaking as he spreads out the colorful shawl. I grab his hand and squeeze it as hard as I can. Cora's head slips out, hanging below me. I weep, knowing that I *have* to summon the strength to continue. I reach down. "Give me the blanket! Give me the blanket!"

Shango places the blanket in my hands. The contraction comes in like an attack.

"One . . . two . . . three . . . four . . . Come on, breathe with me," I hear Mama say.

Clouds form in the sky, ominous and mighty. I wail up to the heavens.

I push once again, and my baby drops out into our arms. Shango's shaky hands cover her with the rainbow blanket. She has not made a sound. Shango holds her upside down and taps her on her bottom. Still no sound. Panicking, he looks up at me with tears in his eyes. He hands me our lifeless child.

"Use your winds," I hear Mama whisper in my ears.

I place my mouth over Cora's and gently blow my winds into her. The rains pour down on us as I cover her with my body. I see the slightest movement on her forehead, then suddenly her eyes pop open and she lets out a mighty cry. We wrap her tightly into the rainbow blanket and rock her between us in the falling rain.

# CHAPTER 31

Chantilly's blood never fully washed out of the rainbow blanket. In fact, it left behind a bright red misshapen heart, just like Kitari's birthmark. We wrap the shawl around Cora as we stand streetside for Chantilly and her father's burial procession. I paid the funeral parlor handsomely to keep Chantilly's secret. They refused to bury her in her peacock dress until I bribed them.

The riot went on for three days after that night. Shango and I hid out at Ellen's house for the duration of the chaos. Everyone else made it home safely. I hold Cora tightly, wrapped in her blanket, thinking of the hatred that took the life of both Chantilly and Cosette, two of the most brilliant souls I knew.

The day is overcast, the sky a muted gray. I don't think the clouds are mine, but I'm too sorrowful to check. A horse-drawn hearse, its black lacquered wood gleaming even in the dim light, slowly makes its way down the curvy streets. The hearse is embellished with intricate carvings and large plumes of black ostrich feathers that sway with the movement of the horses.

Chantilly and her father had no living relatives here, so Ellen planned the entire ceremony. All the ladies are clad in long black dresses with high collars and veils that obscure their faces. Some carry handkerchiefs, embroidered with complicated patterns, to dab at their eyes. Sharon's curly red mane escapes from her veil as she holds on to two of the ladies—Yvonna and Michelle, I think. It's hard to tell with their faces covered. The entire group stands at attention, waiting for the hearse to pass by.

I even recognize some of the men from Chantilly's club. They are wearing black frock coats over their business attire. We follow the hearse on foot as it winds through the busy streets, where the everyday clamor of life pauses in respect. Shopkeepers and passersby remove their hats and bow their heads as the cortege proceeds.

I can't help but notice how different this funeral is from Cosette's, with the second line band and festive music on the streets. The mournful process here is almost too much to bear. Our final destination is a hillside cemetery overlooking the bay. The gravesites are marked by a variety of headstones, ranging from simple wooden crosses to elaborate marble monuments.

A preacher, standing at the head of the grave, reads from a small weathered Bible. I wonder if Chantilly and her father would've wanted sandalwood incense and offerings to their ancestors. Ellen motions for Shango and me to come closer to the coffins as the preacher concludes with a prayer.

"We must pass Cora over the bodies so she will be protected," Ellen says.

The onlookers sing a solemn hymn as Shango passes Cora over Chantilly's and her father's coffins. Cora squirms and almost seems to smile as Ellen holds her up, wrapped in the rainbow shawl. I grab a handful of the rich earth and sprinkle it on the hardwood of Chantilly's coffin.

There is a faint purple glow hovering behind Ellen. When I stare at it, it disappears. I can see it only in my peripheral vision. It almost looks like Chantilly flaunting her silk fan onstage.

Still holding Cora, Ellen turns, smiling, and whispers, "Chantilly knows that you can see her. She wants to tell you that she is still the godmother."

My eyes well up with tears. "Always," I say.

"And forever," Shango adds.

# ENDNOTE

There are many different stories about Oya, but according to popular legend, after nine miscarriages and stillbirths, Oya made a sacrifice on a cloth with the colors of the rainbow. She then gave birth to four sets of living twins and a ninth child. In Yoruba myth, twins are called Ibeji, meaning "born two times." The themes of rainbows and Ibeji are closely linked to Oya and are all connected to the falling rain. May Oya's winds of change continue to bring blessings into your life and blow away that which no longer serves you.

# ACKNOWLEDGMENTS

Thank you:

Sheldon My Love for holding everything down.

Lenard for always supporting me and creating the opportunity for my stories to be shared.

Nicholas Ciani for your continued guidance on my book journeys.

Hannah Frankel and Abby Mohr for keeping me organized and staying on top of me. My whole publishing team for supporting the entire process: Aleaha Renee, Debbie Norflus, Karen Kinney, Shida Carr, and everyone else who played a part in this novel's creation.

Laura Wise, and all of the editors who helped with the process of creating *The Wind on Her Tongue.*

The Simon & Schuster designers who created my beautiful cover.

Jan Miller and Ali Kominsky for being badass agents.

Michael B. Beckwith for being my mentor and spiritual teacher.

My mom, Lorna Kopacz, for practicing spelling words with me in the piano room for hours as a child. I would not be who I am today if it were not for your dedication.

My dad, Maciej Kopacz, for believing in me so much that there was no possible way I couldn't believe in myself.

My second parents, Dot and Selwyn, for always supporting me and the kids.

My ancestors for protecting us and showing the way. Especially Granny and Baba.

My children, Sadie, Tela, and Mayan, for stepping up and taking care of yourselves when I had to write.

Sharon Kopacz for instilling the love of adventure and mystery in me.

Yvonna Kopacz for letting me read the chapters to you as I wrote them.

Michelle Kopacz for being the best audiobook reader ever!

Nikki Kopacz for always finding a way to make me laugh. The title of this book was also inspired by one of Nikki's songs as Ms. ButHerWords, entitled "Thoughts Get Stuck": "Thoughts get stuck in my gut, pushed up to my lungs, vibrating from my tongue, to ears of the young ones."

Jatiana Kopacz for being one of the most kindhearted people I know.

Dani Kopacz for being a beautiful example of self-expression.

Brett and Jove for your business advice and example.

Aiden McKeith for having the conversation with me that sparked the idea for this book.

Risha Rox for your beautiful artwork of Oya.

Yadi Alba for listening to your intuition and connecting me with Lenard.

Synthia Salomon, Nicole Saieva, and the Nyack School District for including my books in the curriculum for AP African American Studies.

Bianca Shorte for getting *Shallow Waters* in your school library.

Allysa Shorte for creating the beautiful dance of Yemaya.

Courtney Shorte for always helping me connect to the right people.

Diana Wilkins and every other professor and teacher for adding my books to your curriculum. Diana, thank you for coming through and doing some copy edits for me.

Casey R. Kelley (@iamcaseyrkelley), Jerid P. Woods (@ablackmanreading), Alicia Bolden (@bolde_books), Kat Trinidad (@booksenvogue), Sol (@thesolreader), Ke Lly (@kellzisbookedup), Seanathan Q. Polidore (@seanathan_the_griot_polidore), Duane Bonaparte (@djayreads), Damien Jackson (@djreadsbooks), Reggie Bailey (@reggiereads), Donna Johnson (@thisbrowngirlreads), and ALL of the other Black Bookstagrammers for your support.

Riva Precil for the beautiful Creole translations.

Sade Tyler for teaching me so much about the Yoruba culture and supporting my books.

Suzanne Potts for the powerful, intuitive editing.

Emily for simply being my muse.

Mara Akil for hosting me at the Writers' Colony in Los Angeles where the idea for *The Wind on Her Tongue* was born.

André 3000 for your album *New Blue Sun*. It was my soundtrack to writing this book.

Daphne Dougé for sharing your mental health journey with me, and how oftentimes the medication made you feel like you'd lost your powers and connection with the divine.

Ayoka Hill, Michelle Mitchum, Jayson Jackson, Sade Tyler, Lee Thompson Young, Velma Love, Margie Nugent, Abiola Abrams, and the many others who have guided me on this path to the Orisha and African Spirituality.

Write On . . . participants—Felicia Watts, Nidia Temple, Jessica Hernandez, Lory-San Clark, Delores Williams, Jazelle Marie, Dolores Raymond, Laura Power, Laura Chung, Sebrena Tate, Diana Wilkins, Marisha Scott, Tracie Anderson, Leila Blackman, Gina Parker Collins, Kristina Casarez, Lori Land, Mang-Yee Reverie, Daphne Dougé, Norisol, Marlene Montilla, Gayah Gillson, Amanda Baudier, Nicolette Cothron, Rena Braud, Nicole Tucker, Nina Woodard, Maly Roberts, Jada Hanson, Oshiva, Dr. Tiffany Williams, Jacqueline Alexander, Ashley Gilchrist, Chanita Lewis-Watson, Charles Chen, Misty Jenson, Rachelle Abston—for writing your creations as I worked on mine.

Sherry Sidoti for generously sharing your beautiful home as my Martha's Vineyard writing retreat.

Tamika Mallory for being the best publishing sibling ever.

Whitney Davis Houston for being my lawyer but really more a friend.

Liani Greaves for letting me write at your breathtaking home.

Angie, Cecilia Gentili (rest in power), and Diana Wilkins for inspiring the character of Chantilly.

Laura Chung for our morning cocoa ceremonies and reading our books to each other.

Céline Semaan for being on your book journey with me, writing chapters simultaneously and crying together.

Colin-Collis Browne for helping me with all of my "legal" matters.

Sila Grey and Luma Rosie for sharing the story of *1001 Arabian Nights* with me.

Val & Jess, the best store in Nyack, and Emma for all of your support.

Malaak Compton-Rock for the fabulous celebration of my book in Martha's Vineyard and getting the novel into the hands of your students from Journey for Change Scholars for Girls in South Africa.

Asia Rainey-Ani for connecting me with Oya and reading that I am her daughter.

Shelah Marie for sharing your story of child loss publicly and touching the hearts of so many. You never know who you will inspire.

My Nyack Witches, Céline Semaan, Nidia Temple, Syntyché Francella, Yvonna Kopacz, and Laura Chung, for inspiring me with all the magic you put into the world.

Doro Erichsen for yelling encouraging words across the fence.

My New Orleans crew—Sharon, Yvonna, Michelle, Nicole (my sisters), Sadie (my daughter), Nidia Temple, Whitney Houston, Yadi Alba, Mona Speaks, Kristina Casarez, and Joi T. DeFrantz, for helping me research Marie Laveau. That drum circle on Congo Square was life-giving.

The Goddess Wisdom Council, Yadi Alba, Cora Poage, and Yvonna Kopacz, for keeping me accountable.

The entire Goddess Wisdom Council family and community for setting intentions with me about my book around bonfires and in oceans around the world.

Vanessa Standard for meeting with me every week and letting me read parts of the book to you.

My soul family Sheila Dennis, Ruba Rizqalla, Elizabeth Santiago, Talitha Watkins, Tracey Kemble, Christopher Gorham, Sharon Leal, Kavindra, Juliana Hawawini, Iesha Reed, Jackie, Bonnie Geronimo, Cathleen Trigg-Jones, Cathleen Benjamin, Laika, Nicole Ari Parker, Resmaa Menakem, Keith Major, and just too many to count. I love you all.

Liz Hines from Salte in Martha's Vineyard for all of your support.

Shelly Roberts for letting me use your house to hide from my kids and write.

Aiden, Deja, Lola, Marley, Sasha, Davis, Xander, Xochi, Althea, for being my reason . . . my reason to write, my reason to share, my reason to shine.

My cousin, Collette Marie, for allowing me to use her namesake for this story.

My entire extended family, whom I listed in my *Shallow Waters* acknowledgments, for shaping me into who I am today. A special shout-out to my new ancestors, Aunty Apple, Uncle Allan, Uncle Eddie, Aunty Soph, Uncle Brother, and Zaria. I feel you with me, protecting me and loving me.

**Anita Kopacz** is an award-winning writer and spiritual adviser. She is the former editor in chief of *Heart & Soul* magazine and former managing editor of *Beauty-Cents* magazine. When she is not writing, you can find her on the dance floor or traveling the world with her children. Anita lives in New York City with her family. She is the author of *Shallow Waters* and *The Wind on Her Tongue*.